Guardians of Time

Books in the *After Cilmeri* Series:
Daughter of Time (prequel)
Footsteps in Time (Book One)
Winds of Time
Prince of Time (Book Two)
Crossroads in Time (Book Three)
Children of Time (Book Four)
Exiles in Time
Castaways in Time
Ashes of Time
Warden of Time
Guardians of Time
Masters of Time
Outpost in Time
Shades of Time
Champions of Time
Refuge in Time
Outcasts in Time

This Small Corner of Time:
The After Cilmeri Series Companion

A Novel from the *After Cilmeri* Series

GUARDIANS OF TIME

by

SARAH WOODBURY

Guardians of Time
Copyright © 2015 by Sarah Woodbury

www.sarahwoodbury.com

To Linda

CAST OF CHARACTERS

David (Dafydd)—Time-traveler, King of England
Lili—Queen of England, Ieuan's sister
Callum—Time-traveler, Earl of Shrewsbury
Cassie—Time-traveler, Callum's wife
Ieuan—Welsh knight, one of David's men
Bronwen—Time-traveler, married to Ieuan
Arthur—son of David and Lili (born June 1289)
Catrin—daughter of Ieuan and Bronwen (born Nov. 1288)

Nicholas de Carew—Norman/Welsh lord
William de Bohun—David's squire
Justin—David's captain
Bevyn—David's adviser
Huw—Member of the Order of the Pendragon
Darren Jeffries—time traveler (bus passenger)
Peter Cobb—time traveler (bus passenger)
Rachel Wolff—time traveler (bus passenger)

1

Dinas Bran (Llangollen)

Christmas Eve 1292

Anna

"Time travel isn't meant to be a get-out-of-jail-free card."

Her mother's words of warning echoed in Anna's head as she prepared herself to *travel* one more time. She'd found a seat near the front of the bus, one of a number that faced inward so she was looking out the opposite windows.

Ten years ago, the first time Anna remembered time traveling, she'd been seventeen, driving fourteen-year-old David to pick up their cousin, Christopher. A wall of snow had appeared across the road upon which they'd been driving, and when they'd crashed through it, they'd found themselves in medieval Wales.

Unlike the other times she'd *traveled,* it wasn't their own lives that had been in danger in that moment, but Papa's. Both that day and this one had been gloomy December afternoons within an hour of sunset. Oddly, the turquoise color of the Cardiff bus wasn't far off from the color of her aunt's minivan either. Today, however, it was raining instead of snowing, and it wasn't Anna driving the vehicle.

The Cardiff bus was both bigger and smaller than Anna remembered. Bigger—because it had been a long time since Anna had seen any vehicle larger than a hay cart, and most medieval ships were half the size of this bus. But it was smaller too, barely seeming to hold, once they'd piled into it, the forty people they were taking to the twenty-first century.

David, in his obsessive attention to detail, had built a well-graveled road expressly for this purpose. From the perspective of anyone who wasn't in on the secret, the road itself looked pretty useless. It started at the bus hanger outside Llangollen and ended at the bottom of a cliff wall. David hadn't completely given the game away because he'd had the road continue past the cliff until it reached a river.

Still, one might wonder why such a magnificent road would end at a spot where there was neither a bridge nor a ford—and no road on the other side. If they made it through this, Math would have to build one.

Of course, David had built the road this way on purpose, and it very much resembled one of those ramps that semi-trucks were supposed to use when their brakes failed while driving down a steep hill. In this particular case, however, there would be no braking involved. The bed of the road was made of rock and hardened earth, not sand, and the goal was to get the bus going as fast as possible by the time it hit the cliff.

Which was what had prompted Mom to comment on the relationship between Monopoly and time travel in the first place.

That had been a few days ago. Anna, Mom, and Lili, David's wife, had been warming themselves on cushioned chairs near the fire in Anna's sitting room, not even pretending to work on the needlework at their feet that was the required pastime of every noble woman in the Middle Ages, even those like Anna who hadn't been born to it.

When Mom had added, "It might not work—" David, who'd been leaning against the frame of the door, had made a chopping motion with his hand, cutting her off. "This is going to work. I know it."

Anna had already had this argument with her mother—and lost—so she'd brought in what she considered to be the big gun—David—and was more than willing to let him make her point for her.

David had been dressed, for once, as the King of England he was, in black leather boots polished so brightly they reflected the firelight, brown breeches and blue coat of the finest wool, and a silk shirt that wouldn't have been out of place in one of the fanciest clubs in London in any century. Or so Anna supposed, since she'd never been in one.

Twenty-four years old in November, David's once baby-round face had slimmed in the past few years as he'd grown into his body—and the pressures of being King of England weighed him down. When he'd arrived in Dinas Bran, Anna had been shocked to see a few strands of gray amidst his normally sandy brown hair.

He'd come with his family to celebrate Christmas—*and* the tenth anniversary of their father's survival at Cilmeri. Dinas Bran had been full to bursting with time travelers and medieval people alike. David had ditched his entire English retinue at Chester Castle in England. His English retainers should have known by now that such behavior meant he was up to something, but as he was the King of England, they had allowed themselves to be persuaded.

"Didn't we decide that uncertainty and fear are necessary to make the *traveling* work?" Mom actually laughed. "Should I be worried that you're not afraid enough?"

"None of us will be feeling any shortage of fear, I assure you." David shifted in the doorway, straightening slightly as his intensity level rose. "You need to get checked out, Mom. Breast cancer isn't something to be screwing around with."

"It's nothing," Mom had said. "Most lumps disappear on their own."

"Most lumps do, and it is *probably* nothing," David said, "but since I'm going, you might as well come too."

"I will come with you, Meg," Papa said.

"Llywelyn, be reasonable. We can't leave the twins alone. Who knows the trouble they'll get into?" Mom put a hand on Papa's cheek.

Papa's hair might have nearly as much gray in it now as black, but according to Rachel, he was fit and healthy, and his blue eyes had twinkled at Mom with compassion and understanding. Even after all these years, the looks that passed between them gave Anna a tingly feeling in her stomach to see how much her parents loved each other. In the need to see that love, some part of Anna would always be three years old, and she knew herself blessed to have found something similar in her marriage to Math.

Who, unfortunately, Anna would be leaving behind.

"Between their nannies, Gwenllian, and me, we are perfectly capable of taking care of the twins for a few days—weeks even, if that's what it takes," Lili had said, "and Wales is in good hands with Math and Ieuan. You're going to have to look for a different excuse not to go."

Lili was heavily pregnant with her second child, which meant Mom hadn't asked why she wasn't going. Mom had time traveled while pregnant three times. Anna herself had done so with her mother when she was a toddler, so *traveling* didn't appear to have any negative effects on small people. Still, the very act meant putting themselves in danger, which nobody, least of all David, was going to let Lili do. Childbirth in the Middle Ages was dangerous enough.

Mom had faced David again, shaking her head hard enough in annoyance to loosen a pin or two from her elaborate upswept hairdo. Brown strands framed her face, and her eyes flashed. "What about England? Don't you think you're being just a teensy bit reckless and irresponsible leaving everyone in the lurch so you can go back to the modern world? You just want a McDonald's hamburger for the first time in ten years."

David had studied his mother and hadn't answered.

Mom's color had been high, and the words she'd thrown at David hadn't been nice—or even true. Then she'd looked away. "I'm sorry. I'm really sorry. I shouldn't have said that. I don't believe it. I'm just—"

"Scared." Papa brought both hands down onto Mom's shoulders. "As we all are. But that doesn't mean we shouldn't go forward anyway. You must see a physician. More to the point, you must have one of these—" he made an impatient gesture with one hand, "—scans."

"If it were just you, Mom," David said, "I'd consider waiting to see if the lump goes away. You say it's tender, which cancer generally isn't, and Rachel tells me lumps like yours happen all the time to forty-something women who've nursed four kids. You are an unlikely candidate for breast cancer anyway. I believe her. But I've been thinking about this for a while, and now that Shane is sick—"

His voice had broken off as they all considered the real reason—the driving reason—that David was contemplating this trip. Shane, a tow-headed seven-year-old who'd come to the Middle Ages on the Cardiff bus with his parents, Jane and Carl, had what Rachel feared to be childhood leukemia. The disease was eminently curable in the twenty-first century. Not so much in the thirteenth.

David, in fact, had confessed to Anna that he was taking Shane to the modern world regardless of what anyone else thought or said against it, even if he had to hold Shane in his arms and jump off a cliff alone as he'd done with Ieuan a number of years ago.

In the end, Mom had agreed to come. She'd even seen the wisdom in taking the other bus passengers back with them. Now, Anna's overriding concern was to have them all survive the attempt. Like David, Anna assumed it was going to work. *It had better work!*

From the front of the bus where he'd been standing near the driver's seat, checking names off a list, David lifted a hand to get the attention of the passengers. "Everybody buckle up!"

Anna got to her feet instead. "I should stand beside you, David."

"Sit, sit, sit!" David flapped a hand at her. "You're fine where you are, Anna." And then he added in an undertone, "You and Mom should wear your seat belts in case this doesn't work."

"That is not what I wanted to hear from you," Papa said, but then he smiled and his tone softened. "We're with you, son. Whatever happens." He draped one arm across the back of Mom's seat and bent one leg to rest his ankle on his knee. He was looking far more relaxed about the trip than Anna might have expected.

In fact, Papa had been with David from the start. Mom had *traveled* with Papa and Goronwy a few years ago to save Papa's life. He saw it as a fair trade that he would be doing the same for her. Besides, the shadows behind his eyes told Anna how worried he was about Mom, as they all were, even if they told themselves the worry was for nothing. More than any other disease, cancer was a terrifying proposition, incurable in the Middle Ages. Anna saw it as a parasite growing inside her mother, and she just wanted it *out!*

David actually managed a smile. "It's just that Anna has never done this alone, and Mom isn't going to lose both of us in one day if this doesn't turn out the way we want it to."

"I thought you said it was going to work." Shane's mother, Jane, looked up at David from her position in the driver's seat. The Cardiff bus had been lovingly repaired by several of the more mechanically-minded time travelers, Jane among them, so it seemed oddly appropriate that she would be the one to drive it into the cliff today.

Since she would be at the very front of the bus with him, Jane was risking her life almost as much as David was, though if they crashed, she at least would have an airbag to protect her. David was going to stand beside her, his hands gripping the metal bar that ran horizontally across the dash. He'd have no protection if the bus ran head first into the cliff instead of time traveling. He would be thrown through the windshield and killed.

"Oh my God." Mom, who was sitting in a seat that faced front, but adjacent to Anna, suddenly put both hands to her face, her fingers spread wide to cover her mouth and cheeks. "This is insane. I cannot believe I let you talk me into this."

"It's our fault Shane is here, even if we didn't mean to bring him." Anna said. "We can't let him die when we could do something about it."

"Then if that's the case, I should be taking him by myself." Mom straightened her spine, revealing her innate courage that was never far beneath the surface. "Nobody else needs to risk it."

"Anna offered to do the same thing, but I told her no." David unbent from his post behind Jane's seat and came closer. "It isn't just about Shane any more. We need information and whatever supplies we can get so we can reverse engineer what we can't yet make. At a minimum, Rachel says a high-powered microscope would do wonders. What's more, by taking the bus today, everyone who came with you on it can go home. One shot deal. Do not pass go. Do not collect two hundred dollars."

"I think that's what the game tells you to do when you're *going* to jail, not escaping it," Mom said, though she managed a smile to mask her worry.

Anna had certainly been annoyed at times over the years with David's intense sense of purpose and what amounted to tunnel vision when he was sure he was doing the right thing. Today, however, his earnestness was endearing—in large part because what he believed to be right definitely *was*.

David reached for his mother's other hand. "Maybe you're right. Maybe this time we will all die in a great tragedy like when the White Ship went down in the English Channel and King Henry lost his son and the flower of English nobility in one go. You're right that time travel isn't to be used frivolously, but this isn't frivolous."

"It isn't like David's been running down to the corner store every five minutes," Anna said.

"Yeah, well, Mom's right that sometimes it feels like I am," David said. "Even if I didn't stay, I did *travel* only a few months ago when I dropped off Lee."

David was referring to one of the bus passengers who'd turned out to be a terrorist, possibly for an offshoot of the Irish Republican Army. Lee had been involved not only in the bombings in Avalon in Cardiff, which had brought Anna, Mom, and the bus to the Middle Ages in the first place, but also bombings at Canterbury Castle and Dover Castle in September.

In his confrontation with Lee, David had inadvertently returned to Avalon and, as he said, *dropped Lee off*. It was a huge relief to be rid of Lee, but they all retained a nagging anxiety about what kind of trouble he might be causing wherever he was now.

Since the *traveling* was keyed to David's needs, not Lee's, Lee wouldn't have ended up some place remote like the Arctic or the Sahara Desert. He'd have fallen into North America or Wales, where he could do a great deal of harm.

"If people are going to stay here, they have to truly choose it—and not because they're afraid to die on the way back. You don't have to go. I can't make you. But regardless of your choice, *I* am going." David's voice went soft. "I can't have them on my conscience any more. I have to do this."

Mom gazed down the length of the bus and finally nodded. "More than anything, children like Shane need to grow up where they were born and live with all the advantages that life can give them."

Bursts of laughter came here and there from the bus passengers as they situated themselves. Some of the people climbed to the upper level of the bus, which Anna thought brave of them, given what they were about to do. This was sure to look much worse from up there.

Anna herself wasn't sure she really wanted to see the bus crash at all, though she was probably required to do so since she was one of the people who had to fear for her life in order for the time travel to work. She prodded David's toe with hers. "They're happy to be here."

"I'm really glad to know that. I thought they would be, once they started thinking about all the people and things they'd missed over the last year. I just hope—" David cut himself off.

"What do you hope?" Mom said.

David licked his lips. "I just hope that what they're going home to is still there. You guys left Cardiff in kind of a mess. Who knows what damage those terrorists have done in the last year?"

"That would be their fault," Anna said, knowing where her brother's thoughts had headed, "not yours."

David gave a disparaging click of his tongue. "Even I am not so full of self-importance as to think I'm in any way responsible for the problems of the modern world, but I did give Lee back to them. It's been three months! A year in the Middle Ages was probably the best thing that ever happened to Lee, because it allowed him to elude the authorities to the point of dropping completely off the radar."

"All set, my lord." Callum appeared in front of David, with his wife, Cassie; and time travelers Darren Jeffries and Peter Cobb in tow.

When Callum had arrived in the Middle Ages, he'd been a capable, even superior, MI-5 agent, but one suffering from his experience in war and too honorable to be happy serving employers who had less honor than he did. A few months in David's service had given him purpose, focusing his energies and intelligence and turning him into one of David's closest confidants. Now, as the Earl of Shrewsbury, he was one of the most powerful men in England to boot.

Leaving space for Callum to sit directly behind the driver, Cassie set her backpack on the floor in front of her, took the next seat down, and buckled up. She wore jeans, a sweater, and a leather jacket, all of which fit her well since they were hers. She, along with those of them who were planning to return to the Middle Ages once their work in the twenty-first century was done, had stored their medieval clothing for the return journey in the back of the bus.

At the moment, Anna's mother wore the modern clothes she'd borrowed from Cassie's aunt's house last Thanksgiving when she and Anna had *traveled* on Thanksgiving Day. Though David himself hadn't had the pleasure of that experience, he meant to model this trip on that one: on Christmas Eve, the authorities would be short-staffed, thinking more about presents and ham dinners than tracking rogue time travelers across the planet. The only real drawback was that it meant missing Christmas with their children.

Just like last time too, Mom wore the Pendleton wool coat she'd borrowed from Cassie's aunt, which should keep her as warm as the thick wool cloak she normally wore. Anna wore the clothes she'd borrowed too, including the puffy purple parka she'd had to forgo once they'd returned to medieval Gwynedd. Peter Cobb wore casual clothing, but Callum and Darren were looking extremely handsome, dressed as they were once again in their MI-5 suits and trench coats. Anna knew for a fact that Callum had secreted his gun at the small of his back, making it almost a given that Darren had too.

That left Papa and David in best-they-could-do medieval replicas of modern garb, which was pretty hilarious and ironic when Anna thought about it. Both wore wool pants over their regular leather boots, a linen shirt, and a wool sweater over the top. Somewhere David might still have the clothes he'd come to the Middle Ages wearing ten years ago, but it wasn't as if they would fit him.

"Is everyone here?" Anna looked up at Callum.

"According to my list, they are," David said.

Mom clasped her hands in front of her lips and studied David and Anna over the top of them. "You do know that to return a busload of people from the Middle Ages to the twenty-first century is *completely* mad."

"Yup," Anna caught her brother's eye and saw the same recklessness in his expression that had suddenly swept over her.

"You have no idea where we're going to end up," Mom said.

"No, we don't," Anna said.

David's chin firmed. "But I sure do hope we run into Lee."

At which point Anna thought, but didn't say, *be careful what you wish for!* In David's case, wishes had a disconcerting tendency to come true.

2

Anna

Anna kept her eyes fixed on Math, whom she could see through the window as he stood outside the bus. His tousled black hair was wet from the rain, and she was noticing only now that she couldn't do anything about it that it had grown longer than she usually let it. She reminded herself to give him a haircut when she came home.

Then she smiled at him, though she felt her eyes fill with tears as she did so.

Anna had said goodbye to her boys earlier, not wanting them here to witness whatever came next. Cadell had stood solemnly before Math as he'd explained that David was taking the adults to Avalon and that Cadell would need to protect his cousins in their parents' absence. Bran knew she was taking a trip, which Anna did occasionally. Usually, it was to medical clinics in the region or to collect herbal remedies from across Britain, some of which were remarkably effective and rivaled—or even were better than—modern drugs. Unfortunately, none could address her mother's cancer or Shane's.

Lili and Bronwen had also remained behind with Arthur, Gwenllian, and the twins, none of whom needed to see what happened with the bus—whatever that might be.

It was already later in the afternoon than David had anticipated leaving. They were coming off a large Christmas feast in the hall at the university in Llangollen. The party had been for villagers, students, visiting scholars, and bus passengers alike, in lieu of any celebration up at the castle tomorrow. David was hoping that people, in general, wouldn't mind that the feast had been held on Christmas Eve instead of on Christmas Day.

The festivities had actually begun before noon, but while they'd intended to spend a couple of hours at the gathering, they hadn't planned on it being nearly dark by the time they set out. This close to the solstice, the sun set at 3:30 in the afternoon. Yet Anna and Math hadn't felt they could leave until the feast was well and truly over. At least none of them had to stay to clean up—one of the many perks of being part of the Welsh royal family.

Anna blinked back her tears again, and when they wouldn't stay away, closed her eyes and pressed her fingers to the corners, willing herself to remain calm. She was about to face death for something she believed in. She was no more willing than David to leave the risk to others.

"Hi there."

She opened her eyes to find Math right in front of her, this time *inside* the bus. He sat down next to her, fumbling with the unfamiliar seat belt buckle.

Anna gaped at him. "What—Math, no—you're supposed to be regent in Papa's absence."

"You're not glad to see me?"

"Of course I'm glad to see you."

Math smirked. "So then don't tell me to get off the bus. I'm coming with you."

"You can't!"

Math tsked through his teeth. "I asked you once if you would return to Avalon if you could, and you said you weren't going anywhere without me. At the time, I told you that I had no intention of giving you a choice. What kind of husband would I be if I let you go alone now under these circumstances?"

Anna put her head on his shoulder while at the same time reaching for his hand. She didn't know what to say, because of course she wanted him with her. But it was reckless and irresponsible of him. And yet, it was only as reckless and irresponsible as David and Papa were being.

Math patted her hand. As she straightened up again, she saw that he and Papa were gazing at each other.

"Did you speak with Goronwy about the change in plans?" Papa said.

"He told me to go. He knows what to do," Math said.

Anna could see the man in question standing outside the bus, his arms folded across his chest and his mustache bristling even in the rain, which—typically for late December in Wales—had started to fall more heavily. Some years it snowed by late December, but not so far this year.

Math squeezed Anna's hand where it rested on his thigh. "I'm looking forward to finally seeing what's on the other side."

"I am too." David touched Jane's shoulder. "I think it's time."

Shane and Jane's husband, Carl, sat farther back in the bus with the other passengers. Even though this was David's plan, everyone had loudly shouted down any notion that he should drive the bus. He'd never learned to drive properly, since he'd been just fourteen when they'd come to Wales ten years ago, and he had driven only a few times since then.

Anna would never have dared to suggest that driving a city bus into a cliff wall was beyond her brother. She wasn't sure if anything was. But if he tipped the bus over before they reached the wall, it might not be enough danger to cause them to time travel, and then they'd be stuck trying to figure out a way to right it before returning to the beginning and going through the whole procedure again.

Nobody wanted that. Since Jane was the mechanic, and since they were *traveling* in large part for Shane's benefit, she'd taken on the task.

"Yes, sir." Jane started the engine, which roared to life and then settled into a well-oiled *purr*.

"Nice." David straightened, resolve in every line of his body.

"Wait a minute!"

Anna shifted in her seat to look behind her, and her mouth fell open to see Bridget, a woman in her mid-twenties and the last person Anna would have expected to see rising to her feet and gathering her gear. Her red curly hair framed her face in its usual untamed mane, and her green eyes gazed stonily ahead at David.

Like everyone else who'd come to the Middle Ages on the Cardiff bus a year ago, it had taken time for Bridget to adjust to the medieval world. But as the year had progressed, she'd done better than most. Back in Avalon, Bridget had worked in a shop in Cardiff, and as with Callum, her arrival in the Middle Ages had clarified her purpose in a way the vicissitudes of modern life had not. She'd rejected the malaise of some of the other travelers her age, and made the best of a bad situation.

She'd come to the Middle Ages with little formal education, though Anna knew her to be intelligent and more well-read than many university graduates, thanks to her local library and the internet. Bridget had a strong working class background, which meant she'd connected with the regular English folk in Shrewsbury, Callum's seat, better than Anna or Cassie ever could.

Her secret power was that she was a knitting aficionado, a skill that had been developed in the Middle East for luxury items in silk, cotton, or linen, but hadn't yet reached much of Europe. Shortly after Christmas a year ago, Bridget had set up shop in Shrewsbury, which was the wool capitol of western England, using start-up funds given to her by Callum.

She'd begun producing knitted woolen products, among them hats, mittens, scarves, and sweaters—one of which David was currently wearing. Before spring, she'd hired three employees, and by autumn, with demand growing by leaps and bounds, she'd employed ten.

What's more, Callum had seen qualities in her that had been lost on her society in her old life and turned her shop into the clearing house for his spy network. Rather than having informants make the trek up to the castle to deliver news, thus revealing themselves to anyone who might wonder what business they could have with the earl, they now brought their news to Bridget. In turn, Bridget passed what she learned on to one of Callum's lieutenants: Samuel, the sheriff of Shrewsbury; or Peter Cobb, his right-hand man. Or so she had done until today.

Bridget marched up to David. "What's this about Mark coming back here with you?"

David glanced down the bus towards Mark Jones, the man in question. He was one of the former MI-5 agents who'd come with Anna and her mother on the bus from Cardiff and had found a place in the Middle Ages working for Callum. As Anna watched, Mark raised his shoulders in an elaborate shrug and mouthed the word, *sorry*.

David looked back to Bridget, hesitating before answering and clearly stalling so as to give himself time to figure out how to reply. Bridget kept her gaze fixed on him, and finally he said, "It was the only way to get him on the bus, short of handcuffing him to a rail."

"You didn't tell me I had that choice," Bridget said.

Peter, who'd remained standing near David at the front of the bus, put out a hand to her shoulder. "It's going be okay, Bridget—"

Bridget flailed out her right arm, smacking his hand away. "Don't patronize me."

Eyebrows in his hairline, his mouth forming a *whoo*, Peter put up both hands, palms out, and stepped back. "No, ma'am."

That didn't appease Bridget in the way Peter might have been hoping for because Bridget turned her glower on him. "I don't suppose you're staying either."

Peter's eyes shifted nervously towards David and then back to Bridget. "Er ... no."

Bridget swung back to David. "So why do I have to come at all?"

"I suppose, when it comes down to it, you don't." He cleared his throat. "But you have to be really sure this is what you want because I'm not doing this again. If you get off this bus, you're living in the Middle Ages for the rest of your life."

Bridget turned to look again at Peter. "Are you coming back for sure?"

Peter fell back on his military training, clasping his hands together behind his back and standing at parade rest. "Yes."

"Do you promise?"

Peter looked at her warily. David's eyes were flicking between the two of them, a slight smile on his lips, and then he shifted forward and lowered his voice. "Bridget, I will bring him home if it is at all possible for me to do so."

Bridget chewed on her lower lip, studying Peter, who had the look of a man who knew that *something* was going on, but he wasn't sure what that something was.

"What?" he finally said when she still hadn't moved from her spot—about six inches from where he was standing.

By way of an answer, Bridget took the lapels of his coat in her fists, tugged on him so he had to bend towards her while she stood on tiptoe, and kissed him full on the mouth.

To his credit, Peter responded instantly, wrapping his arms around her and pulling her to him so he could return the kiss properly.

Everybody around them burst into laughter, even David, though he rolled his eyes at Anna when the kiss went on longer than a few seconds. Finally, Bridget and Peter let go of one another, moving apart enough for their gazes to meet.

Whatever Bridget saw in Peter's eyes seemed to decide something for her, because she nodded, turned to David, and poked him in the chest with one finger. "Okay. I'm holding you to that." Then she picked up her hat, gloves, and backpack from where she'd left them on a nearby seat, marched down the aisle to the back door, and left the bus.

Peter's normally pale face had flushed all the way to the roots of his dark blond hair, which he still kept extremely short for ease of care, and his expression was stunned—probably not only at the kiss but also at Bridget's subsequent departure.

"What just happened?" he said.

Grinning wildly, Darren clapped him on the shoulder. "If you don't know the answer to that, my friend, you truly are a hopeless case."

Callum gripped Peter's upper arm. "You should get off the bus. Follow her."

Peter glanced in the direction Bridget had gone and then cleaned the window of steam with his fist in order to peer through the glass. "Don't you need me?"

"We could use you, it's true," Callum said.

"But do you really want to leave it like that?" Cassie said from behind him. "You want to be with her, right?"

"Of course, I do." Peter straightened to look at Cassie. "I'd get off this bus in a heartbeat if—" He broke off, his eyes moving now to David's face.

"If what?" David said.

Peter took in a breath. "If I didn't feel obligated to you, sire."

David shook his head. "For the last few hours, I've had a nagging feeling in my stomach about how few of us are remaining behind. I didn't say anything because it would be unfair of me to ask anyone to sacrifice the opportunity to go home, but it would relieve my mind very much to know you were here holding the fort."

Peter puffed out his cheeks and released a breath but didn't answer.

"Speak, Peter," Callum said.

Anna had spent enough time with Peter over the last year to know that the command was necessary. It wasn't so much that his upper lip was British stiff. He was perfectly talkative when it came to work or an investigation he was conducting for Callum. But he was one of those men who had a particularly hard time conveying to anyone else what he was feeling. For him, showing no emotion and speaking little was ingrained.

He managed it this time, at least to Callum. "Yeah, I'll stay. I'm glad to stay. I was dreading going back almost as much as Bridget, though I didn't realize it until right now." He turned to Darren. "Call my parents. Let them know I'm alive."

"I'll tell them you're working undercover in Botswana," Darren said.

Peter nodded. "That will make sense to them." He blew out another breath and looked around at his friends. "Good luck."

"The sooner you get off this bus," David said, with a smile splitting his face, "the sooner we can get this show on the road."

Peter followed the path Bridget had taken, and David hit the intercom so the people on the second level could hear him too.

"Folks, in a minute we'll be on our way. Just as a reminder of what's going to happen so nobody is surprised: the road winds down the hill, and then it will straighten out and head directly towards the bottom of the cliff. Jane's going to get going as fast as this old bus can travel on a gravel road. We plan to hit the cliff wall at speed, and Jane has promised not to put her foot on the brake." He cleared his throat. "I'd like everybody to fasten their seat belts. The ride might get a bit bumpy."

He paused, releasing the button and studying the faces in front of him. Then he activated the intercom again. "If this doesn't work, I'm sorry. It's been an honor."

And with that abrupt comment, he turned around and placed both hands on the dash in front of him.

Anna knew her brother. His voice had been thick with emotion there at the end, and he'd cut off any further speech because he didn't want anyone else to know how he was feeling. As Jane shifted into first gear and started down the hill, Anna met her mother's eyes. Mom was clutching Papa's hand the same way Anna was holding Math's.

They didn't speak as the bus safely navigated the first two switchbacks, and then the bus started down the straight stretch, picking up speed and jostling everyone as it went. The bus wasn't designed for gravel roads, even one hardened and smoothed as this one had been. Rain pounded on the roof and ran in rivulets down the windows, at a slant because the wind was whipping too and the bus was going fast.

"Mother of God," Math said.

"I can't let David do this alone." Abruptly, Anna unbuckled her seatbelt and staggered towards the front of the bus. She steadied herself with one hand on the metal bar that ran from floor to ceiling behind the driver's seat and grabbed for David's arm with the other.

"Anna! What are you doing?" The tears were gone from David's voice. Now he just sounded horrified.

"We started this together. We're going to finish it the same way." Anna glared at David, daring him to send her back to her seat.

"All right." David brought his hand off the dash and clasped her left hand in his right. "Together."

They both stared out the front window as the cliff rose up before them.

"David." Jane's voice was all fear and warning.

"Keep that pedal to the floor," David ordered.

A hundred feet. Fifty feet. People in the back of the bus and on the upper level, where they had a better view, were openly screaming now. Some were praying. Anna was screaming on the inside, her breath caught so far up in her throat it was choking her. She glanced down at the speedometer, which was in kilometers per hour. It told her they were going a hundred.

And then Mom was behind them, wedging herself between her children, her arms wrapped around their waists. "I'm here, you two." The cliff wall was right in front of them.

Twenty feet. Ten feet.

There was no stopping now, even if they wanted to. They were going to hit the wall. An irresistible force colliding with an immovable object.

"Eyes open!" David's voice cracked.

Anna screamed as the front of the bus hit the stones of the cliff with a resounding *crash*—

But no, like the miracle it had always been and continued to be, instead of hitting the wall they went right through it, as if they were on a ghost bus and had become ghosts themselves. Anna could only guess what it looked like from the outside. For the first time, because she was determined to experience the *traveling* fully, she kept her eyes open wide as David had ordered. But the lights at the front of the bus shone into nothingness.

She clutched David's hand, which she was still holding, felt her mom's tight grip around her waist, and counted through the three seconds of blackness that surrounded the bus.

Then they were through to the other side—and the bus was screaming down a highway going the *wrong* way.

Horns blared from the two lanes of cars coming at them.

"Iesu Mawr!" Jane said, swearing fluently in Welsh as she swerved the bus to avoid the oncoming cars.

The bus's windshield wipers flailed back and forth at high speed. It was snowing here instead of raining, with at least three or four inches already on the ground. Since the road wasn't a true divided highway, the easiest thing for Jane to do should have been to veer into the far left lane, where cars were going in their direction, but a series of giant orange barrels barred the way. The road was under construction, and it looked to Anna as if it was being expanded into a four-lane divided highway. They were driving on the right side of the road, which of course was the *wrong* side for Wales.

Mom staggered away from the dash, bringing Anna with her. They collapsed into their seats, and Anna felt Math's arms come around her waist and pull her close to him. She put her head into his chest, her whole body vibrating.

"We're going to head right back to the Middle Ages if we don't get off this road!" Callum had risen to his feet to stand by David, who was no longer leaning forward on the dash but had moved both hands to the metal pole behind Jane's seat, which Anna had been holding.

"I'm trying!" An oncoming van forced Jane to careen the bus to the far right side of the road. Unfortunately, as was usual in Wales, the shoulder was about three inches wide with a stone wall buttressing it. On an American highway, they could have pulled off the road and stopped, even if they were facing the wrong way. Here, there was nowhere to go.

"As soon as you can." David's voice turned calm. While Callum stooped to look out the windshield, David stepped closer to Anna so he could bend forward to look out the side window of the bus above her head. "Hey, sis. Thanks." He smiled at Anna and put out a hand to her. "It worked."

She grasped his hand. "It did, you idiot. One more time."

3

David

David was forced to admit, in those first moments as they careened the wrong way down the road, that he'd been criminally arrogant, and he didn't need Anna to call him an idiot to realize it. His time traveling had never hurt anyone before—that he knew of anyway. As he watched a car, in its attempt to avoid the bus, narrowly miss the series of orange barrels that ran down the middle of the highway, it staggered him to realize how much trust the bus passengers had placed in him, allowing him to risk their lives on the hope that he could bring them home.

He didn't know where he'd expected to end up. Somewhere in the twenty-first century was as far ahead as he'd thought. If pressed, he'd have guessed that they'd end up in a field or an empty hillside either in Wales or Pennsylvania—or in a pinch, Oregon. That's where they'd always found themselves before. But then, except for when Anna and Mom had dropped the bus into the middle of a medieval battle, they'd never gone back to the modern world in a vehicle capable of causing the kind of havoc the Cardiff double-decker was currently wreaking on the highway.

A deathly quiet descended upon the bus itself, even as car after car swerved out of their way. With the dark and the snow, getting out of this with only a few dings and some scared drivers would be a miracle. Nobody spoke, not wanting to disturb Jane's concentration and muttered cursing as she fought the wheel, the snow, and the other cars to navigate safely through them.

Jane split the difference between the two lanes in order to avoid two cars that veered away by inches, and then, finally, a gap appeared in the traffic at the same time as a roundabout. She swung the wheel so as to follow the roundabout to the left, which enabled her to merge with the traffic on the other side of the barrels. She ended up not only in the proper lane for Wales—though now, to David, since they were on the left side of the road, it was the wrong lane—but also with the ability to exit the highway entirely.

Unfortunately, the sign telling them what exit they were taking was obscured by blown snow, which had adhered to the reflective lettering. David could make out only a C, and an 'on', and on the next line maybe a dd and an ll. That meant they could be anywhere in Wales.

Three minutes later, Jane pulled into the parking lot of a Tesco store, which was roughly the British equivalent to Wal-Mart in the United States. As she braked to a stop, David closed his eyes for a second, feeling his heart ease into a more normal pattern, and pressed his forehead into the heel of his hand. He felt the bus settle as the engine slowed to a low hum.

Jane leaned back in her seat, wiping sweat off her brow, and then looked over at him. "We didn't die."

"Apparently not," David said, "though not for lack of trying."

"That was too bloody close," Darren said in an undertone.

David nodded fervently and turned to look at his family and friends. Nobody was really talking yet, though some of the bus passengers had risen to their feet to look out the windows of the bus, and a couple of people had opened other windows to let in fresh air and snow.

Then Mom let out an unqueenlike guffaw of laughter, and David found himself smiling at her. They'd done it, and they hadn't killed anyone in the process. A major victory. Yes, he'd been arrogant, but once again, he hadn't been badly punished for it.

"What do we do now?" Mark said brightly, articulating what everyone had to be thinking.

It was on David to come up with the answers, though now that they were here, he felt completely overwhelmed by the magnitude of what faced them. It wasn't enough that he'd brought all the bus passengers back to the modern world. He couldn't just drop them off in a Tesco parking lot and leave them.

But then his ears tuned into the babble of voices coming from the seats behind Mark, Rachel, and Darren. Cell phones had materialized in a dozen hands. Earlier, he'd been too busy to notice the little outlets—both USB ports and those for regular plugs—located beside each pair of seats. Most of the passengers had thought to bring their cell phones and chargers against the moment they reached the modern world and could use them again.

From the back of the bus came the sound of someone sobbing, and David moved toward the voice, afraid the woman in question was injured.

Callum reached out a hand to stop him. "She's just called her family. Leave her be."

David stopped. Other people had tears in their eyes too, Cassie among them. She already had her phone to her ear too, and as he moved back to his post behind Jane's seat, he heard her say, "Merry Christmas, Grandad."

His mother would need to call her sister, but David himself had no other family in the modern world, and no reason to feel any emotion about being here other than relief. Still, he could relate—if he'd had a cell phone to call Lili the last time he'd returned to the Middle Ages after being shipwrecked near Cardiff, he would have used it in a heartbeat.

He raised a hand to get everyone's attention. "Was anyone injured on the journey?"

Shaken heads showed all around, including from the woman who'd been crying. David remembered the intercom and pressed it. "You guys okay up there?"

A chorus of *yes!* sounded from upstairs, followed by a moment where the only sound was the murmuring of the bus passengers as they spoke into their phones. David looked at his friends, not sure what to expect next—and then the thunder of dozens of feet resounded throughout the bus. David looked up at the ceiling, amazed at the noise and wondering if the passengers were bending the metal supports as they pounded down the aisle and the stairs towards the exit.

Then, as if on cue, the people on the lower level rose to their feet too, their voices rising in an excited babble. Someone pushed open the back door and stepped out. And then, within two minutes, the bus was deserted except for David's family and close friends.

David gaped in the direction the passengers had gone. He'd prepared a speech about how grateful he was for everyone's trust in him, and how honored he was to have been part of their lives, but there was nobody left to hear it.

"What are they doing?" David said.

Callum gave a cough. "Let them go. I've seen it before when a group of people has been in danger and is finally rescued."

"What do you mean?" David said.

Callum made an *I don't know if I can explain* motion with his head. "It's as if they've lived on a desert island this past year. While they developed a camaraderie with their fellow passengers and might promise to keep in touch forever, the moment they arrive home, it becomes clear that, with few exceptions, nobody will."

"For *desert island* read *the Middle Ages*, and you've got it," Darren said.

"Huh," was all David managed to say.

Mom gave him a rueful smile. "They're home. You can't blame them for being happy."

Cassie pulled her phone down from her ear for a second and frowned in the direction of the last few stragglers leaving the bus. "Really? Nobody is even going to say thank you?"

"We brought them to the Middle Ages against their will," David said, "and we returned them to their world, as was their due. On top of which, I'm not the King of England here. I'm nobody, and they owe me nothing."

Cassie shook her head, still disbelieving, and resumed her conversation with her grandfather.

"You're not quite nobody," Anna said. "Still, I can see how few of them will look back on this year and see it as anything more than a long, not-very-pleasant vacation that required them to rough it most of the time." Anna, in fact, had talked to many of the bus passengers on David's behalf, once he'd become convinced that the time had come to return them to Avalon.

Callum tapped his fingers on his thigh. "I don't think they realize we're about to be the cause of an international incident. We just made a busload of people who vanished off the face of the earth for an entire year reappear."

"Not to mention the fact that they disappeared inside a city bus in the middle of a terrorist attack on Cardiff to begin with," Darren said.

"Even if the world has completely fallen apart in our absence, somebody might just notice our return," Callum added.

"It might be worse than that." David found that his brain was starting to function again. He gestured to Cassie, who'd just said her goodbyes with the promise to call again in a few hours. "Our families might be discreet, but how long is it going to take for news of where this bus has been for the last year to make the leap to the internet? With pictures?"

"My granddad knows not to say anything, David," Cassie said.

"Thanks for that," David said, "but this isn't his first rodeo. The others aren't going to be so circumspect."

Anna grimaced. "You could have ordered them not to talk about it."

"One, they don't take orders from me anymore," David said, "and two, not telling the truth could be worse than telling it. How else are forty people going to explain where they've been?"

"I hope some of them don't end up in a mental institution." Cassie rose to her feet and crossed the aisle so she could plug her own charger into an empty outlet and recharge her phone.

Rachel wrinkled her chin. "That's not outside the realm of possibility, you know."

"I can't help that," David said. "The alternative was not to bring them. That didn't seem like much of a choice to me at all."

"Trying to stay under the radar was part of the reason why we did this on Christmas Eve in the first place." Anna gestured to the bright lights of the Tesco outside the bus. Red, green, and white Christmas lights wound around lampposts and were strung across the front of the store, and pictures of red ribbons and wreaths were painted on the store windows in washable paint. "The whole point was that it would take longer for the authorities to notice."

Callum leaned forward to talk to Jane. "Douse the lights?" And as Jane did as he asked, he turned back to the others. "We should be aware that the press might get wind of us almost as quickly."

Anna made a dismissive gesture with her hands. "Maybe the first thing we need to do, now that the others have ditched us, is to find out where we are."

Mark was focused on his phone, and he held up one finger, paging quickly through the screens. "We're in Caernarfon."

Dad, who hadn't spoken yet at all, expelled a burst of air. "That's luck."

Math spoke in Welsh to his father-in-law. "This—this—*place* is Caernarfon? What happened to the sleepy fishing village?"

"King Edward cleared the harbor of Welsh families and built a great big castle to suppress the populace," Mom said tartly. "He brought in a bunch of English settlers to supplant them too."

In addition to building the castle and importing settlers, King Edward had also made sure that his son, Edward II, was born in Caernarfon in 1284, so that he could call him 'the Prince of Wales', in order to preclude any native Welsh prince from claiming the title ever again.

The current Prince of Wales actually had some Welsh in him, thanks to the Tudor dynasty of the sixteenth century when Henry VII, the descendant of Dad's advisor, Tudur, defeated King Richard III at the Battle of Bosworth Field and claimed the throne. Henry Tudor had marched across Wales flying the red dragon flag, the first to do so since Cadwaladr ap Cadwallon in the sixth century. He'd done it as a blatant attempt to garner support in Wales for his bid for the throne, and it had worked.

Math sat back in his seat with a *huh* look on his face. "I bow to your superior wisdom, Mother." He took Anna's hand again. "I can see why you prefer my world to yours, *cariad*."

David was glad to see that Math was unfazed enough by the *traveling* to muster up some humor, though he was also pretty sure that Math meant exactly what he said.

Now David bent down to Jane. "How much gas do we have?"

Jane looked at the gauge. "More than half a tank."

It was essentially the same amount they'd started with. The bus had come to the Middle Ages with a mostly full tank. Some of the gas had evaporated over the course of the year that the bus had sat in the barn, and they'd used more in test runs, occasional starts of the engine, and as an even more occasional source of electricity. But they'd tried to preserve the gas as best they could because there was more to running a bus on biodiesel than simply dumping some used vegetable oil—made in the Middle Ages from olives or walnuts—into the tank. Oils were expensive imports, so people in Britain fried in lard or butter instead.

"We need to get Shane to a hospital," David said. "That's our first priority. Then we can see about what Mom needs."

"Mom has a strong need for Italian food, maybe some coffee, and definitely chocolate," Mom said, speaking of herself in the third person.

"We need to bring some doughnuts home for Bronwen," Anna said.

Having come with David to Wales in 1285—2013 by Avalon reckoning—Bronwen was the first of the time travelers outside of the family to choose to stay in the Middle Ages. She'd married Ieuan, David's former captain, who'd remained David's right-hand man even after David had taken the throne of England. Bronwen was pregnant with her second child, which was why she hadn't come with them to Avalon. In fact, until David talked to her about the possibility of *traveling* with him, Bronwen hadn't told anyone but Ieuan about this baby.

Bronwen had experienced multiple miscarriages since giving birth to Catrin four years ago. Now, however, she was already four months pregnant, so there was real hope that she could keep the baby this time.

David looked around at the members of this small group who'd come on the journey with him: Math and Anna, Mom and Dad, Darren and Rachel, Callum and Cassie, and Mark Jones. His throat thickened with emotion just looking at them—at how much he loved and trusted them, and the amazing fact that the love and trust was returned.

Sensing what he was feeling—like he had ever been good at hiding from her what was going on inside him—Mom gave him a smile. "We're good, David. Let's get to work."

Callum shifted in his seat in order to plug in his cell phone and jack, and then all those who hadn't yet done so followed suit. David shared a rueful look with Dad, who didn't have a phone either. Even Anna and Mom had them, thanks to the purchases made by Cassie and Callum last year.

"Do you have any extra?" David said to Callum.

"No, but we'll get you one." Callum grinned as he jerked his head towards the Tesco, which proclaimed itself to be a superstore. Then he turned on his phone. "This'll be interesting if someone has my number on a watch list."

"If we're discovered, it'll be my fault more than yours." Mark Jones was rapidly scrolling through a series of screens David couldn't see from where he was standing. "It's harder to hide my presence from my phone. I'd use my laptop, but I can't reach Tesco's wifi from here."

"Er, David?" Brian, one of the bus passengers, had come up the stairs at the back of the bus, and he stood on the top step, shifting nervously from foot-to-foot.

"What's up?" David glanced outside the window. Most—if not all—of the bus passengers who'd left the bus in such a hurry were still mingling in the parking lot. David checked the time on Anna's phone. It had been only a few minutes since they'd left, though it seemed like a lot longer than that to David.

The passengers had had time to make some more calls, stomp around in the snow a bit, and discover where they were, the same as David's family and friends.

And maybe have second thoughts about their abrupt departure.

"Er ... well ... my sister isn't answering her mobile ... and ... well ... I don't really have any place to go. A bunch of us don't, you know ... I mean ..." His voice trailed off into inarticulateness.

Darla, appeared behind Brian. She was one of the bus passengers who'd spent the whole year at Caerphilly grousing about how much she hated the Middle Ages and refusing, to the best of her ability, to participate. Along with her husband and teenage daughter, Darla had responded to David's decision to take everyone back to Avalon with *it's about time!* In David's conversations with his mother, he hadn't listed fear as one of the reasons to return. Yet for one of the bus passengers to take matters into his or her own hands and attempt to force Anna or Mom—or David himself—to time travel had remained a genuine possibility. Lee had done it, as had Marty a few years before him.

"My brother isn't answering either." She turned her cell phone screen outward so David could see it. "The mobile lines are busy or not working."

"It's Wales on Christmas Eve," Mark Jones said. "They're over-subscribed."

Darla shot him a sour look for interrupting. "All of our credit cards are probably cancelled, and it isn't like we have enough cash for a hotel." She glared at David. "I hate Wales. It was the worst mistake we ever made deciding to visit Cardiff on the weekend."

"So you've said," Mom said in a low voice as she gazed at her shoes, "about a thousand times. If not more."

Dad's lips twitched, and David wanted to kick his mother for almost making him laugh.

"How can I help with that?" David said. "I don't even own a cell phone myself—nor do I have any British pounds."

Darla's face twisted into a parody of innocence—eyebrows raised, eyes wide, and a fixed smile. "You have gems and coins. I know you do." The last sentence came out with an edge. She'd managed to hide her underlying anger and resentment for approximately three seconds.

"You want money too?" Anna said.

David didn't share Anna's surprise at Darla's audacity. He was beginning to think that taking the whole lot of them back to Avalon would have been the best idea ever even if he'd died in the process. They didn't deserve to stay if they couldn't see what medieval Wales had to offer.

"It isn't like any of this is our fault." Darla kept up the stare.

Callum dropped his phone into the inside pocket of his suit jacket and headed down the aisle towards the exit. "I'll deal with this."

David decided not to stop him. "Thanks, Callum."

The bus passengers had always respected Callum more than David, regardless of what station David held in the Middle Ages. Callum was British himself, an MI-5 agent, and spoke with authority. Many of them had never been able to see David as anything more than a punk kid.

"Is he going to use his own money?" Jane asked.

"Yes, but it's all right," Cassie said. "Callum and I figured this might happen. We have an account that won't have been cancelled and has plenty of money in it. We can pay to put everyone up." She looked at David. "They're used to relying on you, even as they resent you. We can't just cut them loose."

"I had no intention of cutting them loose," David said, exasperated. "They were the ones who left the bus as fast as their feet would take them off it."

"That was before they discovered they were in Caernarfon instead of Cardiff," Mom said dryly.

"Why Caernarfon, do you think?" Anna said.

"It's closer to Aber." Dad turned in his seat to look out the window, though the bright lights from Tesco's parking lot prevented anyone from getting a good look at the landscape.

Dad wasn't the only one who was pleased at the news of their location. David knew north Wales better than south, in large part because his early years in Wales had been spent here. At that time, Gwynedd had been all that his father controlled.

Plus, as they'd come in, he'd spied a McDonalds on the other side of the highway, and his mouth watered at the thought of a double cheeseburger, milk shake, and fries. Not that eating French fries was such a big deal anymore. Mom and Anna had brought more than the bus back to the Middle Ages a year ago. The first crop of potatoes had been harvested, and although the vast majority were being saved for seed for next year to really get the crop going and he wasn't the potato lover Callum was, he'd been afforded a few bites.

"Why does there have to be a reason?" Shane's dad, Carl, said. "We made it. That's what matters."

"Yes, but in the past we've ended up in a place where—" Mom paused, frowning at how to explain it to someone who might not share her faith.

"Where we were meant to be," Anna said, and when Carl opened his mouth to protest again, she hurried on, "I know that sounds stupid because where we end up has to be where we were meant to be, but it's more that it's the place where we make a difference. Or where things work out in an unexpected, but good, way."

Carl looked almost offended. "It seems like you're asking a lot."

David couldn't argue with that, since it was asking a lot. He would have preferred not to have come through on the wrong side of the highway, but if nobody had died as a result, he could handle things being a bit hairy for a few minutes.

Mom took up the explanation. "Last time, Anna and I ended up in the middle-of-nowhere Oregon, which would have been very disconcerting if Cassie and Callum hadn't been only a few miles away, spending Thanksgiving with Cassie's grandfather."

"Oh." Carl started to nod. "I get it now. That makes sense."

"Often—maybe even usually—we don't know about that good thing until we've been there a while," Mom continued. "Anna and I had to walk quite a way through the woods in the dark and cadge a ride from a total stranger before we found Cassie and Callum out looking for us."

Mark raised a hand. "MI-5's sensors should have detected us when came in. I suggest that we have sat here too long."

"I don't disagree." David bent to look for Callum out the window. He was glad Jane had turned off the lights, though the lights in the parking lot were bright enough that anyone looking could be wondering why a Cardiff bus was sitting in the middle of the Caernarfon Tesco's parking lot with a crowd of people outside of it.

"I know why we're here." Rachel said, copying Mark by raising her hand as if she was in school. "It's because of my dad. He's a physician with an office near Bangor. While he isn't an oncologist, he has the equipment and the skill to take care of Meg up to and including performing a biopsy."

Darren looked like he was the only one to whom that was not news.

"He has his own full-service women's clinic," Rachel added. "His name is Abraham Wolff."

"How will he feel about helping us out on Christmas Eve?" Jane said from the driver's seat.

Shane had crawled into her lap and was now curled into her, fast asleep. The initial signs of childhood leukemia were somewhat nonspecific, and included fatigue, fever, loss of appetite, weight loss, and night sweats. Shane's symptoms had progressed to swollen lymph nodes, bruising for no reason, nosebleeds, joint pain, and occasional trouble breathing. It was the speed at which he'd moved from the first collection of symptoms to the second that had prompted David to act today. A child could die of leukemia in months if un-treated. Shane no longer had months.

"We're Jewish," Rachel said. "Hanukkah ended on the eighteenth."

"And what about your mother?" Jane glanced down at her son's sleeping form.

"My mother divorced him when I was little."

Jane released a burst of air that was almost a laugh. "Understood."

That was good enough for David too. "Do you want simply to show up on his doorstep, or do you want to call him first?"

Rachel looked at Darren, who spread his hands wide and said, "How many bombshells do you want to drop on your father all at once?"

"You mean, which will get the worst reaction—the fact that I spent the last year in the Middle Ages, or the fact that I'm in love with a black man?"

Darren shrugged, apparently finding the question amusing, though another man might not have. "Your call."

"I'll ring him," Rachel said. "He'll need to meet us at his clinic anyway, so it'll save time if we go straight there after we leave Shane and his family at the hospital."

Darren stood up and held out his hand to Rachel, who took it to rise to her feet. He looked back at the others. "Give us a minute."

David lifted a hand, giving permission, though since Darren wasn't his subordinate here, it wasn't his to give. As far as David was concerned, they could take all the time they needed. He didn't doubt that his mother would be in good hands with Rachel's father. David, of course, had known that Rachel's father was a doctor with a clinic near Bangor, but he hadn't mentioned it to anyone else because the odds of appearing in his vicinity had seemed infinitesimal to David. He should have known better.

Then Callum reboarded the bus. Snow dusted his coat and hair, and he brushed it off in the shelter of the doorway before coming all the way up the steps and making his way down the aisle towards the others.

David lifted his chin. "Are we good?"

Callum released a little snort of laughter. "One of the local inns, the Black Boar, had a block of cancellations due to a wedding that's been called off. They were desperate, and I didn't tell them that I was too, so we got a great deal on rooms and meals for three days for everyone who wanted them."

"Do I need to drive them there?" Jane said.

"Buses have been known to drive through the streets of Caernarfon, though it isn't recommended. Regardless, the passengers decided to walk. First breaths of freedom and all that." Callum gave a slight tsk. "It is my impression that they want to get as far away from us and the bus as possible on the off chance that time traveling happens again. They don't want to be caught up in it."

Cassie put her nose up to the window, her hands cupped around her eyes so she could see better. "They're really gone? Just like that?"

"Just like that," Callum said.

4

Meg

Callum shrugged out of his coat and hung it over the back of a chair to dry, giving something of a self-deprecating smile as he did so. "I gave them my mobile number. We may hear from some of them again."

"Yeah, you can bet we will," Meg said, not in an undertone this time and still unforgiving.

David laughed.

Jane stood, Shane cradled in her arms. "He needs the loo. We'll be right back."

"Okay," David said.

They left the bus, heading for the Tesco, just as Rachel and Darren re-entered and sat opposite Meg.

"Everything's okay," Rachel said. "Dad will meet us within the hour at his clinic."

"I'm grateful that your father will see me on Christmas Eve." Meg leaned across the aisle. "But what happens after that? What if it really is cancer?" She could hardly believe she'd only thought to discuss this now, after they'd already come to Avalon.

Rachel had been sitting sideways in her seat, but she turned to face Meg. "That's what I came along for, among other things. Between my father and me, we can perform tests and navigate around any hospital. The rest we'll have to figure out once we have the test results in hand."

"And if I need treatment?" Meg said. "David can't stay more than a few days. England needs him."

"I know," David said, proving he was listening, though he'd been staring out the window at the falling snow as if he wasn't paying attention.

"But I can and will," Llywelyn said, "and Rachel too, for as long as you need her."

Meg slowly nodded. "Oh, I get it. When the treatment is over, I can take everyone back myself." She hesitated. "Unless I can't. Unless I'm dead." She stared stolidly ahead, across the aisle and out the window, though there wasn't much to see since the breath of so many people had steamed up the glass. While Meg watched, Cassie reached out a finger and drew a heart.

"That's only one of many reasons why I'm here too, Mom," Anna said.

"And Lili stayed behind at Dinas Bran to take care of all the kids," David said, "though she's plenty mad at me about that fact."

Llywelyn pulled Meg to him and kissed her temple. "I know this isn't easy, *cariad*. I also know that you're far more afraid of losing Anna or Dafydd than you are of dying yourself. But we're *here*, against all odds, and now isn't the time for worry. If there is one time

I agree with Dafydd even when he's being obstinate and righteous, it's now. Shane had to come to Avalon; you did too. We accept the fate we are given."

As had most of the time travelers, Llywelyn had taken to calling the modern world by its medieval name, Avalon, and Meg had become resigned to the fact that, while in medieval Wales, it was best not to refer to the twenty-first century as anything other than the realm of Arthurian legend. Time traveling—or rather, universe hopping, which was a more accurate description of what they did—wasn't something the medieval mind could accept. It wasn't something the modern mind could accept either, but at least in Avalon, people from novelists to physicists had played around with the idea for centuries.

In addition, because what they were doing was shifting universes rather than actual time traveling, they didn't have to worry about changing the future in the place they were going. David could scatter as much medieval gold around the modern world as he wanted to, or take as much of whatever he wanted from Avalon back to the Middle Ages. Each future had its own trajectory, and what happened in one world had no effect on the other.

As far as they knew, anyway.

Of course, they still didn't know why the *traveling* happened, or how. Meg had learned to live with the uncertainty. Refusing to believe in magic, David shrugged off all questions, saying he didn't know the mechanism and, until he did, he wasn't going to make any declarations at all. It was what it was, and words like magic, science, or God's will were merely filler until they knew the truth.

Which they probably never would.

Even Anna, despite fighting tooth and nail against it at first, had come to accept that Avalon was as good a name as any for the twenty-first century. Since many people in the Middle Ages thought David was the return of King Arthur anyway, it was one of the few ways of talking about who they were and what they did that made sense and wouldn't get them labeled as heretics or witches.

Meg put her chin in her hand, watching the falling snow being flicked away by the wipers, which Jane had left on low while she was gone. Anna and Math got up to stretch their legs, so David took Anna's vacant seat beside her, his clipboard back in his hand and sucking on the end of his pen—one clearly borrowed from a bus passenger since it was a standard blue ball point.

"Who among your people did you tell that you were going to Avalon?" Meg said.

Only half listening, David flipped the paper over, revealing a list thirty items long, which, when Meg looked closer, proved to be items that David intended to look up on the internet. Chief among them were the directions for making a gravity cell battery.

"I told as few people as I could," David said. "I sent everyone I could home for Christmas, with the excuse that I was going to be with my family so they should be with theirs."

"What about Bevyn? Why isn't he here?" Meg said.

"He's keeping Anglesey safe for me," David said. "He can chew me out later for my dangerously reckless behavior."

"And William?"

William de Bohun was David's squire, who showed no signs of growing out of his hero-worship of David or his absolute belief that David was King Arthur returned. William was also one of the up and coming young nobles in England, among a cohort of men and women in their late teens and early twenties who would replace their fathers and mothers in the English House of Lords one day. In fact, it really should have been called the House of Lords and Ladies, but David wasn't going to push the minor point having won the major victory of including women in the first place.

David smiled. "He protested the loudest when I ordered him home, but even he gave way. He's in Hereford with his parents. If I hadn't convinced him I'd be fine without him, he would have been first in line to come with us. He, too, is going to be ticked when he finds out where we went today." David finally looked up from his clipboard. "It isn't as if I mentioned it to the pope, if that's what you're really asking."

"Have you heard anything more from him?" Meg said, because yes, that was what she'd really been asking.

"Archbishop Romeyn remains—ha, ha—" David broke off to laugh at the similar pronunciation of the two words, "—in Italy waiting to learn the details of this crusade the pope wants me to go on. I'm expecting an announcement after Epiphany."

"That would make sense," Meg said. "The pope often issues decrees about then."

"That's because it's winter, and travel is difficult, so if the people the decree affects don't hear about it until spring, it's miles too late to do anything about it." David bit his lip. "I miss Peckham already."

John Peckham, the Archbishop of Canterbury, had died in early December. He'd been instrumental in putting David on the throne of England, and his replacement was another headache David would have to face after Christmas. David had his own candidates, but the canons of Canterbury cathedral would want their say, as would the pope.

Meg contemplated her son, who'd gone back to his list. While on one hand, it was perfectly normal for him to be worked up about *traveling* to the twenty-first century, she read more than that overt concern in his face and posture. He was agitated, and his intensity—never low to begin with—was roiling off of him in waves.

She took a stab at what was bothering him. "You're the King of England, David, amazing as that seems. You don't have to do anything you don't want to."

"Don't I?" David gave a little laugh. "You're right that this thing with the pope and the French king has me pretty worked up. I don't want to go on Crusade this year—next year—ever. I don't want to leave England at all, but I'm particularly worried about being forced to leave out of an obligation to the Church that I don't personally feel, but which I might have to fulfill anyway. I'm hoping that between Romeyn and Geneville, they can figure out a way to get me out of it."

"King Philip of France might not want to go either, and he—more than you—will do what best serves his own interests," Meg said.

"What Geoffrey needs to figure out is how your mutual interests align and a way to present an alternative plan to the pope—
one, in particular, that keeps the peace between England and France."

Geoffrey de Geneville had been a confidant of King Edward, David's predecessor, and David had considered him an ally only since the bombing of Canterbury Castle by Lee earlier that year. Geoffrey was currently in Paris, attempting to negotiate with the King of France. Given that King Philip had attacked England's shores at Hythe with the explicit intent of undermining David's rule—or even overthrowing him—Philip had some apologizing to do. So far, it hadn't happened.

"You don't have to solve all the world's problems today, you know," Meg said. "It will go spinning on even after we get off it, and whether or not you ever bring electricity to the Middle Ages."

"I know," David said, "but the fact that I was coming here was why I was pushing so hard on some things I might otherwise have left alone for a while longer."

"What is your plan for getting back?" Meg said. "That's another question I can't believe I never asked you."

David grunted what was almost a laugh. "I really have no idea. But I can tell you one thing—it isn't going to be in this bus."

5

Bridget

"**D**id you see that?" Goronwy said.

Bridget knew her mouth had fallen open, but she couldn't help it. One of her girlfriends back in Cardiff, before the time traveling, used to gape theatrically at any remotely surprising news. For a long while, Bridget had been convinced she did it on purpose, because it wasn't possible for anyone to be shocked as often as she was. Eventually, however, Bridget decided her friend really was as innocent and (quite frankly) dim as she acted.

"I saw it," Ieuan said, a little grimly. "Now maybe my heart can settle back into my chest."

"I don't believe it." Goronwy's hand was on the top of his head as he held the binoculars to his eyes with the other. He was still staring at the place where the bus had driven into the cliff wall.

"How can you not believe it?" Justin said. "You have been to Avalon, my lord. Did you think God's grace would fail our king now?"

"No. No, of course not." Goronwy dropped his arm.

Peter stood stoically next to the others, his arms folded across his chest. When he'd stepped off the bus, Bridget had gaped at him too and asked what he was doing.

"Staying," was all he'd said, which was typical of him. Getting him to say anything at all, especially when in the company of others, was like pulling teeth.

From the start, Peter had been her liaison with Samuel, Callum's sheriff. In the first few weeks after her arrival in Shrewsbury, Peter had made himself indispensable, building shelves and tables, helping her to carry and organize the wool, and encouraging her plans for selling her wares. In return, she'd fed him, and she'd thought they'd become friends.

Once she'd become an established businesswoman, however, he started to disappear for days on end, often at the behest of Samuel, Callum, or David. During the disaster at Canterbury, he'd been with David, and he'd been gone for nearly a month. When he returned, while he was as polite as ever, he stopped spending any real time with her. She hadn't been able to figure out why, and it had taken her weeks of careful coaxing this autumn to convince him not to leave her shop within thirty seconds of walking into it.

Kissing him had been a mad impulse that if she'd stopped to think about before she acted she wouldn't have done. At the very least, she'd assumed (had she stopped to think) that it wouldn't have had any consequences until Peter returned from Avalon. They would both have had time to think about what the kiss meant to them, and if they wanted to be more to each other than friends.

But now he stood right beside her, as usual telling her nothing about what he was thinking. She wanted to assume that he'd stayed behind because the kiss meant something to him, but she could be totally and completely wrong. She found herself seriously annoyed with him, though that was unfair since it was *she* who'd kissed *him*.

Bridget had only done it in the first place because she'd been angry. Back on the bus, she'd been having an innocent conversation with Meg, who'd noticed her unhappiness and thought it had to do with whether or not they were going to crash into the cliff face and die. "It's going to be okay," Meg had said.

"Do you think I'm worried about this not working?" Bridget had shifted in her seat, tugging on the thighs of her jeans to adjust them. Her clothes hung more loosely on her than perhaps they had when she'd arrived in the Middle Ages, but she was still far too curvy for fashion in the twenty-first century. "That's not it at all. I'm not looking forward to living there again."

Meg pulled up one leg, probably marveling (in contrast to Bridget) at the freedom wearing pants gave her, and twisted in the seat so she was looking directly down the bus at Bridget. "Why not?"

"Why would I be?"

"Hot showers," Meg said.

Bridget had managed a laugh at that. "You can only take so many of those."

"Every day, actually." Meg gestured to her clothing. "Getting to wear pants."

"I look better in dresses."

Meg had pursed her lips, unable to deny what was an obvious truth. Bridget had suitors lined up around the block looking to court her, though she herself had never given a single one the time of day, even if they didn't seem to mind her size fourteen hips. In truth, not only did the value of being stick thin not exist in the Middle Ages, but the concept of overweight applied usually only to rich men who drank so much wine they got huge and suffered from gout.

Then Mark Jones, the former computer expert at MI-5 and currently Callum's chief supply officer, had sat himself in the first row of seats that faced front, his laptop case beside him. He too had lost much of the pudge that had sat around his middle upon his arrival in the Middle Ages and had even learned to use a sword to defend himself. He might never be a warrior—or want to be one—but like Bridget, he'd discovered over the last year that his skills and brain were adaptable, even to a place without electricity. He'd become more than a computer whiz.

Bridget had swung around to speak to him. "What about you? Are you looking forward to living in the twenty-first century again?"

Mark had been focused on buckling his seatbelt, but he'd looked up at her question. "Me? I'm not staying. Didn't you know?"

Bridget had stared at him. "What? We're all staying. That's the whole point."

"That may be your point, and what David told you, but it certainly isn't my plan," Mark said. "I'm coming to help David get what he needs, but then I'm returning with him."

"Why do you get to do that, and I don't?" she'd said.

"I told him I'd come with him in the first place only if I didn't have to stay," Mark said.

Bridget's eyes flashed. "You *told* David that? And he agreed?"

Mark shrugged.

Her lips in a tight line, Bridget had turned to look at David, who had been standing at the front of the bus talking in low tones with Callum and Peter. Bridget suddenly realized that none of them were staying in the twenty-first century, though nobody had thought to mention that fact to her until then.

Now, standing beside Peter with her heart in her throat, Bridget had no idea what to say to him. She'd kissed him, and he'd left the bus. And now the bus was gone, and the two of them were left in the Middle Ages. *What had she* done?

She put out a tentative hand to Peter. "I'm sorry—I mean—if you—" she stopped, knowing she was babbling, and then said with a rush, "I'm sorry you won't get to see your parents."

"It was my choice," he said.

Bridget eyed him, hoping he'd add to the comment. He'd planned to return to the twenty-first century and now—because of her—he found himself left behind. She opened her mouth, trying to think of a way to ask if he wanted to talk about the kiss, though that would surely be the most awkward conversation in history, especially standing on this bluff above the road with Ieuan, Goronwy, and Justin.

But before she could speak, Peter said, "After you left, David asked me if I would be willing to keep an eye on things here, and I said that would be okay with me."

Only 'okay' didn't sound very promising. "Did you ask Darren to talk to your parents?"

Peter nodded.

Bridget bit her lip. "At least they'll know you're alive."

"It might be better if they didn't."

Bridget shook her head. "I'm pretty sure not knowing the truth is worse than knowing it—especially since you *are* alive, even if you can't come home." Bridget already knew that he had one older sister, who was married with two kids, which was good. If he'd been an only child, it would have been much harder for him to stay away.

Peter didn't answer for a second. His eyes were on the other men, who were now conferring among themselves, probably deciding momentous issues of the realm. Then he spoke softly, "I could have stayed on the bus."

With a swell of emotion, both for her and for him, Bridget felt for his hand, and he surprised her by not only allowing her to take it, but to keep it. The action gave her the courage to ask him another question. "Is this trip the reason you stopped talking to me this autumn?"

That got Peter to actually look at her. "Is that what you think happened?"

"After Canterbury, you hardly spoke to me unless I made you."

Peter closed his eyes for a second. "You were going back, and I was never going to see you again."

It was a relief to finally have that bit of truth spoken. "David had already conceived of this plan? That's not what he told everyone."

"I saw it in his eyes every time he talked about one of the bus passengers. About the deaths of Mike and Noah. About Lee," Peter said. "Whatever he told us, or told himself, this has been a long time coming."

"Why did David want you to stay behind?"

Peter lifted one shoulder. "He had a bad feeling that he shouldn't take all of us to Avalon. That one of us at least would be needed here. I was relieved myself—up until the moment the bus disappeared into that cliff face. Now who knows what kind of trouble Darren's getting into without me." He shook his head. "I hate even to think."

That was more words strung together in a row than Bridget had heard Peter say in months.

"Why was the king relieved?" Justin, David's red-headed captain, had approached without Bridget noticing. All she could think about was her hand, which was still engulfed in Peter's much larger one.

"He's worried about what could happen here while he's gone," Peter said.

Justin looked affronted. "He doesn't trust us."

"I'm sure that isn't it," Bridget said.

The rain continued to fall, but Bridget was reluctant to move, even though there wasn't anything more to do or see. Besides, if they left, she'd have to let go of Peter's hand in order to mount one of the horses, of which she supposed she could have her pick, since there were so many extra, now that everyone who'd ridden in on them had gone. She felt the same reluctance in the men, since none of them were making any moves to leave either. It was as if they were held in suspended animation, waiting for the bus to return, even though they knew it wouldn't. At least not today.

Then hoof beats sounded on the road from Llangollen. Everyone swung around to see who was coming. A member of Dinas Bran's garrison reined his horse at the top of the road and dismounted in order to run forward to stand in front of Ieuan. "The queen sends word to King Dafydd—" He looked wildly around.

Ieuan glowered at the man, though David's absence was hardly the messenger's fault. "He isn't here at the moment. What is it?"

The man ducked his head. "Your sister thought that might be the case. She asks that you—all of you—return to the castle. The English ambassador to France has come in search of King Dafydd."

"Geoffrey de Geneville?" Ieaun said. "He's supposed to be in Paris."

"He was traveling with an emissary from the French king. They were ambushed on the road not five miles from Wales, on the high road from Shrewsbury. And—" The man shifted from one foot to the other.

"And what?" Ieuan said.

The man looked pained. "If you could please come with me, the queen can explain everything."

"At once," Ieuan said.

The men dispersed. Bridget took one last look back at the place where the bus had disappeared, but since Peter was still holding her hand, and he was plainly intent on walking to where the horses had been left, she went with him rather than let go. "There's nothing more to see here anyway," she said under her breath, not necessarily for anyone's ears.

For all that she'd founded her own business in Shrewsbury, Bridget felt herself to be an unlikely candidate for someone who would have done well in the Middle Ages. She hadn't been educated at Cambridge like Callum nor had she been in graduate school in history or archaeology like Meg and Bronwen. A bunch of the others had been good in school. She could have told that just by looking at them, even before she learned that Rachel was a doctor or Darren, with years of night school, had worked his way from being a bobby on the street to MI-5.

She didn't have a university education. Her parents had urged her to quit school at sixteen and get a job, and she hadn't struggled against their wishes. School hadn't been so much fun that she saw the point in continuing with it. Nobody in her family had ever gone to university, and it seemed silly of her to think that she would succeed at it either, especially when nobody else could see the worth of it or imagine her working a job that required a degree.

Her first job, then, had been in a handwork shop in Monmouth, not far from where she was born and raised on the English side of the Wye River. She'd worked there for three years before landing a job at a much bigger store in Cardiff, where she'd been for the last five.

She was good at what she did; she knew that. She understood wool, which was more than she could say for ninety-nine percent of twenty-firsters (as she called them), who thought the only important thing to know about wool was that their jumper had just shrunk in the wash.

But she didn't speak medieval Welsh, old English, or anything better than schoolgirl French. She certainly didn't know Flemish, which would have been very useful once she set up her own shop in Shrewsbury, since the Flems (as she called them) seemed to have cornered the market in medieval textiles.

She'd had a job in Cardiff that she enjoyed for the most part. She'd found it inherently satisfying to find the perfect yarn, the perfect fabric, or the perfect pattern for a customer to make her happy, but she'd never imagined how much better it might be to make a difference to so many people. It was a heady feeling, and one that she hadn't wanted to give up, even if Bridget had never intended to start an entirely new industry in the medieval world—nor provide a central spot for Callum's spy network to meet.

When David had approached her about returning to the modern world, her first reaction had been to jump for joy, just on principle. She'd started cataloging all the things she was going to do (most of which involved food), but then the more she'd thought about it, the more her stomach had twisted in dismay. She'd made a special trip up to Shrewsbury Castle where David had been staying just to tell him she'd changed her mind and wouldn't go.

But then David had looked at her with that puppy dog gaze of his that implied sympathy and superior wisdom all at the same time, and she'd bowed to his request after all.

With her hand warm in Peter's, Bridget told herself that maybe it was time she stopped making these kinds of mistakes. For practically the first time in her life, she had listened to her own heart instead of letting other people's ideas about what was best rule her.

Getting off the bus had been the right thing to do.

6

Bridget

Dinas Bran was an enormous castle, spread across the top of a hill a thousand feet above the valley floor and the village of Llangollen. Back in her old life, on holiday with a few girlfriends, Bridget had hiked up to it. At the time, it had been impossible for her to envision an actual castle from the ruins that remained. Lord Math (Bridget couldn't think of him as anything other than 'lord', even if she could call Anna by her first name) had rebuilt the castle after it was destroyed by the English and made it twice as fine, according to those who'd seen the old one, with a great hall, guest quarters, barracks, a stable, and two kitchens.

However, Bridget found the lack of running water unforgivable. She would never, ever, get used to latrines, no matter how long she lived in the Middle Ages. Just last night, Bridget had drunk a little too much in anticipation of their departure today, and she'd begged David to put the invention of toilets and showers at the top of his agenda. Having drunk almost nothing himself, he'd laughed, saying that they weren't that hard, and he'd see to it.

And now he was gone. Arrogant little bugger.

Stretching the full length of the summit of the mountain, the castle was surrounded by a high curtain wall and a series of ditches and ramparts dating from Celtic times. Anyone who approached the castle had to wend his way through the ramparts in order to reach the gate. Even Bridget, who'd grown up in Avalon, had no trouble imagining archers shooting down at her from the top of the walls on both sides. She craned her neck to see them but couldn't in the fading light.

"Don't worry. They're there," Peter said from beside her.

Another good sign as to Peter's intentions was that he hadn't left her side yet. Even when Justin slowed his horse to confer with Peter about who might be responsible for the attack, Peter hadn't abandoned her and had even included her in the conversation. Of course, it was just business, and since her shop was the clearinghouse for news from the whole of western England, she might have as much to say on the subject as he.

Though she didn't. She had no idea who might have ambushed an emissary from France. David had his nobles pretty well under control as far as Bridget knew, and while she didn't know the Welsh situation as well, she'd thought Llywelyn did too. Apparently, she'd thought wrong.

Bridget tagged along with the others, uncertain of her right to listen in on the conversation with the ambassador, but she figured if someone didn't want her there, they'd tell her. Peter had helped her dismount, and though he didn't take her hand again, he didn't object to her company either. They entered Math's receiving room behind Goronwy and Ieuan, though Bridget hung back against the wall. She still wore her modern clothing and thought it best that she didn't call attention to herself.

Geoffrey de Geneville paced impatiently before the fire, while the heavily pregnant Queen of England tried to appease him.

Though Bridget had seen Geoffrey de Geneville only once, she'd heard about him in great detail from some of the other twenty-firsters. Tall, thin, and white-haired, with fine clothes and a haughty manner, he was everything a medieval lord should be. He'd lost his heir not long ago, however, and Bridget's impression of him was that he wore his grief around him all the time like a cloak.

"My lady, I must see the king!" Geoffrey was saying at the very moment Ieuan pushed open the door.

"He's gone to Avalon, Geneville." Ieaun didn't even look at Geoffrey as he spoke but strode towards his sister. He caught her hand and kissed the back of it. Then he glanced at his wife, Bronwen, who sat a few paces away from Lili's chair, her hands folded in her lap. She'd been looking at the floor while Geoffrey had been speaking, but she looked up at Ieuan's approach, her eyes flashing. He gave her a nod, which Bridget interpreted to mean *all is well*. And Bridget supposed it was—from a certain point of view.

Meanwhile, Geoffrey's face had transformed into a look of stunned surprise, and he took a hesitant step forward. "What did you say?"

Ieuan smiled grimly and didn't repeat himself. He'd spoken loudly such that Geoffrey had to have heard him. "It was an urgent matter, which the king could not put off any longer. I can't say when he will return, but it will be as soon as he can." He made a dismissive gesture. "It should make no difference. We should treat whatever is the matter here the same as if a crisis occurred in Windsor while he was at Canterbury."

"He chose to leave at the Christmas feast in hopes that it was during these few days that he would be the least missed," Lili said. "I suppose we can't be surprised that something like this would happen the moment he turns his back."

Geoffrey barked a laugh that held no trace of amusement. "King David left for the same reason King Philip chose to send Jacques and me on this journey this week of all weeks—out of the hope that we'd be less conspicuous."

Lili added, for the newcomers' benefit, "The emissary's name was Jacques de Molier. Geoffrey reports that he is dead."

Bridget started at that. Up until now, she'd been on the receiving end of news and information, but she hadn't ever encountered a situation as earth-shattering as this. She knew, as did everyone else in the room, that the death of the emissary of France on English soil was only a step or two from open war.

Then Lili gestured to her brother. "Please tell Ieuan what you remember of the attack." Lili might be female and pregnant, but her right to be heard in this conference was undisputed. Goronwy, too, had moved to stand near her chair as an indication of his support.

David might be gone, but his authority—and thus hers—remained intact.

Geoffrey threw out a hand in a sign of impatience. "Not enough! At Molier's insistence, we rode in his carriage, which I despised, mind you. With only some five miles to go, we were looking forward to food and warmth, but then one of the men at the head of the company shouted a warning. I stuck my head out of the window to see what was the matter. Upwards of a dozen men had emerged from a nearby wood. They wore black masks and no lord's colors.

"I tried to hear what my guards were shouting to each other, but Molier was babbling away about barbaric English roads and how he'd warned King Philip not to trust King David. Not to speak ill of the dead, but his hands were fluttering! At the very instant I turned to him to tell him to be quiet, the carriage's horses reared and bolted. As they did, one of the rear wheels came off entirely, which I know only because I saw the scene afterwards. Then the carriage overturned, and I hit my head. That's all I remember."

Geoffrey raised his hands and dropped them in a gesture of helplessness. "I awoke alone in the wreckage of the carriage. I dragged myself from it only to find the carnage on the road. All of my men were dead, along with Molier himself and the three Frenchmen he'd brought with him. A surviving horse cropped the grass in an adjacent field, still with saddle and bridle. I mounted him and rode in haste here."

Ieuan had listened to Geoffrey's story with a finger to his lips, and now he dropped his hand. "A very bad business. Did you check all the bodies? There were no other survivors?"

"That's sort of where this gets worse," Lili said, with a rueful smile.

"Worse?" Ieuan said.

Geoffrey grunted. "We were traveling with James Stewart, who was among the riders. I heard his voice above the initial fray, but neither he nor his horse were in evidence when I awoke."

Bridget took a step forward. "James Stewart, the High Steward of Scotland?"

Up until now, she hadn't said anything. It wasn't her place, but the words had burst from her. Her ancestry was Scottish, and she knew more about Scottish history than English—or Welsh for that matter. Both in Avalon and here, James Stewart had managed to retain his title, even though he'd supported Robert Bruce's claim to the Scottish throne over its current occupant, John Balliol.

"The same," Lili said, with a nod in Bridget's direction, hopefully indicating that she hadn't been too out of line in speaking, "not to mention the fact that he's Earl Callum's friend. The hope, of course, is that James got away, but I would have thought he would have made his way here by now if he had."

Geoffrey shook his head. "It strikes me as more likely that he was captured. If he were injured, these bandits would have chased him down and murdered him too. They had no compunction about killing all of my men! And Molier's!"

"Why was James Stewart riding with you?" Goronwy asked Geoffrey.

"Under other circumstances, it would not be my place to say." Geoffrey grimaced. "England and Scotland have been allied recently, and I would hate to undermine that hard-earned trust, but—" He broke off.

"Now is not the time to equivocate," Lili said. "Tell them what you told me."

"James Stewart heard a rumor that John Balliol had sent an embassage to Pope Boniface regarding the current conflagration between England and France. Balliol desires to underscore that Scotland does not support King David's more rebellious tendencies and to assure the pope that Scotland remains steadfastly obedient to the Church."

Goronwy's eyes narrowed. "King Dafydd has heard nothing of this from his own ambassador, Archbishop Romeyn."

Geoffrey spread his hands wide. "I understand that Stewart's knowledge of this ploy came from the Scottish end, not the Italian."

Ieuan scoffed a laugh. "Is Balliol hoping to take Carlisle while Dafydd is on Crusade? He prostrates himself before the pope now in the hope that Boniface turns a blind eye to war on England later?"

"It sounds absurd on the face of it," Geoffrey said, "but we already knew that Balliol is allied with certain interests in France—men who are unhappy with the way King Philip himself has encroached on his vassals' lands."

Goronwy gave a growl of disgust, deep in his throat. "And now Stewart is missing, and Molier is dead." He was speaking French with Geoffrey, a language they both spoke perfectly.

"As we speak, Cadwallon and Samuel are leading companies in pursuit of the bandits," Lili said. "More men, led by Hywel, stand guard over the ambush site and the bodies of the dead."

Peter stirred beside Bridget. Samuel, as the Sheriff of Shrewsbury, was his direct boss. Callum had promoted the former English soldier to oversee his lands in his absence. But since Samuel's responsibilities were far broader than police work, more often than not, investigations fell to Peter. Back in Avalon, Peter had been a member of the peacekeeping forces in Afghanistan and the Sudan, where roadside ambushes had been common. This attack had occurred on the high road from Shrewsbury in medieval England but, despite the transposition in time and place, perhaps wasn't so different as all that.

Of the other men Lili had mentioned, Cadwallon was King Llywelyn's captain, another medieval man not included in the adventure to Avalon, and Hywel was one of Math's liege men at Dinas Bran. Bridget had heard what she was sure was only part of his story: born a shepherd, he'd been a stable boy at Castell y Bere ten years ago when he'd saved Anna's life before the English had burned the castle to the ground. He'd been in the right place at the right time, and he'd risen to the occasion. He'd proved his worth since then, and his rise, by medieval standards, had been meteoric—though not unheard of these days. In their quest to find able men, David and Callum looked far more to a man's capacity than to his birth.

David had been right to be wary of depriving his kingdom of too many men who had authority, Peter among them. Bridget found herself a little irritated at his foresight. He hadn't been right to make her go back to Avalon with him, but it looked like he'd been right about everything else.

Ieuan knew it too, which was why he turned to Peter now and gestured him forward. "My lord Geneville, this is Peter Cobb, Samuel's lieutenant. He has more experience than anyone here with investigating crimes like this one."

It had never occurred to Bridget before Ieuan used the word that, speaking in French, *lieutenant* made perfect sense. It meant, quite literally, *one who stands in the place of another*, and thus made sense to everyone in the room. Regardless of what role they were playing, they were all standing in the place of another.

"Peter, please tell me whatever you need to proceed," Lili said.

"First I need a little more information." Peter bowed in Geoffrey's direction. "My lord, do you know how long you were unconscious?"

Geoffrey made another expressive motion with his hands. "A quarter of an hour, perhaps? It didn't feel like long—certainly what light there was hadn't changed. The attack happened less than two hours ago."

"Then we can't be far behind them," Peter said. "The fact that you awoke and came here immediately may in the end save James Stewart's life."

Geoffrey shook his head. "I could do nothing else."

"Was your purse stolen?" Peter said.

"Yes," Geoffrey said.

"What about the emissary's?" Peter said.

"Yes to that as well. The bandits took all our gold, along with the letter from King Philip to King David," Geoffrey said. "And, of course, they took James Stewart."

"That is where they made their mistake," Goronwy said.

Geoffrey turned to him. "In what way?"

"We see before us, on one hand, basic theft," Goronwy said. "On the other, diplomatic intrigue."

"I hadn't thought of that," Geoffrey said. He didn't sound offended, merely curious that another man could have had an idea that hadn't yet occurred to him.

"You were left for dead," Peter said. "It could be that we were meant to assume the men who attacked you were simple brigands. We might still be thinking it if not for the abduction of Lord Stewart."

"It was foolish of them to murder Molier too," Lili said, with a bit of tartness in her voice. "Any time a man of his stature is killed, one has to assume it wasn't an accident."

Geoffrey's chin bobbed in Lili's direction in a mini-bow. "They are criminals, and thus fools by definition."

"My lord," Peter said to regain Geoffrey's attention, "perhaps it isn't my place to ask, but knowing the answer could move us towards understanding the reason for the ambush, if it wasn't, in fact, theft. Can you tell me what was in the letter from King Philip to King David?"

Bridget smiled to herself at Peter's eloquence and tact. It was one of those mysteries about him that he could be so talkative when he was involved in an investigation and nearly silent the rest of the time.

Lili nodded her assent. "Tell him, Geoffrey."

Geoffrey pressed his lips together for a second, thinking, and then said, "As I hope you are aware, King Philip was less than pleased with the outcome of this autumn's events. He regrets the ill-fated invasion at Hythe and what it has done to his relations with England, as well as the subsequent falling-out with Pope Boniface. He had written to King David to ask for a conference. Since David has been installed as the Duke of Aquitaine, Philip suggests a meeting where France borders Aquitaine, at the Bremond estate at Saint-Aulaye on the Dronne River."

"Thank you for that, my lord." Peter bowed again. "One wonders who gains most by preventing such a meeting."

"It is, in the main, too early to say," Geoffrey said.

Goronwy turned to Lili. "While Scotland isn't that far away, I'm inclined to look closer to home for whomever is causing this mischief. We shouldn't place blame without evidence or rule anyone out just yet."

Geoffrey gave a snort that from him came out dignified. "It's more than mischief, Goronwy."

Lili canted her head. "I can't imagine Balliol has condoned an attempt on his own High Steward's life. As both of you say, we should make no judgements as yet."

Geoffrey and Goronwy bowed. Bridget didn't get the sense that the two men had been really disagreeing, but rather that they enjoyed their back and forth as an intellectual challenge. David encouraged this type of interplay among his advisors, so that all sides of an issue could be examined without hard feelings on any side.

Then Lili gave a low moan and shifted in her chair, a spasm of pain crossing her face.

Bronwen saw it too and was at her side in an instant. "Are you okay?" she said in Welsh.

Bridget's Welsh was poor, but the 'okay' was unmistakable so she could guess the rest.

Lili gripped Bronwen's hand and nodded. "Just tired of sitting."

Goronwy was already at Lili's other side, and together he and Bronwen helped her to her feet.

Bridget herself shifted, tired of standing and sensing it was a good time to leave. She nudged Peter with a finger to the small of his back.

He nodded imperceptibly before putting his heels together and bowing to Lili and then to Geoffrey. "If you think of anything—

anything at all—that might help me in identifying those responsible, please don't hesitate to say so."

"Of course," Geoffrey said.

Peter moved towards the door, lifting his eyebrows to Bridget as he passed her. She curtseyed and turned on her heel to follow him out the door. They crossed the great hall at a rapid walk, making for the door that would take them into the courtyard. The hall was nearly deserted, even at this hour on Christmas Eve. Was it just last night that it had been full to bursting with friends?

It was only now that it hit Bridget that in allowing the bus to go to Avalon without her, she was not only turning down her last chance to see her parents ever again, but she would also never see any of the bus passengers again. Some of them, like Darla, had been unpleasant, but many had been kind, and she had liked knowing that others in this world shared her experiences.

Once outside, Peter headed for the multi-storied guest hall. Unlike the keep, the guest hall was built in wood, though with a stone fireplace that ran up the back wall where the building met the inside of the curtain wall. It was as warm and comfortable as a medieval house could get, especially because it had a semi-modern chimney, which was properly vented so the sitting room didn't fill with smoke. The ground floor had ten small guest rooms, with more on a second level reached by a narrow flight of stairs. Most of the time travelers had been housed last night in Llangollen, but as Callum's employees, Peter and she had stayed at the castle: Peter with Darren, and Bridget with Rachel.

Peter paused at the bottom of the stairs. "I know time is pressing, but we have to change out of these clothes before we go any further."

Hardly able to believe that he wasn't telling her to stay behind, Bridget went up the stairs and pushed open the door to her room. She and Rachel had shared a narrow bed, and the room was so small there was only a foot between the bed and the walls on either side. Bridget had been happy to share, though she missed the loft where she slept above her shop in Shrewsbury. The town had grown in population in recent years as prosperity had come to England under David's rule, and it was full to bursting inside its walls. Callum had set her up in the middle of a winding street, sandwiched between a baker and a wool merchant.

Moving quickly because Peter would be waiting and she didn't want him to change his mind and leave the castle without her, Bridget stripped off her modern clothing and dressed again in her medieval garb. Almost all clothing in England and Wales at this time was made of wool—cotton being hard to come by and not very warm—though Bridget herself could afford expensive linen undergarments.

Once dressed, she looked longingly at her insulated, waterproof down parka—really the only piece of modern clothing she preferred over the medieval version—before throwing her wool cloak around her shoulders. Among her belongings she had a down coat, which she'd made herself. But even boiled wool, which was remarkably waterproof with its natural lanolin, couldn't keep a heavy rain from soaking through eventually. At that point, instead of a nice warm insulating parka, she'd just have wet feathers.

She and Peter returned to the stable so quickly after their arrival at Dinas Bran that the long-suffering stable boys had hardly had time to brush their horses. Still, one of them lifted Bridget's saddle from its rest and placed it on the back of her horse. Bridget stood patiently waiting until he finished strapping it to the beast's back, and then, once both horses were ready, mounted with a boost up from Peter.

She held her tongue until they had actually passed underneath the gatehouse before asking the obvious question. "Why are you letting me come with you?"

Peter glanced at her. "I need a partner, someone I can bounce ideas off. You do realize, except for Bronwen, that we're the only twenty-firsters left in the Middle Ages?"

Bridget stared at him for a second. She'd just been thinking about the bus passengers, of course, but— "I hadn't thought that far. What with Lili and Ieuan—"

"I know they both can speak American, and Ieuan's been to Avalon, but when it comes to it we're the only ones who are really in this together. When David said he was taking everybody back, he meant it."

Bridget's gaze went to her gloved hands, which were clenching the reins tighter than necessary. She couldn't say that she'd loved every minute she'd spent in the Middle Ages, but she'd stayed because what she had here was better than what she'd left in the twenty-first century. Like Peter, before she'd stepped off the bus, she'd had to ask one of the other passengers to let her mum and dad know she was okay. It wasn't that she never wanted to see them again. She was concerned about them and knew they'd care that she was missing.

But she hadn't ever been convinced that they loved her all that much. She'd been born long after a much older brother and sister, each of whom had children of their own before Bridget herself had come along as a surprise to her mum, who by then was already past forty. Another child—perhaps pretty or less prone to dreaming—might have been doted on, but Bridget had always felt like her mother did nothing but sigh over the inconvenience Bridget had brought into her life. And her dad spent every evening after dinner (which was eaten in front of the telly) down at the pub. Growing up, Bridget had been put to bed most nights before he came home, or put herself to bed when her mother couldn't be bothered.

From the moment David had explained his plan to her, Bridget had entertained two opposing fantasies about what would happen when she showed up on her parents' doorstep on Christmas Eve. In one, her family cried tears of joy to see her, asked about her adventures, and sat riveted through her tale of life in the Middle Ages. In the other, after a perfunctory hug from her mother, her father told her not to make up stories and went back to watching his programme.

Maybe it was a failure of imagination on her part, but she had little doubt which of the two scenarios was genuinely the more likely.

7

Math

Though darkness had fallen, hiding the world outside from his immediate view, Math was still recovering from the crash that wasn't. In his mind's eye, he could see the bus hit the cliff wall, which he knew, as surely as he knew his own name, would kill the woman he loved most in the world, only to have it vanish as if it had no more substance than a puff of smoke.

As Jane directed the bus down the road, having left the other bus passengers to their own devices, Anna sat with her hand in his. "You okay?"

"Ach. I'm fine," he lied boldly. "It's you I'm concerned about. You're still shaking."

"It's one thing to time travel by mistake," Anna said. "It's quite another when we do it deliberately. I've actually never done it on purpose before."

"Your brother has, however, and is a madman," Math said, more calmly than he actually felt.

"I heard that," Dafydd said, though he didn't turn around. He was bent over beside Jane at the front of the bus, peering out the windshield. Snow fell in fat flakes, which the wipers flicked away.

"What about the time it doesn't work?" Anna said.

"O ye of little faith," Dafydd said.

"We will cross that bridge when we come to it," Meg said, glancing at Dafydd and then back to Anna. "Let's not borrow trouble."

Dafydd spun on his heel to look at his mother. "You need to call Aunt Elisa."

"I do, but I kind of wanted to know a bit more about what we're doing first." She gestured to the others, most of whom were focused intently on the screens of their phones.

"Give us another minute." Callum craned his neck to look at something on Cassie's screen.

Math had glanced at Anna's phone, but nothing about it made any sense to him. If, for some reason, they had to stay here longer than Dafydd intended, he'd learn how to use one. But until that day, he'd rather focus on his surroundings.

He'd grown familiar with the bus over the last year, such that it had ceased to be more than a curiosity, but its low growl as it moved along the road had him rethinking his complacency. When he'd ordered the road to the cliff built to Dafydd's specifications, he'd been unable to picture exactly how Dafydd's plan was supposed to work. Now that he was here, Math could understand why it was necessary to make the road as smooth as possible. They were moving faster than Math had ever moved in his life, and yet he was sitting still, holding his wife's hand. The bus hardly rocked.

The lights and trees beyond the bus flashed past. Math felt a little queasy, in fact, looking at them, and he bent forward to look out the front window instead. Red lights from vehicles in front of the bus shone in the darkness. He sat back, shaking his head. "I am a stranger in a strange land."

"Funny you should say that," Meg said. "It's the title of a book about a human raised on Mars who comes to earth."

Math smiled. "I was quoting Exodus."

Meg laughed. "Of course you were." She tipped her head to Dafydd. "Do you know where we're going, kiddo?"

"The hospital first," Dafydd said. "It's nearer to Bangor than Caernarfon and on the way to Rachel's dad's clinic."

"I can't believe we're finally home," Jane said from the driver's seat. "It's like a dream come true." She glanced at Dafydd. "Thank you."

Dafydd bent his head in silent acknowledgement.

"I would agree that it is like a dream," Math said. "I keep waiting for the moment when I wake up back in my own bed in Dinas Bran."

"Let's hope it doesn't turn very quickly into a nightmare," Anna said.

Meg pulled out her own phone from the bag at her feet—a *backpack* Anna called it, for good reason as it had big wide straps that fit snugly over the wearer's shoulders. It was the same bag Dafydd had retrieved years ago from where Meg had left it near Hadrian's Wall. She took out a 'phone jack', which Math knew about from a primer Anna had given him as she'd packed her own phone into her pack, and plugged it into the side of the bus.

Then she looked at Dafydd. "Are you sure our phones are untraceable?"

He raised both shoulders in an exaggerated shrug. "You're asking me? I wasn't here last time. You bought them in Oregon a year ago, barely used them, and then disappeared. If the US government wants us, and they are willing to put effort into tracking us through those phones—and leaving a trace on them that could be picked up a year later—then more power to them. We'll see who's awake on Christmas Eve."

"MI-5 may be aware of us too," Callum said, somewhat absently as he was still reading on his phone. "We're going to have to bin these and get different ones."

"That'll be a trick on Christmas Eve," Meg said.

"Tesco's open," Cassie said. "A sign on the front of the store said they're open for a few hours tomorrow too."

"Damn American influence," Callum said with a smile directed at his wife, who was, of course, an American. "They ruin everything."

"What about identification?" Dafydd said. "I don't have any."

"It's only you, Math, and Papa who don't," Anna said. "I brought my driver's license. Even though it has expired, I thought it might do in a pinch."

"In England, the authorities aren't allowed to ask for identification unless you're suspected of a crime," Mark said with the same absent tone Callum had used. He was focused on his laptop, which he'd hooked up to his phone by a long cord. Math knew that Mark had kept his laptop charged thanks to the electric power available in the bus barn, just so he could use it the minute they arrived in Avalon. "Checking for weapons is different."

Dafydd spread his hands wide. "If they stop the bus, they'll find my many weapons, but I'm just a student who forgot his ID at home."

Anna coughed and laughed at the same time. "Anyone who believes that is an idiot."

"It's how I've been treated whenever I'm here," Dafydd said. "I can't see why it'll be any different this time."

"Ideally, you won't get separated from us this time," Callum said, "so it won't be an issue."

Jane exited the motorway and, a few moments later, stopped the bus near a well-lit complex of buildings with the words 'Ysbyty Gwynedd' emblazoned on a large sign at the entrance. Ysbyty was a word Math hadn't known until Rachel had introduced the concept of a hospital and suggested he build one in Llangollen. His hospital was called 'Ysbyty Gwynedd' too.

Anna patted his knee. "Why are you smiling?"

He pointed with his chin to the sign. "I like the continuity of it."

"Right," Dafydd said. "This is where you guys get off."

Math peered at the hospital entrance. A man in green was standing several paces away down the sidewalk, a white stick that smoked and glowed orange between his fingers. He was watching the bus with interest, smoke pouring from his nostrils as he breathed out. Math stared at him, confused as to what modern devilry this could be. Then, with a flick of his fingers, the man shot the stick into the snow and strode back towards the glass doors at the front of the hospital.

Jane stood up. Carl had taken Shane in his arms for this part of the trip, and he stood too. But even though the bus had stopped and the hospital was only a stone's throw away, he hesitated.

Dafydd canted his head. "What else do you need from me? Just name it."

"Nothing." Carl shifted Shane more to his left shoulder so he could stick out his right hand to Dafydd. "You've done more than we ever—" he stopped, his voice choked with emotion.

Dafydd clasped his hand. "It is the least we could do."

Carl looked around the bus. "I want to say this to all of you. The others may not be grateful. They may think they deserve more than you've given them, but every one of you risked your lives for Shane, and I want you to know that we will remember you forever. I'm only sorry we may never see you again."

"You never know." Meg stood up and hugged him, kissed Shane's cheek, and then hugged Jane.

"If you find yourselves in trouble, call us," Jane said as she held Meg's shoulders and looked into her eyes. "We might be able to help."

"Thank you."

The other women hugged her, and then the men shook hands all around. Math eyed the hand Carl offered him before accepting it for what it was. He didn't understand how the custom of shaking hands instead of clasping forearms had started. The whole point was to know if an enemy—or a friend—had a weapon up his sleeve, not whether or not he could break the bones in your hand if he squeezed hard enough.

When Carl reached Llywelyn, he surprised Math—and maybe even himself—by giving him a real bow. None of the bus passengers had ever been very good at bowing, worse even than the Americans, who found obeisance amusing more than anything else.

"Sire," Carl said. "Good luck. Seven hundred years on, everyone here in Gwynedd would be rooting for you if they knew what you were trying to do."

"Thank you," Llywelyn said.

They left. Dafydd followed them down the steps and stood in the doorway until they had crossed the parking lot and entered through the front doors of the hospital. Then he came back up the steps.

"All right." Dafydd clapped his hands together once. "How we doing? Dad?"

Llywelyn waved a hand at his son. "Don't worry about me."

"Math?"

"Other than being nearly killed, all I've seen so far of Avalon is the inside of a bus where everyone speaks a language I understand," Math said. "Ask me later."

Anna nudged Math and said in an undertone. "The King of England is back, and he's running a meeting."

Math suppressed a smile.

"Callum?" David said.

Callum had looked up at Dafydd's initial query to Llywelyn and now answered him. "You might be interested to know that three days after the new year both Wales and Scotland are voting on independence from England."

Rachel's mouth fell open. "Really? How did that happen? They weren't even talking about it a year ago."

"In the aftermath of the bombings and, apparently, riots this last year, the movement has gained momentum," Callum said.

Llywelyn smirked. "The people of Wales have finally had enough, have they?"

"Took them long enough," Math said.

Dafydd shot an amused look at both Math and his father before turning to Mark. "What have you found?"

Mark's fingers had been flying all over the letters on his laptop from the moment he opened it. "Working on it."

Math didn't ask what he was working on, and neither did Dafydd.

"Moving on, we need to figure out what we're doing first. Now that we're here, do we split up or stick together? I just don't know how much time we have before we'll be tracked down."

"We need new phones," Darren said, "especially since I left mine in the vehicle Callum and I abandoned in Cardiff a year ago."

"I agree," Callum said. "We should buy some spares too."

"What we shouldn't be doing is riding around Gwynedd in a Cardiff bus," Rachel said. "We stand out."

"Thus, the aforementioned international incident," Dafydd said.

"My father's clinic is just down the road," Rachel said. "How about we go there, and while my father sees to Meg, the rest of you buy what we need. I'll ask my father if it's okay to borrow some of his equipment to take back with us. That's probably easier than trying to buy it."

Cassie laughed. "Borrow permanently, you mean."

Dafydd nodded. "That works. We'll leave Mom, Dad, Anna, Math, and Rachel at Rachel's dad's clinic."

"Who's going to drive? I'm afraid that won't be my contribution to this endeavor," Math said dryly.

"I'll do it." Cassie moved around Dafydd and plopped herself in the driver's seat. "What does this thing run on, anyway?"

"Petrol," Callum said, "but it takes a special nozzle. We can't simply fill it at any station."

"Good thing Wales is a small country, then." Cassie buckled the seat belt and shifted gears. "Left hand manual drive is always fun." She glanced back at Rachel. "Point me in the right direction?"

Dafydd moved aside and sat down in Cassie's vacated seat, while Rachel took his place behind Cassie's chair in order to direct her to Abraham Wolff's clinic. Dafydd looked past Anna to Math. "I'm really glad you're here, Math, because I'm counting on you and Dad to keep Anna and Mom safe."

"I don't know what good I'm going to be," Math said. "I don't understand this world at all."

"There are forces that could be working against us—powerful forces that include governments and mercenaries," Dafydd said. "Not to belabor the point, but every time I come to the modern world, I'm reminded of my ninth grade education and relatively young age. All anyone sees when they look at me is an overgrown kid. *The King of England? Don't make me laugh.* I have no more authority than you do. If we're going to leave you and Dad at the clinic with Mom and Anna, you need to keep your eyes open. Act as if we've taken an enemy position, and we don't know what their next move is or the resources they have to counter us."

Math nodded, surprised and also pleased at what Dafydd was asking of him. "I will not fail you."

"You never have." Dafydd sat back in his seat and closed his eyes for a moment.

When Math had made the impulsive decision to board the bus, he'd assumed he would be an appendage to Anna—useless, really—and good only for holding her hand. But he still wore his sword, and he knew how to use it. He had no qualms about using it.

Anna nudged Dafydd, who still had his eyes closed. "We're here, aren't we?"

Dafydd opened his eyes to look at his sister. "We are. It was the right thing to do."

"Exactly," Anna said. "Don't worry so much. Everything's going to be okay."

Math thought Anna was being just a wee bit optimistic, but he had to admit that so far things had gone more smoothly than they had any right to expect. The drive to the clinic from the hospital was short—not so much in distance, but because the road was so smooth and the bus could go so fast that what would have taken an hour in his world took minutes here.

Math deliberately hadn't paid attention to the scenery passing outside the bus because he became nauseated every time he looked out the window. Then Cassie slowed the bus and turned into yet another parking lot. She killed the engine and doused the lights, and then everyone exited the bus.

As Math stepped off the bottom step and helped Anna down, even though she didn't need his help, he looked around with interest. He even went so far as to bend to the road, sweeping away the layer of snow to get at the hard black stone beneath. It was so smooth it explained instantly why the bus could maintain the speed it had without jarring the passengers' teeth out of their heads.

They stood next to a two-story building. Lights shone all around it—not torches, he understood, but light glowing from within glass bowls and powered by electricity—an endless source of energy upon which everything in this world depended.

Cassie had parked the bus alongside the stone walkway that surrounded the building. Low cut grass, covered today in snow like everything else, filled the space between the walkway and the side of the building.

Math looked up into the sky and blinked his lashes against the snow that continued to fall. It was the only thing in the scene that was in the least familiar to him, and it was comforting to know that it still snowed in this world.

Anna squeezed his hand. "You'll be able to see the landscape tomorrow. The mountains and the sea will look the same, even if nothing else does."

Then a vehicle many times smaller than the bus—even smaller than the 'car' in which Bronwen had driven David and Ieuan into Wales—turned off the road and parked beside the bus. A man of small stature with hair and beard shot with gray opened the door. He stood half-in and half-out of the vehicle, gazing at Rachel, who took several steps towards him.

The man then closed the car door with a clunk and stepped onto the sidewalk in time to catch Rachel in his arms as she threw herself at him. "Dad!"

Abraham Wolff rocked back and forth, holding his daughter and crying himself while she sobbed into his shoulder. Some of the others looked away, studying the trees surrounding the clinic, as if by watching they would be interfering with the reunion, but Math observed them closely. He'd known, from Anna, that the love between a parent and a child in Avalon was no different than Math's love for his sons, but he was interested to see it for himself.

After a minute, Rachel collected herself and relinquished her tight hold on her father. She wiped at her eyes with her fingers, while holding out the other hand to Darren. "This is my friend Darren, Dad." And then she introduced everybody else.

Abraham Wolff eyed Darren, and Math didn't think Rachel's father was confused for a single heartbeat about who Darren was to his daughter. Still, he greeted him cordially enough, with a firm handshake.

"Let's get inside." Abraham walked towards the front door of the building, a white square held in his hand.

As he swept the square across a black box beside the door, a high-pitched wail sounded in the distance, like a donkey screaming but far higher and more piercing. Math spun around, his hand on the hilt of his sword. "What is that?"

"Sirens," Dafydd said.

Abraham held the door open. "Are they for you?"

"Could be." Dafydd tipped his head at Math. "Get them inside and let Dr. Wolff work. We'll take care of this."

Llywelyn gripped his son's upper arm. "What are you going to do?"

Dafydd glanced over at the others, who remained outside the building. "I'm pretty sure we're about to lie through our teeth."

8

David

Everyone gathered around Callum to await his instructions, which David found both amusing and interesting. He was glad he had a big enough ego to withstand what he could have perceived as a slight. In the Middle Ages, he was the focus of any conference, but in the twenty-first century, Callum was their leader—and David was completely happy with that fact.

"What are we going to tell them?" Cassie said.

Mark Jones held up his phone to get their attention. "I'm already seeing talk in some of the chat rooms of the more fringy conspiracy groups. The Welsh Nationalist site is going crazy."

"What are they saying?" Callum said.

"They use a lot of code, but there's a definite reference to *him*."

"And who might that be?" Darren said.

"The man who is the return of King Arthur," Mark said, with an eye on David, "who will unite Wales against the Saxons. Who else?"

"Nobody is going to take such a claim seriously," David said.

Mark made a *maybe* motion with his head. "Regular citizens aren't likely to give credence to something like that, but there are people in the Security Service who actually know what's going on. They know about you and your father." The 'Security Service' was the official name for MI-5. Sometimes Callum and the others also referred to it by its in-house name, Box 500.

The sirens came closer and resolved themselves into a single echoing screech emanating from one car. It came around the corner from the direction Abraham Wolff had driven, turned into the parking lot, and braked to a halt sideways across the back of the bus. The driver seemed to be under the illusion that the placement of his minnow of a car would stop the whale of a bus from going wherever it wanted to go.

Two officers got out of the police car. One was a short, stocky gray-haired man in his fifties, not dissimilar in appearance to Abraham, though without the beard. He headed towards the front door of the clinic where David and his friends waited. His partner, who'd been driving, was closer in age to David, and he walked around the far side of the bus, disappearing for a moment from David's view.

Callum held his MI-5 badge in readiness and, instead of waiting for the older policeman to reach him, stepped out in front of the others and held it up.

In the United States, Callum would have said *federal agents!* but here the appropriate words were, "We're with the Security Service."

Darren, Mark, and Cassie flashed their badges too, while David tried to look inconspicuous, staying in the shadow of the shelter over the front door of the clinic. It was still snowing, and he was cold in his sweater, woolen or not. He wanted a parka like Anna had.

His attempt to hide was unsuccessful, however, since the patrol officer latched immediately onto him, nodding his head in David's direction. "Who's he?"

"A consultant," Callum said, lying baldly as David had predicted.

The man's eyes narrowed. "He's awfully young."

"He gets that a lot." Callum held out a hand to David to indicate that he should come forward. "This is Dr. David Llywelyn, our profiler."

Under the principle that a guilty person would never be so bold, David stuck out his hand to the police officer, who shook it warily and said, "Pleasure to meet you."

David nodded a greeting, deciding at the last minute that he wasn't going to try for an English accent, and it was better to say nothing at all. Likely, these two cops had never even seen one MI-5 agent before, much less four. However this turned out, both of them would be bug-eyed at the dinner table tonight, telling family and friends about the presence of the Security Service in Gwynedd. So much for keeping a low profile.

It was taken as a given by all who lived in Wales that the country was the most neglected region of the United Kingdom. This wasn't just in terms of infrastructure, social services, and resources either. London saw places like Caernarfon as remote and inaccessible, which was why in the Middle Ages the Gwynedd kings and princes had managed to stay independent for so long.

Compared to a country the size of the United States, calling Caernarfon 'remote' was laughable, but the whole of Britain, including Scotland, was the size of Oregon, so people thought on a smaller scale. Likely, the people who lived in Orkney thought they were treated the same way, but they couldn't drive to London in four hours either.

The patrolman jerked his head towards the bus. "We got a report of a bus driving the wrong way down the motorway. The caller said the bus was orange and green, from Cardiff, and until I saw the bus sitting here, I didn't believe him."

"This is, of course, why we're here too," Callum said.

"Since when do the Security Service get involved in traffic violations?" the policeman said.

"May I see your badge?" Darren pulled a notebook and pen from the inside pocket of his trench coat.

The policeman cleared his throat. "Yes, sir." He held it out to Darren, who made a note of the name and number.

Callum nodded. "A person of interest was last seen in this bus."

The younger officer had finished his inspection of the exterior of the bus, and now he stood near the front door with his hand on the top of his head, just looking at it. "This really is a Cardiff bus. What's it doing here?"

A sinking sensation overtook David's stomach. He could practically see the gears turning in the man's brain.

"Never you mind," the older officer said. He'd been semi-hostile up until now, like a commoner might feel about the gentry, but his young partner seemed to annoy him more than Callum did.

The younger officer's brow remained furrowed. "Remember last year when a bus disappeared into thin air during the bombing of city hall in Cardiff? They played that clip over and over again. You know, this bus looks just like—" His eyes widened as he turned to the MI-5 agents.

The older officer scoffed. "What are you going on about?"

But Callum was already holding his badge in the young man's face, and when he spoke, his voice was lower and sterner than David had ever heard him. "This is a matter of national security. You two need to get back in your vehicle and drive away. Leave this to us."

The younger officer looked like he was going to protest. Callum swung around to get confirmation from the partner, and the older man responded as expected, jerking his head and saying, "Let's go."

The younger man obeyed, but his face shone with excitement as he walked back to the car.

Before they got in, Callum said, "Happy Christmas to you."

The older patrolman lifted a hand in greeting. Then his partner started the car, backed it up, and drove away.

Cassie let out a burst of air. "The cat's pretty much out of the bag now, isn't it?"

"I'd say so," Callum said.

"Sorry," David said.

"Why are you sorry?" Darren said. "You're the last person whose fault this is." He turned to Mark. "Can you shut this down?"

"From Cardiff I could. I can't from this laptop, not without the right passwords to get past security." He pointed with his chin to where the police car was now driving away. "You can bet they're on the radio, talking to central command. You know they are."

"This just means we need to work more quickly than we hoped," Callum said.

"It was still a good idea to come here on Christmas Eve, David," Cassie said.

"How can you say that, given that we've already been discovered?" David said.

"They didn't write down our names," she said. "They've got a skeleton staff on duty, and all anybody working right now wants to do is to go home or down to the pub. It'll be all over Bangor tonight that the bus is here—and even more that MI-5 is here—but it might not go beyond Gwynedd just yet."

"She's right," Darren said. "Maybe this hasn't gone as pear-shaped as we think. Even if the officer had written down our names and badge numbers and called them in, most likely he wouldn't have reached a desk with a live person at it."

"We can't assume we're safe, though." Callum pulled out his phone and handed it to David. "Ring Anna and let her know what's happened. Math and your father need to keep a watch in case those bobbies return."

"Okay," David said, knowing that 'bobby' was British slang for police officer.

Callum continued talking. "We need to hide the bus right now, and find ourselves more subtle transportation. What do you have for me, Mark?"

"Preferably a van that seats ten." Cassie swung through the door of the bus and plopped into the driver's seat.

"It'll be tough to find that on Christmas Eve." Darren sat in a seat near the front of the bus.

Anna picked up on the second ring. "What is it?"

"How's Mom first?" David said.

"She's fine. Just getting underway here," Anna said. "The sirens stopped."

David related their conversation with the police officers, and he could hear Anna taking in a breath of disappointment that they'd been discovered so quickly.

"I'll send Math and Papa down to watch the door," she said.

"We'll keep in touch. Call if anything happens. This is Callum's phone, but we're on our way to acquire one for me and replacements for everybody else." David hung up.

"The internet is our friend." Mark had his computer open on his lap again. "I'm working on the vehicle first."

Cassie started the bus and drove it out of the parking lot.

"Do you mind if I ask you about a couple of things?" David said to Callum. "I don't want to sidetrack us but—"

"Are you really asking me if it's okay for you to talk?" Callum said.

"I don't want to distract you with stupid questions about how MI-5 works."

"Until Mark finds us a vehicle, we've got nothing but time. Ask away," Callum said.

"What kind of equipment does Mark need in order to find out if anyone back in your old office is paying attention? And can we get it or get to it? I want to know if the time travel initiative exists in any form anymore. Obviously, just from what that police officer said, they have your disappearance from Cardiff on video. If they played that over and over again all across the world, somebody somewhere should have started asking questions I'd rather they weren't asking."

"I've been sifting through news articles from last November," Mark said. "The government left a great deal out. Reading between the lines, after our disappearance, the time travel initiative didn't die entirely. The Security Service will know we're here and where we are from the flash as we came in."

"Does the bus have a GPS?" David said. "I can't believe this is the first time I thought to ask that."

"We disabled it," Callum said. "You don't have to think of everything."

"Can it be turned on remotely?" David said.

Callum laughed and cleared his throat at the same time. "I misspoke. I should have said that we ripped it out."

"Then there's Lee," David said, above the general laughter at Callum's response. "I would very much like to find out what became of him, if anything."

"I would too," Callum said, "but, sire, concerns about Lee have to be secondary to the greater mission."

David didn't blink at Callum's use of the honorific, just ducked his head. "I know. I'm not asking anything more than what Mark can find in his spare time—which I grant he may not have. But Lee is here, somewhere."

"Because of the flash, there will be a record of his return—and your subsequent and immediate departure," Callum said. "We can find out where he started out, if not where he is now."

"I need a better computer and connection to do any of that," Mark said, "and our colleagues to be asleep at the wheel."

"Burner phones are our first priority, after a new vehicle," Cassie said.

"There's another Tesco on the outskirts of Bangor," Mark said, "and I'm working on a car hire right now." He looked up at Callum. "Same ID as before, you think?"

"Why not?" Callum said. "We weren't tracked on our way through California. It was getting on a plane supplied by MI-5 that got us into trouble."

"Just as long as the accounts are paid and current." Mark stuck his tongue out of the corner of his mouth as he concentrated.

"That should be automatic," Callum said.

"And ... it is!" Mark said as he pressed a key on his laptop with a flourish. "We have a rental van at a garage a few hundred yards from the aforementioned Tesco."

Cassie accelerated towards the major road that would take them east from the clinic.

As they rumbled through the snow-covered landscape, David couldn't help thinking that where he really wanted to be right about now was either pacing the hallway of Abraham's clinic with Math and Dad or at Dinas Bran with his wife and son. He was almost jealous of Bridget and Peter for getting off the bus. Hopefully they were having a cozy time of it right about now.

9

Peter

As it turned out, Peter was not having a cozy time of it—with Bridget or anyone else.

He'd returned Bridget's kiss and held her hand, and all was right with the world—except that instead of sharing a carafe of wine with her before a warm fire up at the castle, he was crouched over the body of the French emissary and his escorts. The temperature hovered just above freezing, and it was raining at the same time, which was pretty much what one expected in England in winter but still wasn't Peter's cup of tea.

"What are you thinking?" Bridget stood to his left, bent over with her hands on her knees.

Peter didn't answer right away; he was distracted by both the body and what was going on with him and Bridget. It left no time for conversation. He knew that he should have been the one to say something to Bridget first, but he wasn't sorry she'd taken matters into her own hands. It was a relief to have their relationship clarified.

The emissary lay within the shelter of the ruined carriage, which was half-tipped onto one side. At first Peter had thought the carriage had crushed the man, but none of his limbs were directly underneath it.

In deference to the weather, Molier wore a thick wool cloak over his finer wool garments, which included shirt, pants, under tunic, overtunic and knee-high boots. All in extra-large.

To tell the truth, the emissary was one of the fatter medieval people Peter had encountered, the very definition of what a rich burgher might look like, though he was a politician instead.

As Peter patted at the man's torso, shifting him slightly, his hands came away bloody. More blood stained Molier's clothes and the ground underneath him, but as Peter moved around the body, he couldn't find any wound beyond a swelling to the back of the man's head.

"Hard to believe bandits could be operating this close to Dinas Bran—on Christmas Eve no less—without being detected sooner," Bridget said, "and even harder to believe that they would just happen upon, as their first target, a caravan including the emissary from France and the High Steward of Scotland."

Peter realized at that point that he still hadn't answered Bridget's first question and, in fact, had forgotten she'd asked it.

"Don't forget Geoffrey," Peter said hurriedly, having decided that he didn't want her to give up on talking to him entirely, so he'd better contribute to the conversation.

Bridget nodded. "He's a powerful man in his own right and has David's ear."

"If this was a simple robbery, everyone could have been subdued with the promise of free passage once they'd given up their jewels and gold." Peter glanced over at Bridget. Her green eyes were alight with interest, and she was showing no signs that she minded standing over a dead body with him in the pouring rain. "This was *meant* to look like a highway robbery gone wrong."

"Theft doesn't always mean hanging in David's England. Murder does," Bridget said. "They have to know they're for the gallows if they're caught."

"Which is why I find it hard to believe they'd go so far as to kill for gold they can't spend," Peter said. "Maybe during one of England's civil wars they could have found refuge in the land of an opposing faction, but England is at peace, and Wales is no haven for robbers."

"So what can these men possibly be thinking?" Bridget said. "David isn't going to be happy to learn that his roads aren't safe, and even worse, to have to inform the French king that his emissary is dead on English soil. That, along with the abduction of James Stewart, means they've caused an international incident."

"Fortunately, we have at least a day until David finds out about it, and we'll do what we can before he gets back to discover who did this and why. And get Lord Stewart back." Peter knelt in the mud of the road by Molier's head, his hands on his shoulders. "Can you help me shift him?"

"He's really heavy." Bridget grasped Molier about the torso, struggling to help Peter turn the emissary onto his back. Then she frowned. "Look at this!" She lifted up several layers of the man's clothing to reveal a thin mail vest hidden underneath his linen shirt, adding many pounds to his already significant girth.

In so doing, Bridget also found the wound that was the source of all the blood. The emissary had been stabbed by a thin blade that had cut through the links of his mail along the base of his left rib cage, thus confirming Peter's opinion that the emissary had been the target of the attack. But between the mail, the many layers of fabric, and Molier's girth, the knife had missed his heart. It had gone in but had turned aside at the ribs. Still, Molier had bled copiously.

Then Peter frowned. The blood on his hands was fresh, and the wound was still seeping. That made no sense at all. Dead men didn't bleed.

"You said, 'we'," Bridget said. "You said *we* have at least a day."

"What?" He glanced up at her, confused for a moment about the topic of conversation. Then he shook himself. "I meant 'we'. Like I said before, I assumed any attempt on my part to get you to return to your shop would be wasted, so I thought I'd save my breath."

Without waiting for an answer from Bridget, he returned his attention to the emissary's body and almost fell backwards in surprise as the man expelled a puff of air. Peter pressed with two fingers into the man's thick neck. He thought he caught a pulse but was afraid it was the beat from his own forefinger, so he placed his ear to the man's chest. The heartbeat came faint but steady, and Molier's chest rose and fell a few millimeters as he breathed.

Peter sat back on his heels. "He's alive."

Bridget didn't waste words in shock or surprise, which was one of the things Peter liked about her. Instead, she straightened and waved her arms to get the attention of Hywel, who'd been waiting for them when they'd arrived, and Justin, David's captain, who'd ridden with them to the ambush site to provide support. Rather than feeling resentful not being included on David's trip to Avalon, Justin seemed to be putting an extra strut in his walk at the trust his king had placed in him and David's wisdom in leaving him behind.

"How could someone—us included—not have noticed that he was alive earlier?" Bridget said.

"Nobody was able to feel his pulse on account of all the fat," Peter said.

Hywel and Justin hurried over. "What is it?" Hywel said.

"This man's alive," Peter said. "We need a stretcher."

While Hywel hared off to arrange for the emissary's transport, Justin stared at the body. "That's good news." He paused. "Isn't it?"

"I'd say so," Peter said. "I highly doubt King David would have preferred him dead."

"Now we just have to keep him alive," Bridget said.

Hywel gave a piercing whistle to gather his men, who'd been posted on the perimeter of the ambush site, and two men-at-arms stripped a side board off the carriage. The board only had to carry the emissary to one of the carts, which they'd brought for the purpose of transporting the dead to the village of Llangollen.

"You'd better bring one of the carts closer," Bridget said to Hywel. "We're going to need more than two men to lift him into the bed, and they aren't going to want to have to carry him more than a few steps."

"I hope the horse has the strength to pull him," Justin said, a dubious expression on his face.

"What about the dead?" Hywel said.

"The dead can wait," Peter said. "Take the emissary to the village and then return for the rest." Molier wouldn't have to be driven all the way up to the castle. He could stay at the hospital Math had built in Llangollen, which meant he'd reach help all the more quickly.

Bridget felt at the back of the emissary's head. "You know, I don't think he's really that injured. He might be unconscious more from being hit on the head than from the loss of blood."

"The healers will straighten him out," Hywel said, with all the confidence of a man whose home was the medical center of the known world.

"The cold air may have saved his life," Peter said to Bridget. "It slowed the bleeding, and then his extra layers of fat and clothing protected him from freezing to death."

He and Bridget stepped back to allow Hywel and his men to load Molier into the cart. As it turned out, it took five men to lift him. Once mounted, Justin hesitated, his horse's bridle in his hand. "Sir—"

Peter made a dismissive motion with his hand. "You and your men should provide an escort just to make sure Molier gets there in one piece. Even now, someone could be watching, waiting for a chance to finish the job."

"Someone should stay behind with you," Justin said. "You need an escort too."

Peter frowned, trying to come up with a reasonable explanation that would appeal to Justin's medieval mind for why everyone should leave him and Bridget alone. The truth was, Peter didn't want Justin looking over his shoulder, and he'd meant what he'd said to Bridget: he wanted a partner, like Darren would have been, not simply a companion to ride beside him—to protect him or whatever Justin thought he needed.

Justin was a very capable commander—even a knowledgeable tactician—but he wasn't an investigator. Bridget didn't have the experience in war that Justin had, but she was smart, more creative than Peter himself by far, and he wouldn't have to translate modern concepts for her. He'd always known how soothing he found it to be around her but hadn't appreciated it fully until all of the other twenty-firsters had gone away.

"What if the king returns and you're not there?" Peter said. "He would not thank you for leaving Lili unattended, even if she is safe at Dinas Bran."

Justin ground his teeth, clearly torn between duty and duty. After a moment of thought, he said, "I'll leave you Simon, one of my men-at-arms. He speaks English and has a quick mind. Given King David's disagreements with the King of France, I doubt the bandits are Welsh and you won't be heading into Wales."

"That'll work," Peter said. "Thanks."

The rest of Justin's company mounted and began making their slow way back up the road to Llangollen. It had been nearly four o'clock in the afternoon when the bus had left, and darkness had been coming on. It was full dark now, and their only light was the torch Simon held in his hand.

Thankfully, it wasn't raining as hard as it had been, and a swift breeze was blowing down from the north. The air was colder, which might even mean snow if the clouds didn't disperse before morning.

Peter walked to his saddlebag, pulled out a water skin, and handed it to Bridget.

She drank and passed it back. "What more are you hoping to accomplish tonight?"

"Somewhere, out there, James Stewart is alone and without friends." Peter gestured with the water skin to Simon, including him in the discussion. "I don't think any of us should be sleeping until we find him."

Bridget gazed around at the darkened landscape, her brow furrowed. "You know, it's odd that the bandits attacked during the day."

Simon took a drink from his own flask, which Peter was fairly certain wasn't full of water, and wiped at his mouth with the back of his hand. "I don't know about that, ma'am. It was either attack in the light or not at all."

"Why do you say that?" Bridget said.

Simon shrugged. "They attacked the carriage only five miles from Dinas Bran, which was Molier's destination. If the bandits had waited any longer, they would have had to enter Wales, territory they might know less well, and the ambush site would have been even closer to the castle. They would have increased their risk of being seen."

Peter could see what Justin meant about Simon having a good head on his shoulders.

Bridget tipped her head to one side as she thought about what Simon had said. "If your intent is banditry, you wait until dark and attack whoever happens by. If your intent is to kill the emissary and/or capture the High Steward of Scotland, as it seems was the case, then you have to attack at the moment available, regardless of the hour of day."

"So," Peter took another sip of water. "Who gains from the emissary's death?"

"It's equally likely that Stewart was the target, isn't it?" Simon said.

"And what about Geoffrey?" Bridget said.

"Geoffrey didn't suffer a knife wound to the chest," Simon said. "He was collateral damage. The bandits might not even have known he was Molier's traveling companion until they saw him in the party. The same could be said for Stewart."

Bridget bit her lip.

"What is it?" Peter said.

Bridget took in a breath. "I'm just thinking about bits of news that have come into Shrewsbury in recent weeks. I'm wondering now if they aren't more credible than we initially thought."

Peter frowned. "What bits of news? You never said anything to me."

"You haven't been around much, have you?" Bridget said, and then gave him a smile which he hoped meant she didn't mean anything by the jab. "You were collecting the bus passengers and escorting them to Dinas Bran, and the information was delicate enough that I decided I had to speak directly to Callum."

Peter glowered at her. "Don't make us wait, Bridget."

"I hate even to say anything, but we've heard some chatter—" she put out a hand, "—not with any hint of an attack like this, but—"

"I'm sorry," Simon said. "May I ask what you mean by 'chatter'?"

"Think of it as gossip," Bridget said, "or simply as talk about a particular subject or event. When you hear about it more often than you might expect to or come across the same rumor from multiple sources, we call it 'chatter'."

At Simon's nod, Peter returned his look to Bridget. "So what have you heard?"

"You're not going to like it," Bridget said.

"Tell me."

"An alliance where one might least expect it," she said.

"Who?" Simon and Peter said together.

"Between King Philip of France and Gilbert de Clare, Earl of Gloucester."

10

Math

"What exactly are they doing?" Math said to Llywelyn as Anna and Meg followed Rachel and Abraham into another room.

He understood the need to wait outside—he was just the son-in-law, after all. In the medieval world, he had no business being present at the birth of his own child, even though he had been, much less at a breast exam of his mother-in-law.

"You're asking me?" Llywelyn said, in a perfect imitation of Dafydd. Then he cleared his throat. "Meg explained that they're going to take a picture of the lump with various devices, which will tell them something about what the lump is made of. If they're still worried, they might do a biopsy, which is a way to take a sample of it."

Math knew he looked horrified but couldn't help it. He almost didn't dare ask, but asked anyway. "How do they do that?"

"A big hollow needle, apparently."

Math shivered. "No point waiting here by the door, is there? Dafydd and the others have left, so we should patrol the perimeter in case those officers of the state return."

A grateful look crossed Llywelyn's face. "We should. This is a mission like any other."

Thinking about military tactics had been a way of life for Math since he was ten years old. He'd been pleased to learn that much of the principles he'd been taught had been confirmed by Callum and Peter. One of these was not to split up. Two men together kept each other awake, could spell one another, shout when one was in trouble or down, and were harder to disable.

Math kept a hand on the hilt of his sword as they exited the waiting room, which he recognized from his hospital in Llangollen. They had taken the stairs to the second floor of the building, where Dr. Wolff's examination room was located, and after a quick survey of the associated empty offices and corridor, they followed them back down again.

"How are you finding things so far?" Llywelyn said.

"I haven't seen much of anything yet," Math said.

"True." And then, "It's the perfection that always strikes me most."

Math nodded. "The lines are straight, the walls aren't just whitewashed—they're *white*—and there isn't a scuffmark to be seen."

Llywelyn grunted. "You haven't looked closely enough yet, but they're there. This world does love a straight line, though, I'll grant you that."

"Anna has told me that centuries-old buildings are prized here for being—what was the word?—*rustic,*" Math said. "They value what is old."

"That's something in their favor, then," Llywelyn said.

"Why would they value what is old when they can make this?" Math gestured to the solid walls and doors surrounding him. "I could hold off an army from this building, and yet it sits in an entirely indefensible location with no guards, no people. It's *empty* at night."

They'd reached the main corridor. When they'd followed Rachel's father into the building earlier, the front doors had locked behind them. Self-locking doors meant Math didn't have to worry about anyone sneaking inside except on the coattails of someone who had a key. Then again, it meant he and Llywelyn couldn't get back in if they went out either.

"They build everything this way. And since their country is at peace, they never think about being attacked," Llywelyn said. "It takes some getting used to."

"They have more money than-than—" Math struggled to think of a way to convey his thoughts.

"Than sense." Llywelyn smirked. "What we could do with what they have and think nothing of."

Math was finally starting to understand the quiet desperation he felt in Dafydd when he talked about what Avalon could offer the Middle Ages. "*Things*, as Anna has said many times."

"Things," Llywelyn agreed.

"I would like to see one of these bathrooms Anna goes on about," Math said.

"I thought I saw a sign—" Llywelyn broke off as lights flashed across the doorway, and the sound of a motor indicated someone had entered the parking lot.

Llywelyn signaled with his hand, indicating they should both move back around the corner of the corridor. Math heard the clunking sound of a closing car door and feet crunching the snow.

He and Llywelyn crouched on opposite sides of the corridor, which formed a 'T' with the one that led to the front doors. As the footsteps came closer, Math peered around the corner. A light shone directly in his eyes, and he pulled back his head, blinking away the glare.

He waited a moment, watching the light dance against the walls, and when it disappeared, he carefully looked towards the doors again. A man in a trench coat, a nearly exact replica of the one worn by Callum, shone a light—'a 'flashlight' to Anna and a 'torch' to Callum—all around the doorframe. Beyond him, snow continued to fall, and flakes coated his head and shoulders, just from the brief walk from his car to the sheltered doorway.

"Who could that be?" Math half-moaned, half-whispered the question. "Why can't these people leave us alone?"

"The authorities must have thought better of the policemen's departure and sent this new man to ask more questions," Llywelyn said.

"We're not going to answer any," Math said, a little grimly.

"There you are!"

Both men turned at Anna's voice. She'd come down the same stairwell they had.

Math put a finger to his lips. "Shh."

"What is it?" Anna crouched against the wall beside Math, speaking now in a whisper. "I've been looking everywhere for you, even the men's bathroom in case you were discovering the wonders of a flush toilet."

Math jerked his head in the direction of the front doors. "A man is outside. He is dressed like Callum."

"Oh no," Anna said. "What's he doing?"

"Nothing yet," Math said.

"We don't think he knows we're here, though Dr. Wolff's vehicle is still parked out front." Llywelyn was standing, but he had hadn't crossed the gap between them because it would expose him to the view of the man outside.

Anna's face fell. "If he's MI-5, he can run the license plate and discover in two seconds who owns it." She leaned past Math, seemingly to look around the corner, but Math caught her arm to stop her.

"He's just looking right now. The bus is gone, so there's nothing to see."

"Those policemen must have called their superiors immediately," Anna said. "I would have thought they would have been intimidated enough by Callum to do as he said, since he's MI-5 too."

"Sadly, it doesn't appear so," Math said. "Maybe they found courage in a cup of mead."

"I don't think anyone drinks mead here anymore," Anna said.

Of all the changes that could have occurred in seven hundred years, that surprised Math the most. "What do they drink then?"

"Um—" Anna was distracted by the light bobbing around the hall, directed into the building by the man at the door. "Beer, I think."

"That's an English drink," Math said.

Anna gave him a dark look. "You remember the English won, right?"

"Do you have news of Meg, Anna?" Llywelyn said.

Anna looked past Math to her father. "Actually, yes. That's what I came to tell you. Mom's had the mammogram. It's amazing how quickly things can go when you don't have to wait for anyone else to go first. There's a lump there—kind of a big one, actually. Dr. Wolff is doing an ultrasound right now. The next step would be a biopsy."

"And then we'll know if it's cancer?" Math said, because Llywelyn looked so stricken he had to have been afraid to ask.

"The cells have to be sent to a lab—or should be—but both he and Rachel said they'd look at them with the equipment they have here, and they'll be able to give at least a tentative answer."

Math knew what a 'lab' was because Rachel had one in Llangollen, and he was opening his mouth to ask what equipment said 'lab' might have that Rachel's father didn't when the front door rattled and banged.

"Open the door. I know you're in there!"

The three of them looked wide-eyed at each other. Math put a hand on Anna's arm. "Don't move."

Crouching, he peered around the corner again. The man now stood facing the parking lot, his hands on his hips, clearly frustrated.

Llywelyn took the man's moment of inattention to dash across the corridor to reach Math and Anna. "Can he get inside?" he asked when he reached them.

"I don't know English law, but in America, police need a search warrant because this is private property. They can't just go barging in." She shrugged. "But again, that comes from American television police procedurals, not any real knowledge on my part."

"We've been here only a few hours, and already I can't understand a word you're saying," Llywelyn said, though he squeezed Anna's shoulder as he spoke to take the sting out of his words.

"The answer to your question is, 'I don't know'," Anna said. "I'm just sorry someone was paying attention on Christmas Eve after all. Or was lucky enough to find out about the Cardiff bus so quickly. Maybe that agent lives in Gwynedd."

"I don't like it when my enemy gets lucky," Llywelyn said. "It makes me wonder what other mistakes I might have made."

"It doesn't matter now," Math said. "We can't allow him to arrest us."

Anna pulled out her phone. "It's time to call Callum, don't you think?"

Math grimaced. "I hate to disturb him. He and Dafydd are doing important work."

"What about Abraham?" Llywelyn said. "It's his clinic. He could send the man on his way."

"We can't expose him to MI-5!" Anna said. "If the police had returned, I'd ask him to come down here in a heartbeat, but what if the man takes him away?"

Math found a growl forming in his throat. "Your father and I could take him easily."

Anna shook her head. "I know you can, and it might be easier just to let you. We could lock him in a closet until Mom's done, but that would only cause trouble for Abraham down the road. Callum knows how these people think. He can tell us what to do."

Math's discontentment rose further. He had his sword, but no authority. At home, he would have walked right up to the doors and sent the man on his way. Llywelyn, as King of Wales, could have done the same—as could Anna for that matter. But this world was too big and, while the modern Prince of Wales might have had that kind of authority, among those of them here, it was only Callum who could tell a fellow agent what to do. It was the lesson in powerlessness that David had been trying to teach. Math hadn't understood what he meant until now.

"What if we ask Callum and Dafydd to return, and they are thrown in irons instead of us?" Math said. "This could be a trap for Dafydd."

"I can't talk to these people, Math. Nor can you. Even Anna is an outsider as an American," Llywelyn said. "I know my son, and you know your brother-in-law. He would want Anna to call."

Nodding, Anna pressed the screen on her phone.

Callum answered almost immediately. "Is everything okay?"

"There's a man in a suit and trench coat like you wear outside the door," Anna said.

"Damn," Callum said. "We're in the middle of something here—"

"The door!" Llywelyn dashed away.

A gust of cold air wafted down the corridor, and Anna passed Math the phone at the same time that she called out to the agent, who had pushed the door open. "Hi! We were just coming to talk to you."

"What's happening?" Callum said into Math's ear.

"He opened the door," he said.

"Keep me on the line," Callum said.

Anna caught the edge of the door and stood directly in the doorway so the man would have to push past her in order to enter the building. "May I help you?"

"What can you tell me about the bus that was here?" the man said.

Anna frowned and didn't bother to pretend she had no idea what he was talking about. It wasn't snowing so hard that the great ruts weren't clearly visible in the snow, though they were starting to be filled in by new flakes. "Nothing."

"But you saw it?"

Anna shrugged. "It came. It went."

Although Math was pleased to discover that he understood the English the man was speaking, thanks to being married to Anna for most of the last decade, he wasn't in a position to involve himself in the conversation in a way that would make sense, so he didn't try. His eyes went instead to the vehicle beyond the sidewalk, parked such that Dr. Wolff's little car wouldn't be able to leave.

"Did you notice that it was a Cardiff bus, not one from Bangor?" the stranger said.

Anna put on a puzzled expression. "Why would a Cardiff bus be in Bangor?"

"That's what I wanted to ask you," the man said. "You're saying you have no idea where it went."

Anna raised her shoulders in an elaborate shrug. "I didn't see anything. My mother has a lump in her breast, and the doctor is doing a biopsy of it right now."

The agent frowned and shifted from one foot to the other. "Er—"

Math was quietly pleased to discover that men in Avalon weren't any happier than medieval men to hear about the private doings of women. He had to stare at a point three feet above the man's head to keep his expression blank. It really wasn't fair of Anna to pretend she knew nothing about the bus, but if it made this agent leave without any more questions or Math having to resort to violence, he could accept it.

"Was there anything else you needed?" Anna said brightly. "I really would like to get back upstairs to my mother."

She started to back away, but that was a mistake because the man in the suit pushed between the door and the frame, his eyes now on Math. "Is that a sword you're wearing?"

Math looked down at his sword, and then up again at the stranger. He should have left his sword on the bus, but he hated not having its comforting weight at his side.

"Oh, that?" Anna said. "We've come from a medieval feast to celebrate Christmas Eve. My husband wanted to dress the part."

Math was astounded that Anna had come up with an exact description of where they'd been and why he was wearing a sword that wasn't even a lie.

The man in the suit continued to edge sideways, trying to get all the way inside. Math stepped forward and put out an arm to prevent him from doing so. The man retreated slightly. There must have been something to Anna's idea that the law didn't allow an officer to enter a private building without cause or unless he was invited. Math still had the phone in his other hand, though he'd put it surreptitiously down by his side so the agent wouldn't realize Callum was listening.

"And you decided to stop on the way home for your mother to have a biopsy?" the agent said.

Anna shrugged. "It was when the doctor could see her."

Llywelyn then came into the light and said in his heavily accented English, "Excuse me, could you tell me your name?"

The man reached into his breast pocket, pulled out a wallet not unlike the one Callum and the other MI-5 agents carried, and held it up. Anna looked closer, and Math peered over her shoulder. A piece of paper said his name was Rupert Jones, and he was associated with something called *The Guardian*.

Anna blinked. "You're a reporter?"

Math studied the man. *A reporter.* He'd heard of such an occupation. Darren, in particular, had made several sneering comments about 'the press' in Math's hearing. Dafydd had brought the printing press to the Middle Ages, and books and broadsheets were becoming more common. Wales and England had the beginnings of what Math understood had become a huge industry in Avalon.

Math stepped back and put the phone to his ear, turning sideways so he could still pay attention to the stranger but could also talk without being overheard. "He isn't MI-5. He's a reporter named Rupert Jones."

"Ask him how he tracked the bus to the clinic," Callum said.

Math put down the phone and repeated the question to Rupert.

Rupert gestured to the parking lot. "I have a police radio, which also confirmed that the bus is definitely the one that disappeared a year ago in the bombing at Cardiff city hall."

Anna frowned. "Maybe you're looking at an alien abduction."

Math didn't know what that was and, apparently, Rupert didn't either because he ignored the comment. "One of my contacts was on the motorway earlier and saw it appear out of nowhere with her own eyes."

If that was true, Rupert's friend had truly been in the right place at the right time and, depending upon how close she was when the bus appeared, she was lucky to be alive. It also meant, now that Math thought about it, that Rupert might have a bigger role to play in what was happening here than it first appeared and wasn't merely an obstruction to what they were trying to do.

"Tell me your name again?" Rupert had his phone in his hand and looked like he was prepared to write something into it.

"Anna and Math Rhys," Anna said before Math could stop her. He heard a tsk coming from the phone, which meant Callum would have preferred she'd made up a name too. "We're just visiting."

"Did she tell him what I thought she just told him?" Callum said.

Math put the phone back up to his ear in order to answer. "She did."

"Get rid of him!" Callum said, and then added somewhat under his breath, "A reporter. Jesus Christ."

Math grimaced, but Callum was right that it was time the conversation ended. He put his hand on Anna's shoulder and spoke in Welsh. "Go. Let me deal with this."

Anna looked at him warily, but with a tug on her elbow from Llywelyn, they got her moving away, back down the corridor.

Rupert's attention became fixed on Math. "You're not from around here, are you?"

"I assure you, I was born in Wales and have lived here my whole life. Now—" Math studied Rupert, who didn't exactly wilt under his gaze, but some of his aggression seemed to leave him. He might have thought he could bully Anna, a woman, into giving him the information he wanted, but Math was a different story. "I know that you have no cause to enter here, and my wife and I have far more pressing issues than answering questions about things we have no answers to."

Rupert glared at him, frustration rolling off him in waves. Math started to close the door, but Rupert jammed his foot into the gap before Math could close it all the way. "All of you know more than you're saying. I was hoping, sir, that you could explain the flare-out."

"The ... what?" Math said. The corridor was freezing now, and snow had blown in such that it had accumulated in the doorway to an inch in the time they'd spent talking.

"The bus vanished from the middle of downtown Cardiff on a Saturday morning over a year ago. The flare-out was caught on video. Research shows that a change occurred in that location at the subatomic level." Rupert was still wedged into the doorway so Math couldn't close the door. "Do you have anything to say besides 'alien abduction'?"

Math's eyes narrowed; this wasn't making Rupert go away. If anything, he seemed more interested than before. "No."

Rupert grunted and then reached into a side pocket of his jacket to pull out a small rectangle of paper, which he handed to

Math. "Ring me if you have any information that might help track down the bus."

Math took the paper automatically, with no real idea how it would help him contact Rupert, but he slipped it into his pocket anyway. "Of course."

He paused as it struck him that Rupert's tone had changed completely. He was giving way—except Math didn't believe for a moment that Rupert was giving up. More likely, he was trying to appease him, and when Dafydd and the others returned, he would be right behind them, following them to wherever they went next. Callum wouldn't thank him for allowing that.

"You might consider a trip to Caernarfon. That's where the real action is tonight."

"Caernarfon." Rupert sneered. "Right."

He didn't believe Math, of course. It had been a faint hope that he could divert Rupert, even if telling him that answers lay in Caernarfon had been the truest thing Math had said so far.

Then Rupert's phone rang, and he stepped back from the door to answer it. This gave Math the opportunity to close the door, but he hesitated in order to eavesdrop on Rupert's conversation.

"What did you say?" Rupert barked into the phone, one hand to his other ear to better hear the person on the other end of the line. Then he looked up, his eyes fixed on Math. "The Black Boar Inn in Caernarfon town? Right." He disconnected the call.

"I told you the action was in Caernarfon tonight," Math said, with a grin he couldn't help.

His grin faded, however, as he closed the door. Rupert was already walking quickly to his car, excitement evident in every step.

11

Bridget

"Why didn't you say anything about Clare and King Philip of France when we were back at Dinas Bran?" Peter said. "Lili and Geoffrey need to know."

Bridget shrugged, feeling hard pressed and helpless. "I couldn't talk in front of all those people, and I know Callum said something at least to David before he left. We put the pieces together only a few days ago, and he had no chance to talk to anyone about it until we all arrived in Dinas Bran. Clare is in Ireland and Philip in Paris, so it wasn't something David or Callum thought they could do anything with right now."

"Excuse me, ma'am," Simon said. "I may not be understanding you correctly, but are you suggesting that King Philip would somehow arrange to kill his own emissary to King David? That doesn't make sense."

"It does if Philip is looking for an excuse to go to war with England, this time with perceived right on his side," Bridget said.

Simon made an expressive gesture with his hands that reminded Bridget of Geoffrey. "Clare holds lands in Aquitaine and has benefitted from David's control of the region, not to mention David's rise to throne of England. He has no reason to help Philip."

"I know it seems that way," Bridget said. "I don't want to be dramatic, but we know from past behavior that Clare has always looked after himself first and foremost. Remember the Barons' War."

Bridget didn't have to elaborate to Simon or Peter about that. England's Barons' War was recent history here. Twenty-five years earlier, Clare, Simon de Montfort, and Llywelyn had become allies with the plan that, upon the defeat of King Edward, they would split Britain among them. Clare, however, only a few months after signing the treaty, switched sides, turning against Montfort and ensuring his death and defeat. What Clare did seemed crazy to Bridget, since Montfort was winning at the time. Edward must have promised him something really good, though it was hard to imagine what could have been better than half of England. Perhaps Philip had done the same.

"Clare and Philip have never been closely connected," Peter said. "Even if Clare decided to betray David, doing it with Philip defies reason, no matter what Philip might have offered him."

"Maybe," Bridget said, "but if David has to go on Crusade with King Philip, he leaves his throne unattended."

"That might be good for King Philip if he wants David close by so he can murder him, but why would it be good for Clare?" Simon said.

"He could be king, given the right backing," Bridget said. "He's one of England's most powerful barons."

"He's England's most powerful baron, full stop," Simon said.

"Still, I have a hard time believing Clare would be so half-arsed about it," Peter said. "He strikes me more as the type to arrange his scheme so everything falls into place at the same moment."

"If you don't believe Clare would betray David over his power in England, how about Ireland?" Bridget said.

Peter grunted. "That's more likely."

"Before David goes off on Crusade," Bridget said, "he really is going to have to deal with what's going on there."

"If the issue is Ireland, however," Peter said, "it isn't just Clare who could rise up against David when he starts reining his barons in."

Sometimes Bridget could hardly believe it was she who was having this conversation with Peter. The word 'poorly' wasn't an adequate description of how she'd done in school, which was one reason she'd left at sixteen. She'd loved reading, but she'd had to sneak her books up to her room underneath her coat and many homework assignments had been left undone because her mother hadn't liked seeing her with her nose in a book all the time, thinking it a bad way to attract a man.

Once she'd left school, her mum couldn't stop her from reading a thousand free ebooks on her mobile phone, and access to books was probably the one thing she missed most. She hoped that someone on that bus would think about loading up a phone with books.

They would need electricity to power it, but if put in airplane mode, it wouldn't have to be charged very often.

When she'd mentioned to Callum that she couldn't really be the person he wanted to manage his spy network centered in Shrewsbury, he'd scoffed at her, accusing her of denigrating her talents in an unbecoming way.

"I mispronounce words all the time because I've only ever seen them written," she'd said.

"At least you've seen them written," Callum said.

"I left school at sixteen!"

"And our esteemed King David left at fourteen."

Bridget had shaken her head. "He doesn't count. He's a genius."

Callum had looked her in the eyes and replied, "Here, you can become what you choose to be. Like he has."

It was probably those words from Callum, more than anything else, that had made her get off that bus. Even if things didn't work out with Peter, it had still been the right decision to stay.

Peter waved a hand, as if smoke instead of conversation had obscured the air. "Does Clare have estates close by?"

"No," Bridget said.

"That isn't helpful," Peter said.

"It isn't, is it?" Then her brow furrowed. "But you know, it wouldn't have to be a place he owns. He could be visiting an ally, staying as a guest somewhere. What if he's working with the Mortimers? They're close by at Montgomery."

"A conspiracy that includes King Philip, Clare, *and* Edmund Mortimer?" Peter said. "I don't believe it."

"You don't want to believe it," Bridget said.

"Do you know how many little hamlets we're talking about searching through?" Peter said. "It's twenty-five miles as the crow flies just from Llangollen to Shrewsbury."

"I know." Bridget said. "Clare's all the way down in Gloucester, but he could have sent men this far."

Hoof beats pounded on the road, a much louder sound than had heralded the arrival of the messenger from Lili back at the bus hanger at Llangollen. They turned to see a company of ten coming up the southern road. It was Cadwallon returning from the hunt. He reined in and dismounted.

"What do you have for us?" Peter said.

Bridget didn't object to him taking charge. For all that David intended for women to take their place in society as men's equals, they weren't exactly there yet. Cadwallon would feel more comfortable reporting to a man, and truthfully, while she knew a great deal about the local region and its politics, Peter was the detective.

"Many riders travel this road every day," Cadwallon said, "but nobody saw a company of masked men. Nobody knows of any marauders holed up in the forest attacking travelers—not within ten miles of this spot."

Peter studied Cadwallon for a moment. Bridget didn't know what Peter was thinking, but she had to struggle to keep the dismay out of her expression. Like Justin, Cadwallon was more than able as a commander. Given his long recovery from William de Bohun's attack many years ago, he had the respect of his men. He was loyal, brave, and true, which was exactly what King Llywelyn needed in the captain of his *teulu*. But he didn't have a devious mind, and he wasn't the best man to send to track down criminals. He couldn't think like them if his life depended on it.

"Did you ask if anybody saw an unusual number of riders on the road, in groups or alone, whether or not they wore masks?" Peter said.

Cadwallon frowned. "I suppose several people mentioned an unusual number of riders on the road. I didn't think anything of it because they weren't masked, and it is Christmas Eve. Many people are traveling today."

"Did they say where the men were going?" Bridget said.

"A farmer's wife near Chirk mentioned seeing riders along the road towards Whittington," Cadwallon said.

"You traveled far," Bridget said, trying to make Cadwallon feel better about the fruitlessness of his search.

"Many miles, but not all in one direction," Cadwallon said, half-apologetically, as if it would have been possible for him to cover more than ten or fifteen miles in the few hours since the attack. "Lord Samuel was charged with riding east and north. We headed west first, and then turned south before doubling back and riding up the road from Shrewsbury."

Cadwallon's English was passable, but Lili had been wise to send him to search primarily in Wales for sign of the bandits rather than England.

"Thank you for your help," Peter said. "We'll take it from here. I'm sure Queen Lili and Lord Geoffrey would like a complete report."

"Surely you're coming back to the castle too?" Cadwallon reflexively checked the sky. It was covered with clouds and completely darkened.

Bridget pulled her hood closer around her face and cinched tighter the scarf under her chin that held it in place. She was glad for her wool mittens too. Various people had told her that she would eventually get used to being cold all the time, but it hadn't happened yet, and she didn't believe now that it ever would. She'd started her store in part so she'd have better access to higher quality wools to keep herself warm.

"We'll head south," Peter said.

Cadwallon raised his eyebrows. He could probably count on one hand the number of nights he'd spent in England in his whole life.

"Please tell Samuel which direction we're going," Bridget said. "Maybe we can get as far as Whittington tonight. It's what? Five miles from here?"

"A little more by the road." Peter nodded at Cadwallon, who departed with his men.

Bridget watched him go. "Poor Cadwallon. It never occurred to him that the bandits would have removed their masks."

"I'm glad to know there are men like him in the world. It gives me hope for humanity." Peter boosted Bridget onto her horse and then mounted his own.

Simon held their only torch, its bottom end tucked into the spear rest near his right knee, and the light flickered in the wind. He urged his horse a little faster, taking the lead in order to light the road ahead. Bridget allowed her horse to pick its way among the ruts and rocks, staying just to Peter's left so his sword arm remained unhindered by her presence. Silence fell between them. She and Peter seemed to have exhausted the topic of their search for now until they had more information to go on, and she struggled for something else to say.

Finally, she decided she had nothing to lose by taking the bull by the horns and pressing him on the only thing they hadn't yet discussed. "Are we going to, you know, talk about what happened?"

Peter frowned. "What do you mean? We've been talking about it."

"Not about the ambush. About the fact that I—" Bridget made an exasperated sound, "—kissed you." The last words came out in a whisper, and she glanced ahead, hoping Simon hadn't overheard her. She'd felt relaxed and comfortable with Peter today, but if he didn't say something soon about how he felt about her, she was going to scream.

"Is there—" he stopped. "Are you sorry?"

"No!"

"Oh, good. I'm not either." Peter clicked his teeth at his horse, directing him to skirt a puddle that took up the full width of the road.

Bridget had to fall back to follow him, shaking her head and glad, for once, that he wasn't looking at her. All the stewing around in her brain she'd done in the last few hours about this gesture or that reference, fearing that he regretted his decision to stay in the Middle Ages—and it turned out he was totally oblivious to anything she was feeling.

Peter slowed his horse to wait for her to clear the puddle, which again was a good sign, and as she came abreast, she decided to try one more time. "Are we, you know, *together*?"

"Er—" Peter flicked his gaze in her direction for approximately a third of a second. "Is that what you want?"

Bridget rolled her eyes. "Yes."

"I do too." He relaxed into his saddle. "So then it's settled."

Bridget shook her head. If she'd known it was going to be that easy, she would have kissed him months ago.

12

David

When Callum's phone rang, David had been examining Tesco's Christmas display of chocolate, all of which was on a fifty-percent-off sale now that it was Christmas Eve. The Tesco was afraid it wouldn't sell out in the last few hours before the store closed.

"We should buy it all." Cassie started to load up her cart, which already had in it—among other things—ten cell phones; a host of pills, lotions, and other medical supplies; three boxes of lip balm for Bronwen; neodymium magnets in various sizes; ziplock bags; every pair of reading glasses in the store; dozens of packages of rubber bands, and duct tape. A second cart held two laptops, a wireless printer, and several reams of paper.

David grinned. "Think what an amazing gift one of these will make to a visiting dignitary." Then he paused. "I almost hate to ask, but … you're sure—now that you're here—about coming home? If you do return, this is the first time you will have truly chosen it."

Cassie stopped, a box of chocolate held in each hand. "I know. Callum and I have talked, and we're ready to go back." She canted her head, as if she was thinking this through at the same time she was speaking to him. "Maybe it's growing up on the reservation as I did, but the border between this world and the medieval one is more blurred to me than to some of the others. I don't feel like this decision is forever—and even if it is, I'm at peace with it."

"And your grandfather? What did he say?"

"We'll be talking more, but he told me that he knew it was me before he even picked up the phone," Cassie said. "To call him on Christmas means a lot to both of us. Thank you for giving me that opportunity." She smiled at him with tears blurring her eyes again.

David found himself swallowing hard. "Don't think I'm not grateful to you both."

"I told my grandfather that Callum and I are going to name his grandchild, if it's a boy, after him."

David was so stunned he couldn't actually speak.

Cassie laughed. "And don't worry, I wasn't thinking of Grandad's English name, which is Arthur, but his Indian name, 'gentle spirit'. That's 'Gareth' in Welsh."

David shook his head. "You two sure know how to keep a secret."

Still grinning, Cassie said, "How big, by the way, are these generators you want? With all this and them too, will everything fit in the van?"

"Oh sure," David said, hardly aware of what he was saying. He was more thrilled than he could say that Cassie and Callum were finally going to be parents. He was going to tease Callum about it at

absolutely the first opportunity. "They're like a foot and a half wide—
"

"A reporter." Callum spoke sharply into his phone. "Jesus Christ."

Cassie, Darren, and David gathered around Callum, who was listening intently. Mark had been left in the rental van, surfing the web on Tesco's wifi, with the promise that Cassie would bring him tea and biscuits. The Cardiff bus had been safely disposed of, left in a turn out—what Callum called a 'lay by'—on a remote road between Bangor and Y Felinheli, a little village to the west.

Up until now, everyone had been in a good mood. David now knew the source of Cassie's happiness, while David himself had been riding high on what he was pretty sure was a combination of pleasure at being back in the modern world, at surviving another brush with death, and at the illicit nature of their current existence..

But now he deflated like a popped balloon. "Oh no."

Darren's mouth turned down. "That can't be good."

Callum put the phone's mouthpiece to his chest. "Math's talking to him right now. I told him we'd get there as soon as we could, but I hope we don't have to. We need to buy what we have and get back to the van."

The modern world was set up for buying things. They'd lucked out with this Tesco, which had a broader inventory than some Tescos, and it even had a self-checkout. That meant they didn't have to talk to anyone about their odd assortment of purchases. Twenty minutes later, with Callum's bank account several thousand pounds lighter, they were back in the van. Built to seat fifteen passengers, it fit on the narrow Welsh roads hardly better than the giant Cardiff bus.

Cassie sat at the wheel, as was appropriate given her superior driving skills and the fact that she'd scored higher than Callum on the Security Service exam. David busied himself with his phone. Even for his fourteenth birthday ten years ago, before he'd first come to medieval Wales, his mom hadn't given him a smart phone. It was 2020 now, however, and he hadn't seen a single dumb phone on the entire rack at Tesco. Maybe nobody made them anymore.

"What do you have for us, Mark?" Callum said.

Callum had hung up the phone with Math, who'd successfully put off Rupert Jones, and then Callum had given everyone a rundown of the conversation, including the last bit about the events at the Black Boar in Caernarfon.

"What do I have for you regarding what? The acquisition of information that will vault the Middle Ages into the twenty-first century or in regards to that reporter outside the clinic?" Mark said without looking up from his laptop.

"The clinic."

"I'm working on it," Mark said. "Rupert Jones is a legitimate reporter, writing for *The Guardian*. I can't see how our old employer is involved yet, Callum. No way could anyone get here this fast."

"Unless someone was already in the area," Callum said.

"Who? And why would they be?" Darren said.

"Somebody whose parents live in Gwynedd," David said.

"Math took care of Rupert, so how about we focus instead on getting the industrial magnet and that microhydro-electric thingie David wants?" Cassie said over her shoulder.

"I did find an industrial supply depot near Bangor University," Mark said.

Callum had taken the seat in front next to Cassie, and he turned to look at David. "That sounds like the place to start."

David shook his head. "I don't know, Callum. How important can these things be compared to the fact that the bus passengers are talking so much that *The Guardian* has heard of it. Rupert could be there in a half-hour. Our cover is totally blown, especially when someone tells him that Mom needed a breast biopsy. He's going to know who they were."

"That's why we need to let Dr. Wolff do his job while we do ours." Cassie looked into her rearview mirror so she could see David's face. "The bus passengers were never going to do anything else, David."

"I just hoped we'd have more time," he said. "It was a failure of imagination on my part. I thought a great deal about how to get everyone here, but I didn't spend enough time thinking about what would happen to them and us once we did. I spent more time worrying about ending up in China than in Gwynedd, because I thought in the latter case they could take care of themselves."

"You didn't know," Cassie said. "It's kind of hard to plan for something like this."

"At least the local constabulary seems to be neutralized," Callum said, "for another hour, anyway."

Cassie pulled the van behind a row of parked cars, many of them stopped half on the sidewalk to get them farther out of the main flow of traffic. The streets here, as everywhere in Wales, were half the width of American streets. Even as deserted as the roads were at six in the evening on Christmas Eve, David found himself having to close his eyes every time they passed a parked car on the left or a moving car on the right. It was even worse when they had to do both at the same time.

"Where to?" Cassie said.

"Mark and I could use an internet café with the ability to print stuff out," David said. "If we do nothing else here, I need to kill a tree or two."

"And I'm looking for anonymity before I hack fully into the Security Service," Mark said.

Cassie looked from Mark to Callum. "Is that really necessary?"

David put a hand on the back of Cassie's seat. "I want to give them Lee if they don't already have him."

Cassie half-turned in her seat. "That's what this is about? Some kind of vengeance?"

David didn't even know how to answer that and gazed at her, a sickness in his belly that she would think that of him.

Fortunately, Callum answered for him. "Not vengeance, Cassie. Justice."

David cleared his throat. "While I'd rather not blow our cover for nothing, I still care about this world and everyone in it."

"Yeah, I get that. Okay. Sorry, David." She put out a hand to him. "I'd prefer to forget all about Lee."

"He's here, somewhere," David said. "Mark says there haven't been any bombings since Cardiff, but that's not to say there won't be, now that Lee's been back here for three months. I find it unlikely that he isn't planning *something*."

"Maybe we caught him when he came in," Darren said, and David knew he meant 'the Security Service' as the 'we'. "There would have been a flash that could have led us to him."

"A double one, actually," David said, "since I came and left again. In fact, those flashes could have led any number of organizations to him. If they were paying attention, which they might not have been."

"But we've done it again now," Callum said, "which could be getting everyone excited, Christmas Eve or no Christmas Eve."

Mark held up one finger. "I have a better idea than an internet café, and it will solve all of our problems in one go."

"What is that?" Callum said.

"University of Bangor," Mark said. "I went to school with a graduate student there, Evan Thomas."

"In what?" David said.

"Computer science," Mark said, and then at everyone's pleased looks added, "Yes, he's a hacker. I told you he could solve all our problems at once."

"Let's go before Anna calls back and tells us that Mom's done and they're ready to be picked up," David said. "I want to be able to leave as soon as we hear from her."

Mark accessed his laptop again, and then he picked up his new phone to dial his friend.

"It's Christmas Eve. He might not be there," Callum said.

"You don't know him like I do," Mark said. "He'll be there."

Sure enough, Evan picked up on the first ring. "What?"

Mark laughed. "Evan, it's Mark Jones. You at the university?"

"Of course."

"Tell me where."

"Room 221. Off Dean Street. You coming here?"

"Yes."

"You can't get in the door without a key. I'll come down."

"Be there in two ticks," Mark said.

"You didn't tell him there were a bunch of us," David said.

Mark smirked. "People don't mean very much to Evan. He won't care one way or the other, and it would only confuse him."

Nothing was very far away in Bangor, though traffic had picked up slightly now that it was the dinner hour. A few stores were open late for last-minute shopping, though none of these could sell David an industrial magnet for creating electricity.

He stared out the window. "I'm beginning to see the flaw in the plan in terms of actually bringing home technology," he said to no one in particular. "It's Christmas Eve. No wonder my mother was concerned about us stealing what we needed."

"We weren't going to be able to walk into a shop and buy the generator anyway," Cassie said. "That industrial supply place isn't going to be open tonight, tomorrow, or the next day. We have to break in, in which case we need some time to scout it out."

"I can help with that," David said.

"Alternatively," Callum said, "we could find a dealer, who may or may not have one on hand. For now, while you, Darren, and Cassie surf the internet, Mark and I can see what's happening at MI-5."

"If the press is here, and if the bus passengers are talking in Caernarfon, MI-5 can't be far behind," Cassie said. "I'd like not to have David end up in a windowless room again."

David scoffed. "You and me both, thank you very much."

They reached Evan's building, which turned out to be made of gray stone, a hundred years old, and one of many similar looking buildings along the block. They piled out of the van: David lugging the reams of paper; Mark and Darren with the three laptops, two of which had been newly acquired; and Callum with the printer.

"Let's try to keep a low profile, everyone," Callum said. "David is the only one who looks like he might belong here. Slouch like you're a graduate student, David, but otherwise I recommend you don't say anything."

David grinned, hoping that Callum would someday give him that kind of order when they were in the Middle Ages, just for laughs. Callum wouldn't, though. He'd missed his calling as an actor, because he played whatever role was necessary to any particular scene. To-night he was the Security Service commander. Two days from now, when they were back in medieval Wales, he'd be David's valued retainer once again.

Evan, when he appeared to let them into the building through the front double-glass doors, turned out to be a tall and lanky twenty-something, with straw-like hair and a face full of brown freckles. He wore tan corduroys and a blue-striped, buttoned-down shirt. He also, oddly, sported a string cowboy bolero tie like David hadn't seen since he'd lived in Oregon. David couldn't think of a single reason why the tie would be in fashion anywhere on the planet. Maybe that was the point.

Mark and Evan shook hands, and then Mark introduced everyone else, though he left off the part where David was the King of England in an alternate universe, and Evan was already turning away before Mark was halfway through the introductions. Evan ushered them inside and then up to his office, which, if the number of desks was any indication, he shared with three other people, none of whom were present.

Evan took a seat behind one of the desks and turned to his computer, not even bothering to gesture them to the other chairs. Mark, Cassie, and Darren sat anyway, but since there were no more seats, David braced himself against the frame of the door, which he made sure was securely latched, and Callum perched on the edge of one of the desks.

"What's going on?" Evan typed into his keyboard for a second, but when nobody answered, he finally swung around to look at the motley assortment of strangers in front of him.

"We need your help," Mark said.

Evan made a *sheesh* sound under his breath. "You're MI-5 aren't you? You've the entire world under surveillance by now. Why would you need my help?"

Callum cleared his throat. "What we want from you is a bit under the table."

Evan had been leaning back in his chair, his hands clasped across his chest, but now he shifted forward, looking genuinely interested for the first time. "Who are you?"

Callum canted his head. "As you said, MI-5."

"Is this where you tell me that if I help you I'll be serving my country?" Evan said, mockery in his voice.

"You would be," Callum said.

Evan scoffed again and looked at Mark. "Don't tell me you've gone rogue. You of all people?"

Mark turned to Callum. "If we want his help, we have to tell him the truth."

"To my recollection, telling modern people the truth doesn't usually turn out well," David said.

Evan folded his arms across his chest and again reclined in his office chair, which he must have unwound as far as it could go because he was lying almost horizontal. "I get the truth, or I don't help."

"We need to know what MI-5 knows about us," Mark said without waiting for Callum's or David's consent. "I can hack in with my old codes, but it'll send up a red flag the second I do it. Does that sound like something you can help us with?"

"You're kidding, right?" Evan said. "What is this—some kind of a trap?"

"Not for you," Callum said. "We all *worked* for MI-5, but we've been out of it for a year. Unfortunately, we now need access to information we can't get elsewhere. That's why we came to you."

"If you're caught, you'll go to jail," Cassie said brightly.

Evan spun around to his computer. "The whole point is to not get caught." But then he reached back towards Callum and snapped his fingers. "This is a test, right? Let me see your badge."

Callum obliged, though not before shooting a look at Mark, who raised his eyebrows and shrugged.

"You're right," Mark said. "This is a test."

"You want to prove to your superiors that MI-5 is hackable— which it completely is, by the way." Evan's fingers were already moving across the keyboard. "What do I get paid for doing this?"

David shifted slightly against the frame of the door, but then forced himself to stop moving. Nobody else was making an effort to correct Evan's misconception, and he didn't feel like it was his place to say anything. He was the low man on the totem pole. This wasn't his world anymore, and he didn't feel that he had the right to interfere.

"I'll be sending you an S-7 form in the new year," Mark said.

Evan made a guttural sound at the back of his throat, implying disbelief, and remained focused on his computer—which was actually a bank of three oversized monitors. "Get me a job, will you, after I graduate. I'd be happy to hack for MI-5 all day long."

"Done," Mark said.

David frowned at Mark's certainty, but he still kept his mouth shut.

Mark stood up to look over Evan's shoulder.

Callum stood up too, though not to look at the computer. "Is there some place we could set up our stuff other than in here? Some place we could spread out?"

Evan was focused on what he was doing, but he took a second to wave a hand before returning it to the keyboard. "Sure. Down the hall. Computer lab with everything. My code is 1282."

"Thanks," Callum said without commenting on the significance of Evan's code. He put his hand on Mark's shoulder briefly, silently telling him he was leaving, though David wasn't sure Mark noticed. Then Callum shooed everyone else out the door.

Fifteen minutes later, his new laptop on the table in front of him and having spoken to Mom and Anna twice more, David was hard at work on the internet. Military technology aside, David's highest priority was getting his nascent communication system up and running. Thanks to huge advances in the last few years in metallurgy, he was a few months away from being able to broadcast a speech to half of England. Once you understood the theory behind it, a radio was an incredibly simple device to make, even without stripping the cars for parts. They had turned out to be easier to produce than the telegraph, since he didn't have to string wire across the whole of the country. Tonight, he was looking for any information that might augment the work.

Each of the others had a list of twenty similar topics—the result of long sessions with various bus passengers over the course of many months where they'd brainstormed for everything they could think of that was buildable in the Middle Ages with the resources they had. David didn't need to vault the Middle Ages all the way into the twenty-first century—the seventeenth would do well enough.

Unfortunately, David felt like he'd only gotten started on his research when Mark came flying down the hall and skidded to a halt in the open doorway. "We're here."

At first David was confused by Mark's use of the word 'we', but Callum stood so fast his chair tipped over; he didn't have to ask who Mark meant. "Where? Outside this building?"

"No. In Caernarfon."

And then David's phone rang again.

13

Meg

... ten minutes earlier.

"Who are you calling, Mom?" Anna said.

Meg tipped the phone away from her mouth for a second. "My sister."

"You haven't already? I thought David told you to call her hours ago."

"I didn't want to until I knew more about what was going on with me, and then I when I called her home number, nobody was there," Meg said a little more tartly than she intended. "I had to call Callum to get her cell phone number. I need something to distract me while we wait for the results."

Which was about the truest thing Meg had ever said. When she'd found the lump in her breast months ago, she'd ignored it, since there wasn't anything she could do about it anyway. She'd had lumps before, as nearly every woman of a certain age eventually did, especially one who'd birthed and nursed four children.

But the lump hadn't gone away, and she found herself constantly suppressing the urge to touch it, which was hardly something the Queen of Wales should do in polite company, given its location. It was just always *there*, and she'd grown to hate it. If there was any indication it was cancer, she hoped Dr. Wolff could cut it out today.

From the very beginning, Dr. Wolff had been relentlessly cheerful, but as the evening had progressed, he began to look less like Santa and more like a stern professor. Rachel hadn't been kidding when she'd said her father had a full service women's clinic. On the way upstairs, she'd passed birthing rooms, examination rooms, a laboratory, diagnostic imaging, and a childcare facility. Now, here she was in a section of the building with every piece of equipment necessary for diagnosing breast cancer.

She'd had the mammogram first, but when that hadn't shown anything amiss, and that the lump appeared normally fibrous, he'd gone and done an ultrasound anyway.

After the ultrasound, however, although he spoke reassuring words, she didn't think he could help the deepening 'v' between his eyes. Rachel had said he was only doing a biopsy because it wasn't like he could tell her to go home and come back in three months. But his expression, coupled with the way he was taking the whole Middle Ages thing in stride, had her more worried than pretty much anything else he could have said or done.

When he'd stuck the biopsy needle into her breast, she'd heard a popping sound, which he said was normal, but at this point, she wasn't willing to believe that anything about the lump was normal. The biopsy took only a few minutes, after which he'd patted her hand, nodded at Rachel, and then disappeared into his inner sanctum to look at the cells under a microscope. After bandaging the incision point and getting Meg ice for the swelling, Rachel had gone after him.

Meg was officially terrified, though she was trying to hide it for Anna's sake.

By now it was nearing eight o'clock in the evening. Meg hoped the others were faring better than she was. David had kept in constant communication with both her and Anna. Every time she'd spoken with him, she'd reassured him that things were progressing smoothly, whether or not it was true. At least they'd had no more visits from the police or the press.

Elisa picked up on the third ring, and almost before Meg had said hello, she said, "I knew it! I knew it was you!"

Meg found herself smiling. "Merry Christmas!"

"Where are you?" Elisa said. "Please don't tell me you're outside our house in Pennsylvania."

"No, actually. We're in Gwynedd."

"So are we!" Elisa crowed so loudly into the phone that Meg had to hold it away from her ear lest she be deafened.

She put the phone back to her ear. "Really? Where?" Elisa sounded like she was practically jumping up and down with excitement.

"The Black Boar. It's a hotel in Caernarfon. More of an inn, really. It's about a thousand years old."

Anna gasped, having overheard because of the volume coming out of the phone. "Mom, that's where the bus passengers ended up!"

"Elisa, we're only a few miles away in Bangor." Meg's heart had started to pound. "Why are you here?"

"Christopher has been asking to spend Christmas in Wales since he was ten years old. He's seventeen now, you know. If we were going to do it, this year seemed like finally the time. The real question is why are *you* here, Meg?"

"Medical stuff."

"Just a second. I can barely hear you because there's a ton of people in the restaurant, and they're talking really loudly. Meg—" Elisa paused and lowered the volume on her voice, "—I don't know how to tell you this, but we're listening to some of what they're saying, and—" She paused again.

"What are they saying, Elisa? Just tell me."

"Something about a bus? Elen's eyes are the size of dinner plates because we heard David's name mentioned along with 'thank God we're back'. Is that about you? What's going on?"

Meg closed her eyes. When Math had come back from the interaction with the reporter, saying that Rupert had received a call from the Black Boar Inn in Caernarfon, Meg had been counting the minutes until someone said something that led him back to the clinic. To her. It didn't sound like that had happened yet, even though Rupert had to have reached Caernarfon by now. Maybe he, like Elisa's family, was listening, even egging the bus passengers on, trying to get the whole story out of them before they thought better of their frankness.

Meg opened her eyes again, and her attention was caught by an inspirational poster that showed an eagle suspended in an over-saturated blue sky as it flew among white-peaked mountains. Except that the inspirational quote wasn't, in fact, inspirational. A rabbit had been caught in the eagle's talons, and the message, instead of saying something about soaring like an eagle or reaching for the stars, said, "Sometimes standing out in a crowd is the last thing you want to do."

She gave a gasp of laughter, and the humor was enough to break through her dismay. "It's complicated, Elisa. Believe me when I tell you that the best thing you guys can do is not get involved and not talk to anyone. Let me call David and get back to you. Stay where you are. We should be almost done here, and then we will come to you."

Meg dropped her hand to look at the screen so she could hang up the phone, but Elisa's voice echoed out of the speaker, "Wait, Meg!"

Meg put the phone back to her ear. "What?"

It was Ted who answered. "Four men in suits just entered the restaurant. Believe me, when I say I've seen their type before."

"Have they seen you?"

"No," Ted said, "or at least no more than anyone else. We're kind of tucked into a corner here. There are a lot of people between us and them."

"Good," Meg said. "Hopefully, they wouldn't know you to look at you, though if they get the register from the hotel, I have to believe it'll take approximately ten seconds for someone at MI-5 to flag your names. Nobody is going to think it's a coincidence that you're here at the same time we are."

"What should we do?"

"Have you finished your dinner?" Meg said.

"Yes. We were just about to go up to our room when you called. It's one in the morning back at home. Though—" and Meg could hear the frown in his voice, "—Christopher went off to the bathroom and hasn't come back."

If Callum were here, Meg would have passed the phone to him, but since he wasn't, she would have to do her best. Her first thought was that she had to stay confident if she wanted Ted and Elisa to feel the same.

"When he returns, smile, get up, and make your way to the door, just like you would any time you leave a restaurant. You can keep talking on the phone if you like because it means you don't have to make eye contact. Maybe Elisa and Elen can go in front. Kids are a good distraction."

"You really think we can walk right past them?" Ted said.

"Is there a back door?"

"Not that I can see," Ted said.

"Do you have a car?" Meg said.

"Yes, but the keys are in the room."

"You have no choice but to get to your room, then. Nod as you pass them, man-to-man," Meg said. "I am so sorry to have you guys caught up in this again."

"We came to Wales of our own accord," Ted said, "and you never asked to go to the Middle Ages."

Elen's ten-year-old soprano piped up. "I think it's awesome."

Despite the tension, Meg laughed. She was looking forward to meeting her niece.

"Elen has been listening to Christopher a little too much." Ted laughed into the phone too, which Meg thought, as a whole, was a good thing, if distraction and nonchalance were what they were going for.

Then Ted said, *"I really think we need to buy now before the price goes any higher."*

"Excuse me?" Meg was befuddled by the total non sequitur, until she realized that he wasn't talking to her at all but to a mythical stock market colleague.

Ted's voice normalized again. "Sorry about that. One of them just walked past our table."

"Anna's calling David right now," Meg said.

Anna had walked a few paces away and was talking quickly into her phone. She hung up. "They're on their way. I'll tell Math and Papa to let them in."

Meg nodded to Anna, who disappeared. She herself stood and started getting dressed, trying to put on her shirt while still keeping the phone to her ear.

"Where in the hell is Christopher—" Ted stopped.

"What is it?"

"More men in suits. I really don't like MI-5's fashion sense."

"The agents aren't all bad, you know, despite the hard time they gave you," Meg said. "Callum, the one who came back to the Middle Ages with us, is a close friend and the Earl of Shrewsbury."

"We've talked to him," Ted said. "I can't wait to see you guys, but I need to hang up. I'll call as soon as we're safe."

"Okay." Meg hung up, her heart pounding. Then the door to Abraham's lab swung open to reveal Rachel with her father right behind her.

Meg faltered. In the midst of the conversation with Ted, she'd managed to forget all about why she was here in the twenty-first century in the first place.

Rachel saw the expression on Meg's face and held up both hands in an appeasing way. "It's okay. You're okay. The lump is a fibro adenoma, which is not cancerous."

Meg sagged against the table, head down, hardly able to believe it. A huge weight lifted off her chest, and she felt like she could breathe for the first time in weeks. Then she looked up. "What do we do about the lump?"

"Nothing," Rachel said.

"What happens if I get another lump?" Meg said.

Rachel smiled. "Let's cross that street when we get to it."

Meg narrowed her eyes at the two doctors. "You do realize that I'm going back to the Middle Ages, right? It isn't as if I can return every few months."

"We all have little abnormal bits inside us all the time. It's part of the human condition," Abraham said. "You just happen to know about one of them."

Meg sighed. "I suppose." Then she studied Abraham for a second. "So, you believe where we're from?"

"My Rachel wouldn't lie to me," he said, "and, because I have spent the last year trying to find her, I have known for some time that what happened to her was outside the range of normal."

"Like me." Meg gave a mocking laugh.

"What?" Rachel had turned to her father. "You never said anything about that."

Abraham tipped back his head, and a spasm of pain crossed his face. He wasn't feeling physical pain, Meg didn't think, but the achingly familiar mix of fear and love and worry he'd felt for his daughter this whole last year. Meg herself knew that pain very well. Some of it was ever-present in the very fact of being a parent. The rest was a product of having a child go missing.

"Through my connections at the Cardiff hospitals," Abraham said, "I tracked down witnesses to the Cardiff bombing and spoke with anyone who would talk to me about what happened. I have a friend who is a detective in Cardiff, and he got me the official—and unofficial—reports. I spoke with reporters at length, and one in particular, Rupert Jones, who has been on your trail since you and Lly-welyn came here three or four years ago."

"Dad—"

"He was downstairs just now, I know." Abraham put out a hand to his daughter. "I would have done anything to find you. You have no idea what it's been like."

"But I do," Meg said. "I lost David and Anna when they were in their teens, and it was a year and a half before I found them again."

"Except you knew where they might be," he said.

"Yes, I grant you that. Though knowing might have made it worse because I knew what it was like there, and they were all alone."

"Or not, as it turned out," Abraham said.

Meg looked at Rachel, who shrugged. "We've had time to talk while we prepared the results." She eyed her father. "Though he didn't exactly tell me everything."

Abraham was still focused on Meg. "Because you understand, it is my hope that you will agree to my request not to be separated from my daughter again."

"Dad, I have to go back," Rachel said. "They need me."

"I'm not asking you to stay here," Abraham said. "I'm asking you to take me with you when you go."

14

Christopher

Christopher had been seven when David had disappeared ten years ago. The afternoon it happened, he remembered playing at his friend's house long after he normally got to stay. When David and Anna didn't pick him up in time for dinner, his friend's mom fed them corn dogs, which he'd never had before, and he'd eaten two because they were amazing.

The fact that his cousins had gone missing, followed a year and a half later by Aunt Meg, hadn't really affected his growing up. They'd lived on the other side of the country anyway, and since David and Anna were so much older than he was, it wasn't as if they'd been friends.

When David had shown up nearly three years later, at almost the same age Christopher was now, however, he'd heard the real story about their disappearance for the first time. Christopher would have time traveled to the Middle Ages in a heartbeat then, and he'd do it today if he could. He'd thought about crashing his car into a tree himself, but even if he shared a lot of the same genes as David and Anna, he figured he'd just kill himself, rather than time travel. Even if his girlfriend had dumped him last week, he wasn't depressed enough to do that.

This trip to Wales had been his idea because he'd heard from his mom about how Aunt Meg had tried to return to the Middle Ages tons of times, even coming to Wales to try to get it to work. His parents didn't know he was hoping that being here might spark the time traveling in him too. But they'd been here three days already, and Christopher hadn't gotten any kind of time travel vibe from any of the places they'd visited. The old castles were cool, but he wanted to walk into one where people were actually living.

Which was why when he caught the words, 'David', 'bus', and 'Middle Ages' from people at the bar as he passed by them on the way back from the bathroom, he stopped and edged closer to listen, hardly able to believe what he was hearing.

"Nobody is going to believe us, Darla," one older man was saying. "There's no point in taking this any further."

"I tell you, if we talk to the press, we can make a lot of money selling our story," she said. "It doesn't matter if people believe us, really. What about the blokes who go on about UFO's. We've got something way better than that. Look—" Darla opened her purse and showed the man what was inside it.

"Gold, Darla? I thought you told David you didn't have any money?"

Darla shrugged. "What he doesn't know can't hurt him."

Christopher didn't think that was necessarily true, but he looked away to study the calendar tacked to a post by the bar in case either of the people realized he was listening.

Then a third voice spoke. "I can write your story."

Christopher glanced around to see a tall man in a suit and trench coat lean his hip against the ancient, polished wood bar. He was holding out a black wallet, the writing on which Christopher couldn't see from where he was standing, but he didn't dare move closer.

"Rupert Jones, *The Guardian*."

"Let me see that." Darla took the man's credentials and studied them, her face screwed up in concentration. Then she handed them back. "Okay. But we want a fee."

Rupert gestured around the bar. "I'll buy you a drink, and if I think there's something to what you're telling me, then we'll talk about money."

The man with Darla tipped his head. "Sounds fair."

Darla didn't look thrilled, but she picked up her drink and followed the two men to one of the few empty tables in the restaurant, which was too far away and nestled amidst other tables for Christopher to get close without calling attention to himself. Frustrated, he looked around at the twenty other people who were at the bar or near it. These people knew something about David. Christopher had to find out what that was.

"There you are, son." His dad's hand came down on his shoulder in a strong grip. "We have to go."

"Dad—we can't go. These people know something about Dav—"

His father cut him off. "I know."

"You know? How?"

"Your Aunt Meg just called. They're *here*. All of them." His father's eyes were lit up as bright as the Christmas tree in the corner, full of excitement and something Christopher rarely saw in them— almost recklessness.

"She called—"

"We have to get out of here now." His father directed Christopher's attention to four men in suits, two of whom were conferring near the front door, and the other two who were moving casually among the diners. "MI-5."

"Holy sh-crap," Christopher said, changing what he was going to say at the last minute for his father's benefit.

"Exactly." His dad beckoned to his mother and Elen, and they wended their way towards them from their table.

"Are they looking for us?" Christopher said.

"We don't know," his dad said, "but if you've heard what we've heard, most of the people in here were on the Cardiff bus, which Aunt Meg just brought back from the Middle Ages. Hopefully, they'll keep the agents busy so they won't think to check the register until later for other names they might recognize."

"They might recognize you on sight, Dad," Christopher said. Some of the excitement he'd been feeling was giving way to a cold ball of fear in his stomach. His dad had been questioned by MI-5 for hours a couple of years ago. If they were arrested, it might mean that they lost their chance to see David and the others. "There's a back way out of here." He grabbed his dad's arm. "It's on the way to the bathrooms."

It wasn't easy for a family of four to look inconspicuous, especially when three of them—Christopher, his sister, and his dad—were Americans with bright red hair, but nobody followed them into the narrow hallway that led past the bathrooms and then through a narrow supply room that opened into the hotel part of the inn on the other side. The hotel's corridors were twisty and made it hard to see anyone until they were already upon them, but nobody stopped them from leaving the restaurant. Maybe MI-5 wasn't yet as organized as they could have been.

As they trotted up the narrow staircase to the second floor, his dad said, "The inn is so old, this wing was probably added on after the original part was built, and they wanted a way for servants to come and go easily."

Christopher glanced at his father, completely unsurprised that he would take the time to comment on the architecture of the inn while running for his life.

"Our rooms are this way, aren't they—" Christopher cut himself off, turning on a dime and shoving his family back down the stairs they'd just come up.

"What are you doing?" his mom said. "We need the car keys."

"Two men in suits just went into your room," Christopher said.

His father didn't object anymore to Christopher preventing him from going up the stairs, but he stopped on the landing and ran his hand through his hair. "What do we do, Elisa?"

"I need to see Meg," she said.

"There's a fire door down there." Elen tugged on her mother's hand and pointed to the end of the hallway.

"Let's hope we don't set off the alarm when we go through it," his father said.

"I honestly don't care if we do," Christopher's mother said. "We'll be outside, and that's what's important"

"No car, though," his dad said.

"Meg said she'd come to us," his mother said.

"What are we going to do in Caernarfon in the dark on Christmas Eve?" his dad said.

"I know where we could go," Christopher said. "There's a fish and chips slash Chinese restaurant slash grocery store down the block. I saw it when we came past the castle earlier."

"You just ate," his mom said.

"I didn't mean that we should eat there, but it might be open," Christopher said. "As Dad said, where else are we going to go at this hour?"

"Good idea, son," his father said. "Let's do it."

As it turned out, the alarm did not go off as they pushed through the door, and the snow was still falling, maybe even heavier than before. Christopher was from Pennsylvania, so he knew snow, and this wasn't even enough to cancel school. It was pretty, though, and made Caernarfon look like a postcard of Christmas in Wales. White, green, and red Christmas lights were strung across the cobbled streets and around the windows of the stores, though all but the grocery store he'd seen were closed at nine o'clock on Christmas Eve.

Christopher and Elen hadn't changed out of their boots to eat, but Christopher's parents wore dress shoes, which weren't as good in the snow. Thus, Christopher took his sister's hand and stumped through the snow with her, leading their parents away from the inn. Unfortunately, they had all left their coats in their rooms, so they were shivering by the time they entered the store.

Once inside, Christopher's dad pulled out his phone to call Aunt Meg again. "We're safe."

Aunt Meg's "thank God" came through loud and clear. "David's not here yet but he's coming. Where are you?"

"In a shop outside the inn," his dad said. "Fish and chips slash Chinese. Maybe we ought to order something?"

"Honestly, that would be great," Aunt Meg said. "None of us have eaten since we left the Middle Ages."

"You got it. Call us when you get to Caernarfon."

Christopher peered through the front door, which was made of glass. Several more black SUVs rumbled past, though they couldn't get to the inn down this street because it was closed to through traffic. His father, who was still two inches taller than Christopher, peered over his shoulder at the scene too.

"I really, really want to see David, but I never thought asking to visit Wales for Christmas would get us into trouble, Dad."

His father's hand came down on his shoulder again. "Don't apologize, Christopher. Even your mom wouldn't have missed this for the world."

15

Bronwen

"**W**here is Lord Ieuan?" Geoffrey said in French, looking around the room with something like dismay.

"Given the urgency of the current crisis, both he and Lord Goronwy felt that they should be among the men to ride into Llangollen, to question the villagers at the tavern and students at the university," Bronwen replied in the same language. "Most would have been at the feast for much of the day, but if any of the bandits passed through after the attack, hopefully someone will have seen them."

Geoffrey had come a long way in the few months he'd been working for David, but he still wasn't comfortable with having a woman in charge. Maybe he thought it should be him. Bronwen didn't necessarily think it should be her, but with Lili unwell and Ieaun and Goronwy gone to the village, she wasn't going to leave this to anyone else. She'd spent these last eight years during which she'd lived in the Middle Ages rising to whatever occasion presented itself, so she wasn't going to let the Norman baron intimidate her out of doing it again.

Besides, if graduate school in archaeology had prepared her for anything, it was for dealing with older men with large egos who had axes to grind. If a woman in her early twenties was to survive the cutthroat world of academia, she had to learn how to stand up for herself and her ideas and not to allow anyone to shout her down.

Thus, Bronwen stood in the center of Math's receiving room with a circle of men around her, among them Samuel, who'd arrived moments before with his men, having ridden many miles in search of the bandits; Cadwallon; and Justin, all standing, all impatient and frustrated. In contrast, the hall they'd just left was full of jovial post-dinner conversation.

The idea that Math and Anna had gone to Avalon with King David was far less disturbing to Math's people than Bronwen thought it should be—though their acceptance was convenient too because it meant she could focus on the crisis with France rather than on appeasing distressed medieval minds. The people who were the most upset at the bus's departure were those who'd become friends with some of the bus passengers, like Jane and Carl. Rachel, at least, would be returning, so the hospital and medical college wouldn't be bereft for more than a few days.

Convenient also was the fact that it was David's miraculous absence that was the topic of conversation in the hall rather than the real danger of imminent war between France, England, and Scotland if the emissary died or James Stewart wasn't found alive.

"How is the emissary?" Samuel said, now in English, which was the most comfortable language for him.

"I've been sitting with him," Geoffrey said, seemingly fluent in English as well, for all that Norman lords didn't always speak it. "Your healers have cared for him, and he is as comfortable as I can imagine him being, though he remains asleep."

"Breathing, though," Bronwen said to Samuel.

Samuel growled. "We can ride no further tonight, but with your permission, we'll leave at first light for Chirk on Peter's trail."

"Tell him when you find him to proceed very carefully," Geoffrey said. "James's welfare is all."

"Yes, my lord." Samuel put his feet together and bowed. "I was once captive with James Stewart and know his worth."

Currently the Sheriff of Shrewsbury in Callum's absence, Samuel was *the* authority in Shropshire. Bronwen had watched the friendship and trust among this core group of time travelers living in Shrewsbury, consisting of Callum and Cassie, Darren, Mark, Peter, and Bridget. She was happy to know that everyone who'd gone would be coming back from David's jaunt to the twenty-first century. If not for Peter and Bridget staying behind, she would have been the only twenty-firster, as Bridget insisted on calling them, in the whole of the Middle Ages, though to be so wouldn't have been particularly daunting to Bronwen. She'd chosen this life and wasn't afraid to live it.

Even though he wasn't a time traveler, Bronwen always included Samuel in the group in part because Callum trusted him completely but also because he too was a man out of place, if not time. Samuel was Aaron's son and thus Jewish, even if he'd spent many years before David's arrival hiding his ethnicity in order to serve as a man-at-arms for the Earl of Chester, King Edward's brother. Back when David was sixteen, Samuel had rescued him and his men from the remains of King Edward's camp—and found himself included in the Welsh retinue at a level he would never have dared to dream of. David tended to do that to people.

Once Samuel didn't need to hide who he was anymore, he'd found his way back to his father and his religion, even if his lack of strict adherence to the law was disturbing to some of his co-religionists. He'd married his Elspet, a Gentile, after all. He and Rachel had hit it off in that regard, and Bridget knew that Samuel had encouraged her to accept the love Darren was offering. Bronwen wasn't quite sure why Darren and Rachel weren't married yet, but she hadn't asked. Prying into her friends' private lives wasn't her habit.

She was glad, however, having heard her husband's first-hand account of their kiss, that Bridget and Peter might finally stop dancing around each other and get serious.

Bronwen understood the difficulty with committing to a relationship in a foreign place when you didn't know if you were in love with the place, with him, or just so desperate and lonely that having someone was better than being alone. Anna had asked the same questions before she'd married Math. Maybe it was that way for everyone, no matter in what universe one lived. Commitment was hard.

Samuel departed to see to the welfare of his men, and Geoffrey cleared his throat. "May I ask what was the business that had King David and King Llywelyn traveling to Avalon today of all days?"

Bronwen pressed her lips together. She should have known this question would come from someone, and it wasn't really a surprise to hear it from Geoffrey. "I could tell you it was a private matter, but that would hardly assuage your concern."

"No," Geoffrey said. "It wouldn't."

"Queen Meg is ill," Bronwen said, and then called yet again upon the myth of King Arthur to explain the unexplainable. "David brought his mother to the isle of Avalon to be healed."

Understanding crossed Geoffrey's face. "But when will he return?"

"Within a day or two at most," Bronwen said. "He promised."

"Not all who ask to enter Avalon are admitted," Geoffrey said. "Not all who ask to leave are allowed to go."

"They all were admitted," Bronwen said. "Ieuan saw it with his own eyes. And we cannot doubt that David will be allowed to return."

Geoffrey kept his gaze fixed on Bronwen's face. "You're very sure."

"Of David?" Bronwen nodded. "Whether in Avalon or here, you can never go wrong believing he'll do what he tells you he will."

Geoffrey made no attempt to argue with that.

When Bronwen pushed open the door and entered the royal bedchamber, Lili was sitting up in bed with pillows stacked behind her, reading a book to Arthur. Bronwen had made it a personal campaign to have children's books, a few of which Bronwen herself had written in her spare time, be a large part of what was being produced by David's new printing presses. If they were to change the world, the best avenue to do so was through the education of children. Growing up in far flung places, she'd seen with her own eyes how villagers often viewed their school as their greatest asset.

At Bronwen's approach, Lili glanced up and smiled but continued reading. Bronwen waited until Lili finished the book, at which point she tipped her head to Arthur's nanny, asking her silently if she could take the boy away. The nanny obliged, though not before Bronwen got a kiss from Arthur on his way out the door. She didn't, in principle, like relying on nannies and servants as much as they all had learned to. By any definition, parenting standards in the Middle Ages were low. Children were alternately spoiled and neglected, and then thrown into the adult world—often from the age of seven—and expected to make their own way. Under the current circumstances, however, the more adults Arthur knew he could rely on, the better.

Bronwen sat on the edge of Lili's bed. "What's going on? Are you having contractions?"

Lili let out a puff of air. "Yes."

"This is way too early."

Lili didn't answer, just stared down at the blankets covering her legs.

This was like pulling teeth—and unlike Lili. "What does Branwen say?" Hired right after her marriage to David, Branwen was Lili's maid and much loved and trusted by Lili.

"She worries too. And nags."

"As she should." Bronwen leaned forward. "You and I both know that there's no way out of this birth. Only through it. The baby is going to come, whether you want it to or not. We're here for you, for whatever you need. You have to believe that everything's going to be okay."

"Rachel's gone," Lili said. "We will have to do this without her."

"Why would we have to? Everyone gets contractions every now and then. Do you think the baby is really coming?"

Lili rubbed the end of her nose. "It may be that my dates are wrong."

Ice settled in the pit of Bronwen's stomach.

Then Lili added, "There's no may be. My dates are wrong."

Bronwen closed her eyes, willing herself to remain calm. "Last I heard, you were seven-ish months pregnant. Are you telling me that isn't right?"

Lili bent her knees so they made a mountain in the middle of the bed and tucked the covers around herself, all without looking directly at Bronwen. "Yes."

Bronwen tried to think of what to say that wouldn't mean leaping the distance between them and shaking Lili for keeping the truth from her—and from David. "We've all thought you've been looking big, and you're already waddling."

Lili smirked. "Thanks."

"You know what I mean." Bronwen met Lili's gaze. "David doesn't even suspect, does he?"

"He wouldn't have gone to Avalon if he had," Lili said.

"And you wanted him to go."

"Of course I didn't want him to go!" Lili spit the words out, "but he needed to go." Lili looked away. "My mother died in childbirth, Bronwen."

"I know."

Lili shook her head. "It's a burden we all carry. I can see the fear weighing Dafydd down. I don't want to add to his troubles, but in the dark, in the middle of the night, I want to scream sometimes. I can't let the fear go." And then she finally told Bronwen the truth. "I wish I weren't having this baby."

Bronwen's throat was thick with emotion. She swallowed hard, searching for the words that would make this better for Lili, though she knew finding surety and letting go of the fear was something Lili could do only for herself. "We've had this conversation before, remember? That time, you and I were the ones consoling Anna."

"I remember. I was so confident then. I want that surety back. Instead, I've been reduced to a quivering mess by this child. I've spend months lying to my husband on the way to lying to myself." Lili made a helpless gesture with one hand. "Sometimes I look at him, and I just want to wrap my arms around him and protect him from the world. An entire country depends on him, and all these bus passengers only added to his worries. I hated them for that and wanted nothing more than for them to all go home. When he decided that he needed to take them himself, I was relieved."

"But you still didn't tell him about the baby."

"They had to go back, and he needed to take them," Lili said. "When Shane got sick, Dafydd felt such guilt. How could I make him feel more by asking him to value me over Shane, or by speculating about the baby when there was no way to know the truth?"

Bronwen reached for Lili's hand. "Admittedly, it's too late now."

Lili squeezed back. "There's still a chance I could be wrong."

"Did Catriona check you liked I asked her to?" Bronwen said.

Catriona was the chief midwife at the hospital, now completely in charge since Rachel was in the modern world.

"Yes," Lili said.

Bronwen didn't reply, and after a few seconds Lili sighed and rolled her eyes. "I'm slightly dilated, but less than two centimeters," she said, perfectly parroting what had to have been Catriona's words, themselves learned from Rachel. Centimeters were a form a measurement without context in the Middle Ages, and Bronwen briefly wondered if, going forward, they would apply only to childbirth.

"Thus, you're staying in bed until David gets back," Bronwen said.

"So it seems," Lili said.

Bronwen studied her sister-in-law some more. "Being strong doesn't mean you can't ask for help."

"I knew that once," Lili said. "I get lost in being Queen of England and forget how to be myself."

A knock came at the door, and then Gwenllian, Llywelyn's ten-year-old daughter by his wife, Elin, who'd died at Gwenllian's birth, pushed the door open without waiting for permission.

"I can help mind Arthur," Gwenllian said.

Lili patted the bed beside her, to indicate that Gwenllian should join them. At first the girl perched on the edge of bed in a very ladylike manner, but then, after a moment, she crawled under the covers with Lili and put her head on her shoulder. Bronwen hadn't been party to Gwenllian's conversation with Meg and Llywelyn before they left, but she remembered being ten. Gwenllian had to be feeling abandoned.

"They had to leave us," Bronwen said.

"I know," Gwenllian said, speaking perfect American English, "but I wish they'd taken me with them. Other children got to go."

"Only those who are from Avalon and are going to stay there forever," Lili said. "The rest of us had to stay behind."

Because she was small for her age and reserved, it was easy to forget that Gwenllian was nearing womanhood. Her heart-shaped face had thinned in the last six months, and her long blonde curls fell halfway down her back. With her blue eyes, she was the epitome of medieval female beauty, just as her mother had been.

Llywelyn and Meg were already talking about marriage for her, trying to tread a middle way between using her to make an alliance with another royal house and allowing Gwenllian the opportunity to choose her husband. The negotiations between Meg and Llywelyn had been heated, and finally David had stepped in and suggested they give Gwenllian a list of prospective suitors and allow her to make the first cut. Given her beauty and that she was a princess of Wales, men would be falling all over themselves for the chance to win her hand when the time came.

Fortunately, they had a few more years before they needed to make a decision. Right now she was just a ten-year-old girl missing her mother.

"What if they don't come back?" Gwenllian said. "What if Mama—" She stopped, choking off what she'd been about to say.

"I've traveled like they did," Bronwen said. "It's scary when it happens. They were all scared when they left, even if they were trying not to show it, but what does your brother always say?"

"Fear should never stop you from doing what is right, and courage isn't about not being afraid—it's about acting even when you are afraid," Gwenllian recited. "I've heard Callum say it too."

"And they're right." Lili hugged Gwenllian to her.

"So why didn't you tell Dafydd about the baby?" Gwenllian looked up into Lili's face.

Lili bit her lip. "Because I was afraid, and it did stop me from doing what was right. Sometimes adults don't live up to what they say they believe."

"It's called being a hypocrite," Gwenllian said, with all the complacency of the ten-year-old girl she was. "Dafydd told me."

Bronwen gave a small smile. "Sometimes, though, it is just being afraid."

Lili squeezed Gwenllian again. "*Cariad,* I promise I will do better, if not for myself, then for you." But as she met Bronwen's eyes over Gwenllian's head, she stiffened as a contraction overtook her.

Bronwen gently rubbed Gwenllian's arm with the back of one finger to get her attention. "Run and get Catriona. Ready or not, the baby is on its way."

16

Peter

"You've turned melancholy all of a sudden," Bridget said. They were approaching the royal manor at Chirk, needing a meal as well as the opportunity to leave another message for Samuel as to their progress, were he to decide to follow them. Peter had once visited the modern Chirk Castle, back in Avalon before the bombings in Cardiff, but it had been built by King Edward after he conquered Wales, so it didn't exist in this world.

"Just thinking," Peter said.

If he and Bridget were really in a relationship, which he wanted very much, he knew he needed to learn how to tell her more about what was in his mind, but he didn't want to talk about the twenty-first century with Simon present. Peter flicked his eyes in the direction of the man-at-arms, and instead of being irritated by Peter's lack of communication, Bridget nodded.

"Okay," she said. "How far are we going tonight?"

"Let's decide after we eat." Peter should have been tired, given the upheavals of the day, but he was wide awake, and so were Bridget and Simon, who'd stayed a silent shadow, leading the way for the ride from the ambush site. "The steward here always has a good ear to the ground."

Chirk wasn't exactly a booming metropolis, but because of the royal manor, it included a small village. The three of them had to pass the green and the church dedicated to St. Tysilio in order to reach the manor house, which was nestled in the bend of the River Ceiriog. Peter's eyes lit for a second at the thought of sharing what was sure to be a very uncomfortable bed with Bridget.

It wouldn't do, though. Not with standards of propriety in the Middle Ages. Still, if they decided to stay, the manor included two rooms in the back, which would hopefully be serviceable for their needs and might possibly be more comfortable than any bed at the inn in Whittington. It was their decision to arrive so late. They could have returned to Dinas Bran and started in the morning, so they had no business being choosy about where they laid their heads.

In the last year, Peter had ranged all around this area with Darren as part of their service to Callum and to Samuel, as the sheriff, keeping the peace in Shropshire. Chirk itself, though on the English side of Offa's Dyke, had always had strong ties to Wales. While Peter had grown up in a suburb of Bristol, the countryside had never been far away, at least for him. He'd spent his holidays on his grandparents' small farm near Cwmhir Abbey in Wales, where Llywelyn's headless body was said to have been buried in 1282 after his head had been taken to England and stuck on a pike at the Tower of London.

Chirk was around forty miles as the crow flies from Abbey Cwmhir, and Shropshire was the same green landscape he'd grown up with, even if, east of Offa's Dyke, it was somewhat less mountainous than Wales proper. Afghanistan had been dry but mountainous in places, and he'd been far more comfortable with that landscape than the city kids from London, Manchester, or Liverpool.

Peter had been to the manor at least a half-dozen times before, though always with Darren. George, the steward, recognized him instantly as he and Bridget entered the small hall, which was approximately twenty-four by thirty-six feet.

"My lord!" Looking concernedly at their wet clothes, George hurried across the wooden floor. "What can I get for you and—" he paused, eyebrows raised, "—your lady wife?" George only glanced at Simon, who'd come in right behind them, recognizing him as a retainer rather than a knight. "I have a nice table here for you by the fire."

Knowing his place, Simon made his way to the back of the hall, where members of the manor's small garrison were seated. He had a beer in front of him almost before he sat down.

"Thank you, George. We need food and drink."

"And, perhaps a place to sleep for the night?" George said.

Peter glanced at Bridget, who nodded and shrugged at the same time. It *was* late. "If you have it," Peter said. "And how many times do I have to tell you that I'm not a lord and am barely a knight."

Callum had knighted both Darren and Peter, claiming that in order to serve him properly, they needed to have the authority that came with the station. Peter was afraid that other men in Callum's guard would resent them leapfrogging over them, but they hadn't— mostly because Callum treated everyone fairly. Any man who could afford his own sword and horse, and had distinguished himself in Callum's service, could find himself knighted.

Callum didn't care about bloodlines. He'd also knighted Samuel, who had to be the only Jewish knight in the entire realm.

"Of course, sir," George said, ignoring Peter's request as he always did. "This way."

Bridget smiled. "Thank you."

Once seated, Peter leaned across the table towards Bridget. "You understand the deception about our relationship?"

"I shouldn't be traveling with you unless I'm your wife," she said. "I know."

"You don't mind, though, do you?" Peter said. "Being my wife, I mean?"

He had no idea before he said the words that he was going to ask her that question. It had burst out of him without him thinking, and, as usual with women, he'd done this completely the wrong way round. No romance, no flowers or poems, no loving words.

Bridget just sat looking at him, her hands in her lap. She hadn't answered his question of course. What woman would, given the way he'd asked?

"You don't have to answer, but please, don't make a scene."

Bridget gave a short laugh and shook her head. "When have I ever made a scene?"

Then George was back with wine for both of them, followed by a boy carrying a trencher with meat, cheese, fresh baked bread, and onions enough for two.

"George," Peter said before the steward could leave, "have you noticed anything unusual along the road through Chirk today?"

George adjusted the trencher so it lay exactly equidistant from Peter and Bridget. Peter had noticed a perfectionist tendency— almost a military rigidity—in George the previous times he'd visited here. It was always odd to encounter in a medieval person what he would have viewed as a strictly modern sensibility. It indicated, of course, that there was very little about human behavior that was truly modern.

"I don't know if I could say one way or the other. What do you mean by *unusual*?"

Peter swiveled in his chair to survey the room, which was moderately full with perhaps a dozen other people, mostly men, but a few women too, maids or wives. Christmas Eve was a time for community and celebration, no less here than in the modern world. In this case, however, they might all be sitting up late because they would shortly be attending midnight mass at the church. He and Bridget would need to go too.

"I apologize for not being specific enough. What I meant was—has anyone mentioned seeing riders along the road to Whittington today—either more men than usual, possibly passing north as a group and returning south in smaller companies?"

Peter was guessing about the latter arrangement, but if he had been the one to ambush a French emissary and the High Steward of Scotland, that's the way he'd have done it.

George frowned. "The road definitely saw more traffic today than usual, but that would be because of the Scots."

"The Scots?" Peter spoke without emphasis, trying to ask the question without implying that he cared. His stomach growled, and he stabbed the tip of his belt knife into an onion. He hadn't realized he was hungry.

"Cousins to Lord Fulk, come down from the north." George made a sour face. "I can hardly understand them when they speak, though they claim it's English."

"Have some come here?" Peter said.

"A few," George said. "They have plenty of food and drink down at the castle, of course, and I've heard Lord Fulk has sent out hunting parties every day."

"Hunting parties," Peter said. "Really."

George hesitated, swallowing hard. Hunting wasn't a privilege accorded to just anyone, even to a local lord like Fulk Fitzwarin, who ruled at Whittington. The king—meaning David—controlled all forests in England; and Wales should be off limits to any English hunting party.

"I-I-I don't know," George said.

Peter rubbed his chin. "Thank you, George, for being honest with me. I didn't hear it from you."

His expression cleared. "Thank you, sir." He bowed and departed.

Peter ate a slice of mutton, thinking hard. That Scots were at Whittington and James Stewart had been abducted a few miles to the north couldn't be a coincidence.

"I don't know this Fulk Fitzwarin, though." Bridget's brow furrowed. "He must be a by-blow of the Warenne family." Among the Normans, an illegitimate child whose father acknowledged him acquired his father's surname, with the addition of *fitz* before the name.

Peter's parents hadn't been married when they'd had his older sister, though they did marry before his birth, with the odd idea that, while one child wasn't enough to seal the deal, two ought to be. They'd made it work, and he got on with them well enough, though his dad hadn't supported his joining the military. Peter had written and called during the time he'd been in the Middle East and then Africa, but the long months and years of separation had taken its toll on their relationship. With him staying in the Middle Ages for the foreseeable future, it seemed unlikely it was ever going to improve.

"The connection isn't recent as far as I know," Peter said.

The medieval obsession with illegitimacy became comprehensible as soon as you realized that condemning a child for the sins of his parents wasn't actually about sin or damnation, but about money. In England, illegitimate children, even those acknowledged by their fathers, weren't supposed to inherit. When two nobles married, the bargain struck was that the son of the woman would inherit the father's money, and vice versa.

Sometimes a child was acknowledged anyway if he or she was royal—and sometimes even when he wasn't, as seemed to be the case for whatever bastard in the Warenne family had raised himself to the point of inheriting Whittington Castle. David hadn't produced any illegitimate children himself—no Fitzroys were running about Westminster Palace—so, he hadn't chosen to press the issue yet.

In Wales, illegitimacy was ignored by all parties if the father acknowledged the child. And in that case, the child inherited equally with his legitimate siblings—and could even be the chief heir. This policy had been changing in the years leading up to David's arrival in Wales in 1282, as England gained more control over Wales politically. But these days, with King Llywelyn, whose own father was illegitimate, on the throne, traditional Welsh law continued to prevail. David wasn't technically legitimate either, since his parents hadn't been legally married at his birth.

Peter was pretty sure nobody remembered the true situation anymore—or if they did, nobody, *nobody*, would have the temerity to suggest that David wasn't going to inherit his father's kingdom.

Peter lowered his voice again so it wouldn't carry beyond their table. "Do you have any idea what the Scots could be doing with the Fitzwarins?"

Bridget stared down at her vegetables. "The wife of King John Balliol of Scotland is a Warenne, you know."

"I want to believe that's a coincidence," Peter said, "but I can't, not if there are Scots at Whittington, and Fitzwarin has Scottish cousins."

"Could the King of Scotland really have had a hand in abducting his High Steward from an English highway?" Bridget said.

Peter shook his head, his eyes searching the hall for George. "With the Scots, anything is possible."

Bridget made a face. "I'm Scottish."

Peter whipped his head back around. "I didn't mean you!"

Bridget grinned, and laughter filled her face. "I know you didn't. I was teasing."

One of Peter's problems with women had always been that he was too sincere and misunderstood situations like this as a matter of course.

"We should ride to Whittington," Bridget said.

"It would be gone midnight before we got there, and while Fitzwarin would admit us because I'm undersheriff to Samuel, we wouldn't be welcomed with open arms, and we would certainly arouse his suspicions if he has something to hide."

Bridget looked down at her food, which she'd hardly touched. "You're right."

"Besides, we'll be no good to James Stewart or anyone else tomorrow if we haven't slept. We're not in Avalon and can't behave as if we are. But I can tell you this: King David isn't sleeping."

17

David

David wasn't sleeping. In fact, David was pretty sure that none of them were going to be getting sleep any time soon. They'd arrived at the clinic ten minutes after leaving the university. While everyone was pleased Mom didn't have cancer, David found himself somewhat subdued over Abraham Wolff's adamant request to come home with them—and with Mom defending his choice.

"The whole point of this trip was to reduce the number of modern people in the Middle Ages, not add more!" David said.

"I know how he feels to be without his daughter," Mom said.

David opened his mouth to argue more but then couldn't think of anything to say, so he snapped his mouth shut, deciding he didn't actually have to decide this one way or the other right now. They weren't going back this minute.

"There's more," Anna said. "Rupert Jones, that reporter who's gone off to Caernarfon? Abraham talked to him after the Cardiff bombing."

David looked at Abraham in surprise. "Why?"

"I was looking for Rachel," Abraham said simply, "a fact for which I will not apologize. Rupert does not appear to have done his homework, however, if he came to my clinic without knowing it was mine. Or perhaps he spoke with so many people after the bombings that he didn't immediately connect my questions for him in Cardiff a year ago with a clinic in Gwynedd today."

"Good job he didn't," Darren said, "or he would have been far harder to get rid of."

"As it is, we sicced him on the bus passengers in Caernarfon," David said with something like a moan.

"I didn't mean to do more than get rid of him," Math said. "It was all I could think of."

"It is what it is, Math," Mom said, her hand on her son-in-law's arm. "He would have gotten the report from the Black Boar whether or not you ever said anything to him about it."

They all piled into the van, Rachel sandwiched in the very back between her father and Darren, in what had to be an uncomfortable manner.

Darren stuck out his hand to Abraham again. "Sir, Rachel and I are more than friends. I just wanted you to know."

Abraham shook his hand, a smile hovering around his lips, which boded well for Darren. "I know. Rachel told me. I'm glad she has had someone there to care for her."

David eased out a breath. That could have been more awkward. Abraham was at least putting a good face on it, but even David could see the slightly pinched look around Abraham's mouth, indicating that maybe he wasn't quite as accepting of Rachel and Darren as he looked.

Abraham directed his next question to Callum. "How is it that MI-5 could possibly have tracked you so quickly? Surely you're not using your own identities?"

Since everyone on the planet—including, it seemed, Rachel's father—had seen too many spy movies by now, they knew that using credit cards and your own identification was always the first mistake of someone on the run. Callum twisted in his seat to answer. He sat this time in the second row since Cassie was driving again and Mark was beside her, navigating.

"Mark tapped into MI-5," Callum said. "He didn't even have to get in very far to find the chatter about our arrival. Apparently, someone was filming the snowy motorway when we appeared out of nowhere, driving the wrong way down it. There's just no reasonable explanation for that, and even with it being Christmas Eve, the slowest analyst might sit up and take notice of a video showing our arrival."

David added, "For whatever reason, there's a flash—or a 'flare out' as that reporter said—that isn't visible to the naked eye but is picked up by camera and radar. If anyone was looking, they'd see it. The whole point of coming here today was that nobody would be looking, but I guess that was too much to hope for."

"The bus passengers have pretty much given the game away anyway," Cassie said. "I wish we could have stopped them."

David turned to her. "How? The second we arrived, they stampeded for the door. We could have held them by force, but that would have been worse in the long run. I should have given more thought to what would happen when we arrived, but I didn't."

"I didn't either," Callum said. "This isn't all on you."

"David isn't their king anymore," Anna said. "It's actually Papa and Math who concern me most."

"Us?" Math was sprawled beside Anna, his arm across the back of the seat. "We're just along for the ride, as you say."

Dad laughed too. "Meg does not have cancer, so I am the least of your worries."

"You're medieval, Papa and the King of Wales," Anna said. "I'm sure anyone from MI-5 to whatever that private security force was called—" she looked at Callum.

"The Dunland Group turned CMI."

"Right, them," Anna said, "would love to keep you in a locked room."

Dad frowned and glanced at David. "We've talked about that, and I would like to avoid it, if possible."

"You know what?" David said. "You guys should go back right now. Mom got what she came for. There's no reason to stay. I can take everyone else later."

"I'm not leaving until I see my sister," Mom said.

David rested his head against the window. "Right. I forgot what we were doing for a second."

"Better if we stick together, son," Dad said.

"By the way, has anyone heard from Jane?" Cassie glanced in the rearview mirror before returning her eyes to the road. The snow was continuing to fall, if anything more heavily than before. David hadn't seen a snowplow yet and wondered how many there might be in all of Gwynedd, much less the UK.

"I spoke with the physician who admitted him," Abraham said. "He took one look at Shane and called in a pediatric oncologist—a good man whom I've had dinner with a number of times. He left his home for the hospital immediately. They're in good hands."

"What about the diagnosis?" David said.

"The tests were ongoing, but yes, Rachel is right that it is probably leukemia," Abraham said. "The admitting physician was disturbed that Shane had been allowed to reach this point without treatment."

David sank lower in his seat, his hand to his head. "That's my fault."

Abraham lifted a hand. "You didn't cause the cancer, nor are you responsible for the bombing in Cardiff that brought Shane to the medieval world."

"I've told him that at least twenty-six times," Rachel said. "He doesn't listen."

"The story Jane told was that they'd returned to this country today specifically because Shane was ill. I supported her story," Abraham said.

"Will he live?" David said.

"Childhood leukemia is eminently treatable, even in later stages," Abraham said, "though it is too early to say one way or the other in Shane's case, and it would be wrong of me to do so." He eyed David for a moment. "The first thing you learn as a doctor is that you can't save everyone."

"You can try," David said.

"Absolutely," Abraham said, "and I would not argue that you shouldn't."

"We're entering Caernarfon," Mark said from the front seat.

"This is easily the most confusing town I've ever driven in," Cassie said, as she followed an off ramp and then did a loop-de-loop under the motorway to get into the city proper. Christmas lights were strung across narrow alleys, some of which they couldn't have gone down even if they wanted to, given the size of the van. The really old part of the city was surrounded by a medieval town wall, which had fewer than a half-dozen entrances. They turned onto a road that took them along the east side of the city.

"The inn is through that gateway." Mark indicated an archway to the left.

Cassie slowed, but then Mark threw out a hand before she had completed the turn.

"No, no! Don't go in there. The road doesn't go through!"

"Sheesh!" Cassie swung the wheel back to the right, narrowly missing a car parked with its rear angling into the street. "How can it not go through?"

Mark peered at his phone. "It's blocked by a pedestrian-only walkway."

For David's part, he was perfectly glad not to enter there, since they might have had to pull in the mirrors on either side of the van in order to get through the archway.

"It was better not to get so close to the inn anyway," Darren said from the back. "I saw several vans like ours parked along the road."

Cassie crept along at less than ten miles an hour, a perfectly reasonable speed given the falling snow and the four or five inches on the ground. They passed yet another one-way entrance fifty yards on, before finally reaching one that they could enter.

Cassie slowed, the blinker ticking, but then turned it off and continued driving straight ahead.

"Good choice, Cassie." Like Mark, Callum was splitting his attention between the road and his phone, which showed a map of Caernarfon. "I didn't like the look of that road either. Caernarfon has too many one-way streets inside the city walls. We could get boxed in and not be able to get out."

"That was my thought," Cassie said. "The hairs on the back of my neck are standing up."

"Let's go around again," David said.

"Nope. Can't go around. I have to turn around instead," Cassie said, and then grumbled under her breath, "I hate Caernarfon already."

David peered out the window as she executed a perfect three-point turn and drove back the way they'd come. He looked at his mother. "How about you call Uncle Ted and tell him we're here."

"Doing it now." Mom pulled out her phone, dialed, and then turned on the speaker as she waited for Uncle Ted to pick up.

His voice bellowed out of the phone before Mom hastily turned down the volume. "Where are you?"

"We're here. Sort of." Mom peered out the window as Cassie slowed the van and took a narrow street to the right. "We tried to reach the inn, but ended up going all the way back out to the main street. We're parking next to the castle in a big square with a ton of shops. Do you know it? Can you meet us here?"

"We're on our way."

David could hear activity from the other end of the phone, and then Aunt Elisa's voice came on. "This is crazy, Meg."

"I know," she said. "The good news is that the lump in my breast isn't cancer."

"Good God!" That was from Uncle Ted, who'd overheard. "Is that why you're here?"

"One of the reasons." Mom put the phone back on normal and stuck it up to her ear so the conversation became private.

Fortunately, as it was Christmas Eve, they had their choice of parking, and Cassie pulled into an empty space that had plenty of room around it, in case they needed to make a quick getaway.

"When we want to leave, all we have to do is go around the square, end up over there, and take a left," Mark said, looking up from his map. "I think."

They piled out of the van, and once they were outside David elbowed Anna. "That's a Subway."

She laughed. "You're thinking with your stomach again. Mom says Uncle Ted is bringing us food."

"There they are!" Mom ran forward to greet the four people who'd just emerged from a side alley, coming from the town. All four were carrying big white takeout bags.

She and Aunt Elisa embraced, tipping back and forth from side-to-side as they hugged each other. "Wow." Aunt Elisa said as she stepped back from Mom. "You look great."

"You do too." Mom gestured Dad forward. "This is my husband, Llywelyn."

Aunt Elisa shook his hand, and then Dad went on to Uncle Ted, who wrung his hand hard. "Very good to see you again, my lord."

"We are brothers," Dad said, in his pretty good English. "There's no need to speak formally."

David, meanwhile, grasped Christopher's shoulders and spoke at the same time as Christopher. "I never thought I'd see you again." And then they both laughed.

After everybody was introduced to everyone else, Callum began herding them back to the van. "I don't think we should spend any more time out in the open than we absolutely have to." He looked at

Uncle Ted. "I need to know everything about what was going on in the hotel, but don't tell me out here."

David didn't even give the Subway a second glance, since he'd already opened the food bag Uncle Ted had given him and broken off a big piece of fried fish to eat. Once at the van, Mom sat next to Aunt Elisa and Elen, who seemed to be absorbing everything with big eyes. Christopher and Uncle Ted crowded in behind David, and then Darren closed the door behind them.

"Does driving away now mean we are abandoning the bus passengers?" David licked his fingers and spoke into the general chatter that had been ongoing.

Mom picked at her lower lip with her pinky finger. "I can't decide what our responsibilities are."

"I overheard two of them talking to a reporter," Christopher said.

"They were all talking about the bus," Uncle Ted said. "To go back would mean we would spend the night being questioned by MI-5. They're all over the inn. You can't go back."

Rachel nodded. "David, the passengers can take care of themselves. You brought them home. They were going to have to deal with the authorities eventually no matter how well you eased them back into their old lives."

"And we aren't finished with what we set out to do," Anna said.

"I agree with the general sentiment," Callum said. "Going back, exposing yourself to my former colleagues, isn't going to help anyone."

David gave way. "Okay. Let's get out of here for now, Cassie. If for some reason it seems we need to come back here, at least we don't have to jeopardize everyone."

Cassie didn't even wait for David to finish speaking before she shifted into drive, and once again with Mark navigating, wended her way out of Caernarfon. Silence had descended upon the van as if nobody could think of anything to say.

Then Christopher broke the silence. "Hey! Did Dad tell you the news?"

Uncle Ted made a slashing motion with his hand. "Not now, Christopher."

"What news?" David said.

"You know how you're the King of England, right?" Christopher said.

David laughed. "Usually."

"Well, Dad's spent hours doing our genealogy over the last couple of years. He's *obsessed—*"

Uncle Ted put out a hand to his son, trying again to stop him from talking, but Christopher was on a roll.

"It turns out that all of us are royal too!"

David's eyes narrowed. "How so?"

Uncle Ted groaned. "He's exaggerating."

"I'm not!" Christopher said. "It turns out that one of our ancestors was an illegitimate daughter of one of the King Henrys from the Middle Ages."

"Our Middle Ages?" David's voice came out slightly strangled.

Mom, who was sitting in the seat in front of Uncle Ted, broke off her conversation with Aunt Elisa and turned to look at him. "Which King Henry?"

"Mid-thirteenth century, so before your time, David." Uncle Ted made a dismissive motion with his hand. "It was rumored that he had a liaison with a daughter of King Alexander II. Caitir, I think her name was. It was never proven, but I traced your father's ancestry, Meg, to a daughter they were supposed to have had."

It was only when he finished speaking that Ted realized everyone in the van was staring at him in shock. Pleased with the reaction he'd gotten, Christopher added, "We're all descended from the kings of Deheubarth too, so you're a Prince of Wales like eight times over, but by now so is everybody with Welsh ancestry."

Dad started to laugh, and soon not only was it rolling out of him in giant guffaws but most everyone else in the van was laughing too.

Christopher, Aunt Elisa, and Uncle Ted looked from one person to another, bewildered more than anything else. "Why is this funny?" Uncle Ted said.

"I'm descended from King Henry!" Mom was laughing so hard tears streamed down her cheeks, and she wiped them away with her fingers.

David had to hold his stomach because it hurt so much. "I don't believe it."

Finally, Mom calmed down enough to explain that most of England believed she really was King Henry's illegitimate daughter, though she denied it, of course. In the run up to David's crowning, papers had surfaced that proved it.

Uncle Ted looked from one to the other. "Seriously?"

"Coincidence 'R' Us," Mom said.

Mom's words caused David to sober. "Lee."

Callum shook his head. "Lee can wait. Right now, we need food, sleep, and, quite frankly, neutral ground."

"Neutral ground." Anna frowned. "Why?"

Callum sighed. "I don't think any of you should have anything to do with the Security Service, but if we are truly to find out what has happened to Lee, and—as a side note—rescue the bus passengers from whatever scrutiny they are under, one of us should speak to Director Tate."

Silence greeted that statement until David said, not as a question, "And you think that person should be you."

"Do you disagree?" Callum's eyes stayed fixed on David's.

"Strategically, no." His chin resting in one hand, David studied his friend. "We have to think carefully about how you do it, though."

"Agreed," Callum said.

"Come to my house." Abraham spoke up from the back. "It's the safest place."

"There's fifteen of us," David said.

"You haven't seen my house."

Rachel frowned. "Did you move, Dad?"

He smiled. "I bought that old farmhouse we've been looking at for years. The one with the medieval tower that's supposed to be—" He broke off as everyone in the van except Cassie, who couldn't turn around, gaped at him.

"Dad, don't tell me you bought Aber!" Rachel said.

18

David

That was exactly what he'd done. When Dad got out of the van, he stood with his hands on his hips, staring up at the tower, which was all that was left of the expansive royal *llys* (palace) that had once occupied this space. The curtain wall was gone too, as were the tunnels. Mom said the driveway had nearly collapsed the last century, so the tunnels had been filled in.

"I can't say I think very much of what time and English owners have done to the place," Dad said.

Mom laughed and took his arm. "Your people remember you, my love. You really can't ask for more than that."

While the others followed Abraham into the house, Callum raised a hand to catch David's attention, and the two of them hung back in the darkness of the stoop, David still half-in and half-out of the open door.

"On second thought," Callum said, "staying here isn't really a good idea. The bus passengers can name Rachel. A search on her name could bring up her father's address here pretty quickly."

Abraham Wolff pulled the door all the way open. "No, Callum, it won't. Not unless they're looking very hard."

"Why is that?" Callum said.

"My corporation bought the house. It isn't technically in my name at all." Abraham made a rueful face. "Call it a tax dodge if you like, but I'm the only physician in this village, and I see patients in the coach house, which I converted into an office."

"Thank you for taking us in," David said.

"Anything for the kings of England and Wales." Abraham winked and pulled back inside the house to be replaced instantly by Mark.

"Too bad Aaron isn't here," Mark said. "I know it's impossible, but I feel like Abraham is his direct descendent."

"If Abraham has his way," David said, "you'll be able to introduce them."

Callum indicated that they should move away from the doorway and into the darkness of the driveway. "We need to talk about MI-5, David."

"About you exposing yourself, you mean?" David shook his head. "If it weren't for Lee and the fact that my family is here, we'd be gone already. I would really prefer to keep this whole trip under the radar."

Mark sucked on his upper teeth for a second. "It's really too late for that, isn't it?"

Callum nodded. "We bought extra phones. Perhaps it's time to use one."

David released a breath in tacit agreement and walked with them down the driveway until Mark indicated he had good reception on his phone. Every now and then, the glare of headlights from passing cars shone on the motorway that ran in front of the village below them. Beyond that lay the Menai Strait and Anglesey, also lit by tiny lights from the villages built along the shore.

Back in the Middle Ages, David hadn't visited Aber Castle in at least a year, but at one time he'd considered it home. In that universe, the setting was as peaceful as they come. The mountains and the sea had formed a nearly unbreachable barrier that had kept out the English invaders for centuries.

In this world, it was only after David's father's death that Edward had captured Aber. David glanced up at the tower. He agreed with his father: what had been done to it was unconscionable.

The three of them stood together a hundred feet from the house. Mark had his laptop open and was using the mobile phone as a wifi hotspot so that Callum could run the call through the internet instead of the phone service, thus masking the GPS of the phone. David didn't pretend to understand exactly how that might work, but he trusted that it would seem like Callum was making the call from somewhere in Oregon.

"This is the Cardiff number for agents in trouble—not the public number." Mark tapped into his keyboard.

"This late on Christmas Eve, we're sure to get the lowest-ranking flunky in the building," Callum said to David, as an aside. "This is a good thing."

The phone rang twice, and a woman answered. "Box 500."

Callum bent to speak into the laptop's microphone. Mark had had the foresight to turn off the camera. "I need to speak to Director Tate. This is Alexander Callum."

David smirked at the mention of Callum's first name, which he never used if he could help it. David didn't know why, since Alexander was a perfectly respectable Scottish name.

There was a distinct pause on the other end of the line, and then the woman said, "Did you say, Alexander Callum? Director Alexander Callum?"

"Yes." Callum drew out the 's' in a hiss.

"Do you need immediate assistance?"

"I am not in danger currently," Callum said, "but that could change at any time."

"Right. Director Tate is on another line. Can he ring you back?"

"Certainly." Callum rattled off the number the computer gave him.

This time it was Mark who whispered to David. "It's a randomized number that will cease to be valid after twenty minutes."

David shook his head at all that he didn't understand. If he'd spent the last ten years in the modern world, he surely would have been a computer geek, but as it was, his knowledge of computers was ten years out of date. Back at Bangor University, when he'd opened the laptop to try to surf the internet, Darren had had to come over and open the browser because the interface was dramatically different from what he remembered, even from three years ago when he'd come to Wales with Callum and Cassie and surfed the internet from the confines of an MI-5 interrogation room.

David found it frustrating to be nearly as out of his element here as Dad and Math. At the same time, he found himself constantly reaching for his new phone to Google a question that just occurred to him. If he lived here for real, he'd never stop.

In the darkness and the snow, though it was falling more gently in their spot within the shelter of a tree that overhung the driveway, they waited for the callback.

"I can practically see the tech's fingers flying over the keyboard, trying to trace our call," Callum said.

"They won't be able to. I may be rusty, but I'm not out of the game yet," Mark said.

"The question before us," Callum said, "is how they will view my return. It seemed to me the operator wasn't wholly surprised at my call."

"They've interviewed the bus passengers by now," Mark said. "They have to have known you were here, and the fact that you are calling now could be taken as a good sign that you're ready to come in again."

Another minute passed before the call button finally started flashing on Mark's screen. Callum took in a deep breath and then nodded to Mark, who pressed 'talk'.

"Sir," Callum said.

"Can we dispense with preliminaries?" Tate's voice reverberated out of the speaker, deep and commanding—and not unlike Callum's in tenor and tone.

"Certainly," Callum said.

"We've interviewed the bus passengers at the Black Boar. I've personally spoken to Jane and Carl Thomas," Tate said.

"How is Shane?" Callum said.

Tate paused for a count of three, which was a really long expanse of silence over a phone line. "You did the right thing bringing him back."

David felt the breath he hadn't realized he'd been holding ease out of him. *Yes, they had done the right thing.* It gave him some reassurance as to Tate's motives and character that he knew it too.

"Where's the bus?" Tate said, back to business.

"Parked on a rural road, out of the way," Callum said.

"What are you driving?"

"Let's save that for later." Callum then cut straight to the point. "Have you caught the men who bombed Cardiff's city hall and courthouse?"

"What—" Tate paused. "That's what you're calling about?"

"One of the bombers—perhaps even the man behind it—was on the bus with us when we traveled to the Middle Ages. His name is Lee Delaney, or at least that was the name he went by with us. He returned to this world three months ago. You should know that already because of the flash when he entered."

Tate grunted into the phone. "Yes. We did notice that. He came alone?"

It sounded to David as if the words were departing Tate's mouth with extreme reluctance.

"No. There should have been two flashes, one right after the other."

Tate grunted his assent. "We saw that. We didn't know what it meant."

"Did you send men to the scene?"

"We did," Tate said.

"Where'd Lee come in?" David said in a whisper to Callum, who then repeated the question to Tate in a louder voice.

"In the middle of the Menai Strait, near the Caernarfon end. But by the time the Coast Guard arrived, he was gone."

The expressions on Callum's and Mark's faces were as blank as David's had to be. The Menai Strait was a dangerous body of water under many circumstances, but it was also swimmable in some locations. That David had dropped Lee off in Wales meant that he could still be close by. David's stomach churned at the sickening thought.

"Perhaps he swam for shore," Callum said.

"If so, we didn't find him—but of course, it took a while for agents to reach the site, and we didn't know who or what we were looking for until now. I'd like to ask why you believe Lee Delaney was the culprit in the bombings."

"He brought C-4 to the Middle Ages with him," Callum said.

Tate drew in an audible breath and then said, "None of the bus passengers mentioned that. You need to come in."

"I can't do that, sir," Callum said.

"We mean you no harm," Tate said. "Surely you must see that."

"How are the bus passengers?" Callum said, changing the subject. "What have you done with them?"

"We haven't done anything with them. We interviewed many of them tonight, as I said." Tate gave a tsk through his teeth. "The inconsistencies in their stories are large enough to drive a bus through, though they're in agreement that they spent the last year in the Middle Ages. How's David? They did all say that he's here with you."

Both Mark and Callum glanced at David, who gave a short laugh.

"He's fine," David said into the microphone.

"We'd like to meet with you and your father," Tate said.

"I'd love a working relationship with you," David said, "but so far you haven't given me any reason to trust you."

There was another few seconds of silence on Tate's end, and then he said, "Mistakes were made."

"Yeah, lots of them over a long period of time," David said. "Appointing Callum as director of the Project was a great idea, but how long did that last? Two years and then, when push came to shove, you bailed on him."

"Political realities—"

"Become my problem when they're your problem. I understand that," David said. "These days I know all about politics. I'm having issues with the King of France and the Pope, for starters. It would be nice if I got help from you every time I showed up here instead of being chased halfway across Wales—or worse, locked in a windowless room."

"Young man—"

"I'm the King of England," David said. "You may call me 'sire' or not at all."

Callum put a hand on David's shoulder while Mark muted the call.

"Sorry," David said. "He was ticking me off."

"I noticed," Callum said.

"What about a trade?" Mark said. The connection to Tate was still muted.

Callum eyed him. "What kind of trade?"

"Offer to trade me and everything I know about the Middle Ages, including the *traveling* David and his family do, for a couple of microhydro generators and an industrial magnet. I think I should get you guys a couple more Kevlar vests too, since David's is still buried in the rubble at Canterbury. They also need to promise not to prevent your return to the Middle Ages when you're ready to go," Mark said, "and not to interfere with Ted's and Elisa's return to the United States."

David goggled at him. "Mark, no—"

"I want to stay here. Tate will see our agreement to this as a huge concession on our part, but this is no sacrifice for me. I've done okay back there, but in the hours we've been here, I have come to realize that I'm a modern man." He hefted the laptop. "This is what I do. Just as when Callum and Cassie were left behind, I can help you more from here than from there."

Callum pressed his lips together, ignoring the "Callum? Callum?" coming from the speaker, and David said, "Mark—"

"Let me do this, sire."

"You are a grown man, and neither of us command you here," David said.

"And hardly at all there, for that matter." Callum managed a slight smirk, though his eyes remained troubled.

Mark pressed 'talk' again. "Sir, this is Mark Jones."

"Jones!" Tate was all enthusiasm. "You came too?"

David noticed that at no point in their conversation had Tate questioned the existence of their alternate medieval universe. Even with the obvious disappearance and reappearance of the bus, David hadn't necessarily expected such an outcome. People can be stubborn and blind long after it made any sense to be so, and there was no reason Tate couldn't have chosen that route. He had been involved in the cancelling of Callum's project after all.

"Clearly." Mark's tone was wry and also confident. David heard in his voice the belief that he could withstand the machinations within MI-5, and that he was making the right choice. "We propose a trade." And then Mark outlined in detail the brief discussion he'd just had with David and Callum. Rachel had already packed medical supplies, including a simple microscope her father had kept in storage, in the back of the van, so they didn't need help with that. "Do we have a deal?"

"We do. When and where should we meet?" To his credit, Tate didn't hesitate.

"Tomorrow morning. Nine o'clock." Mark pressed mute again in order to say to Callum, "How about in the Tesco parking lot?"

"That's a sucky spot," David said before Callum could answer. "A zillion sightlines and no way to cover them all."

"It'll be deserted on Christmas Day," Callum said.

"Where won't be deserted on Christmas Day?" David said.

"Bangor Cathedral?" Mark said.

"Lots of civilians there." David shrugged. "At nine in the morning on Christmas Day, it'll be the only place in Bangor with people."

But Callum shook his head. "I don't want innocents in harm's way if Tate's motives aren't pure. I have a better idea."

He unmuted the call with Tate. "We'll meet you on the bridge at the motorway interchange just to the west of the Bangor Tesco, heading north right after the exit for Bangor/Caernarfon."

"Callum—" David began.

Callum muted the call again and looked at David. "We'll bring the van and the bus. We can park the bus on the bridge going north and stop the van further down the motorway going the other way so

Cassie can pull past the meeting site, and we can get in and out quickly if this goes pear-shaped."

"Don't tell Tate that last bit," David said to Mark, who then pressed 'talk' again and finished Callum's explanation. Tate agreed and disconnected the call.

Mark gave a satisfied nod. "If Lee is really here, all the more reason to leave me behind because I know what he looks like. I can help catch him."

Callum tapped a finger against his lips. "You always say, David, that you come in where you were meant to. Up until now, I've been assuming we're here because of your aunt's family and Rachel's father."

David nodded. "But now you're thinking we're here because of Lee."

19

Llywelyn

Llywelyn hadn't stood a watch in many years, but at his own request, Darren had woken him at four, as indicated by the timepiece beside the bed. But even if under normal circumstances he was no longer the one asked to guard a castle, it was an hour that was familiar to him. He and Goronwy had been known to rise this early simply to clear his desk and his mind of all that was required for the successful running of his kingdom.

Llywelyn had forced Dafydd and Christopher, who'd stuck like a leech to Dafydd's side, both of them talking nonstop, away from the computer to go to bed at midnight, and he'd checked on Dafydd again before coming outside. He was sound asleep face down on a mattress on the floor on the first floor of the tower. Llywelyn hoped he could stay that way for a few more hours.

He didn't even know what time Meg and Elisa had gone to sleep. At midnight, they'd still been up talking, and Llywelyn hadn't had the heart to shoo either of them to bed. They hadn't seen each other in more than eight years and might never see each other again.

One night without sleep was a small price to pay for the pleasure of reacquainting themselves with one another.

As he stared up at the tower, silhouetted against the night sky, Llywelyn wished Goronwy could be here to see what had become of his beloved Aber. On one hand, it was good to know the worst. On the other, the Menai Strait still stretched before him, even if these modern meddlers had dredged the Lavan Sands in order to allow large ships to pass through the strait instead of taking the time to go around Anglesey. He believed Meg absolutely when she told him that the Aber River still ran to the west, and his mountains still rose up in the darkness behind the castle. His grandfather had claimed the title, 'Prince of Wales and Lord of Snowdon', and it was that legacy that had Llywelyn's boots stuck as deeply in the soil of Wales here as in his own universe.

The snow had stopped falling sometime before midnight, but as Llywelyn stood watching, it started again, silently settling on his leather hat, which he'd borrowed from Abraham Wolff. The hat had a wide, stiff brim, just right for keeping the snow out of his face.

"You can keep it if you like."

Llywelyn turned to see Abraham standing in the doorway, faintly silhouetted against the electric light glowing from the kitchen, which lay deeper inside the house.

"You read my mind." Llywelyn touched the brim with one finger in a silent salute. "I would be grateful."

"Anything for my king," Abraham said in Welsh.

"Do I hear a touch of irony in your voice?" Llywelyn said.

Abraham stepped forward out of the doorway and closed the door behind him. "If you did, it was not my intent. My life has been upended in the last twelve hours since Rachel rang me up, but I am blessed beyond measure to have her back."

"You have my son to thank for that," Llywelyn said.

"Can one not see the father's hand behind the actions of the son?" Abraham said.

Llywelyn laughed. "Only when he's doing the right thing." He sobered. "Which my son does virtually all of the time."

"He bears great responsibility for one so young," Abraham said. "Power over life and death is not to be taken lightly."

"As you know, being a doctor," Llywelyn said.

Abraham canted his head. "I grant you that."

"Your daughter, for whom I must, in turn, thank *you*, knows it too."

"No training could ever have prepared her for the difficulties she's faced, but from my own experience, I know that becoming a doctor taught her how to make the decisions that need making."

"As did Dafydd's training," Llywelyn said, "though there is a goodness in him, an innate righteousness, that defies my understanding."

"I suspect the kingdom is better for it," Abraham said.

Llywelyn smiled again. "I have a friend with whom I think you would get along very well. His name is Aaron. He is a doctor too."

"Rachel mentioned him." Abraham looked away for a moment, seemingly to gather his thoughts, and then he turned back to meet Llywelyn's gaze. "It is a great thing you have done for my people, sire."

Llywelyn didn't need clarification to know what Abraham meant. Jews had been persecuted in Europe throughout history. "Again, you can thank my son for that more than me. It's hardly a triumph on my part to live up to the Christian ideal I espouse."

"I don't think so," Abraham said. "A lifetime of prejudice is difficult to overcome. Few men have the capacity. You could have paid a heavy price for it had the gamble not paid off."

"There's always that chance when one does the right thing. It shouldn't stop a man from doing it anyway," Llywelyn said.

"Ah. See." A smug smile lifted the corners of Abraham's mouth. "I knew I saw the father in the son."

Llywelyn shook his head. "I am neglecting my duty. I must walk the perimeter. Would you walk with me?"

"I would be honored, but I need to visit the clinic," Abraham said. "I have affairs to set in order and a few things to collect."

"I am not going to try to convince you not to come. My children are everything to me too, and the years I was parted from them were more than trying." Llywelyn looked up at the tower above him. "But I must ask, what will become of this place?"

"Aber will go in trust to the Welsh nation," Abraham said, and then at Llywelyn's astonished look, he shrugged. "I bought it because I wanted it and wanted to care for it, but with Rachel gone, I had no heirs. Why not leave it for generations of children to appreciate?"

Llywelyn put his heels together and gave Abraham a slight bow. "I give you the thanks of past generations too."

Abraham waved a hand dismissively, though he was smiling. Llywelyn realized he hadn't seen Abraham smile very often. He put out a hand before the doctor could enter his car, which had been parked on the edge of the circular driveway.

"Darren is a good man, Abraham. As one father to another, I know how hard it is to see your child make a choice you wouldn't necessarily have made."

Abraham stopped, one foot already inside the car. "It isn't that I don't approve of Darren, and please don't think that the color of his skin has anything to do with my objections. It's more that I don't want her to be with him only because she doesn't want to be alone."

"And he's not Jewish," Llywelyn said.

Abraham made a helpless gesture with one hand. "My wife wasn't either, and look what happened. We divorced."

"Marriage isn't easy, no matter the circumstances," Llywelyn said. "I have been very fortunate in that I married women I loved—twice—which isn't necessarily usual in my world. Darren is a good man. He loves Rachel. Give him a chance."

Abraham took in a deep breath and let it out. "I will try. Thanks."

"You gave me my wife back. It's the least I could do."

Abraham laughed and shook his head at the same time. Then, still chuckling, he entered his car and drove away. Llywelyn watched until the red lights at the back of his vehicle had disappeared. Then he started his circuit of the castle.

House.

Chicken farm.

Disgust rose again in his throat at what had become of his beloved Garth Celyn, which was the ancient name for Aber. It was from here that he'd written of defiance to King Edward a month before Cilmeri. He had to acknowledge, years after the fact, that he'd done so out of the same surety that had convinced him to admit the Jews of Europe into Wales when everyone else rejected them. Doing the right thing was its own reward, even if it meant his head on a pike at the Tower of London.

Llywelyn walked all the way around the property, taking his time and looking beneath every bush and up every tree for watchers. By moving slowly, he was able to get a feel for sky and earth. He listened hard for any movement that wasn't natural. It took a while to filter out the noise from the motorway below him, though at four in the morning on Christmas Day, that sound wasn't as constant as it had been the night before.

Then he heard the crunching of gravel on the driveway, and he came back around to the front of the house in time to see Abraham stop the car by the front door.

The good doctor started speaking before the car door was fully open. "The clinic is surrounded. I decided I'd better not try to get past everyone to reach my office."

"We should inform Callum." Llywelyn led the way into the house without asking for more information. He knew why the clinic was surrounded; he just wished this Tate had been as good as his word.

Callum was standing at the counter, talking to Cassie and Darren and drinking coffee. Beyond them, in the darkness of the sitting room, Llywelyn could see the mop of Mark's dark hair sticking out from his blankets where he lay on the floor. He and Dafydd had set up their computers in here last night and had spent hours downloading information and printing it. The backpack Callum had bought at the Tesco in Bangor sat on an adjacent table, full to nearly bursting with the paper that had resulted. Llywelyn hoped Dafydd had found most of what he'd wanted because he feared their time had just run out.

Callum looked over as Llywelyn came in. "We were just about to leave to scope out the rendezvous point well in advance. Would you like to come? I could use your experience."

"We have some new information that changes everything." Llywelyn gestured to Abraham, who'd come into the kitchen behind him.

"Someone, I'm presuming it's MI-5, has surrounded my clinic. That doesn't seem like a friendly act to me."

"No, that's not good." Callum let out a sharp breath. "Tate lied to me."

"He probably wouldn't call it lying," Cassie said. "More like covering all his bases."

"Were he to use a baseball metaphor, yes," Callum said.

"We should change the meeting point to a place we know," Darren said, gesturing with his cup of coffee to indicate the world beyond the house. "Give them a half-hour's notice they can take or leave."

Callum stood with his hands on his hips, looking down at the ancient wood floor and thinking. Nobody interrupted him because they were all doing some thinking of their own. For Llywelyn's part, he couldn't be the least bit surprised that Tate had changed the terms of the agreement. These were the same men who'd locked up his son.

Callum looked over at Abraham. "Tell me exactly what you saw."

"My clinic is on a side road, as I'm sure you recall, but it's visible from a certain spot on the hill above it, which I was driving down when I saw the vehicles: four SUVs and two police cars."

Callum rubbed his chin. "They are taking this seriously. How long before they find you here?"

"If they dig hard enough, not long," Abraham said. "At the same time, my corporation is heavily invested in real estate in this area, so they'll have at least a dozen properties to search. This is also listed as a 'clinic', not a residence."

"You know," Cassie said, "to give Tate the benefit of the doubt, they might be at the clinic because of the bus. The police officers would have told them it was there, and so they started looking for it there. They may not have connected Abraham to us at all."

"All it will take is one of the bus passengers mentioning Rachel's existence," Llywelyn said. "She disappeared a year ago, just like the rest of them."

"Then we can be thankful, again, that it's Christmas Day," Darren said. "Don't forget that Meg's family was checked into the Black Boar, but have now gone missing. Tate is going to assume we're all together."

"Caernarfon Castle," Abraham cut in. "The Prince of Wales is giving the Christmas Day speech from the bailey this afternoon. The whole city will be full of tourists and security forces."

Llywelyn's eyes narrowed. "Did you say 'the Prince of Wales'?" Llywelyn had wanted to meet this English upstart from the moment Meg had told him how he himself had lost his life at Cilmeri.

"So that's what's got Tate in a tizzy." Cassie was nodding her head. "It isn't us. It's protecting the Prince of Wales. Security is higher, everybody's on edge, and now the time travelers are back. No wonder Tate is doing everything he can to find us."

"If he labels us terrorists," Callum said, "he can make any security force, policeman, or reporter, for that matter, do his bidding."

Llywelyn turned to Abraham, for whom his respect had grown with every minute he'd spent with him. "Why do you suggest we meet Tate at Caernarfon if that's where the Prince of Wales will speak?"

"I don't mean for us to meet him in the castle itself," Abraham said. "There's a swinging bridge over the river that runs along the south side of the castle. I know the man who manages the controls for the swing, and I have a friend with a boat. MI-5 could leave the supplies on the bridge, and my friend could take them away in his boat."

Callum stared at him. "They would do that for you?"

"Of course," Abraham said with utter certainty.

"On Christmas Day?" Cassie said.

Abraham shot her an amused look. "Jewish. Remember?"

"Crowds were the reason we rejected Bangor Cathedral as a meeting place," Callum said, "but Abraham may be on to something. Meeting in a public place—especially if none of us but Mark ever has to show himself to MI-5—will allow us to lose ourselves in the crowd. Even if we split up—which we should do in order to scout the area— we can keep in touch by mobile."

"It could be much like when Goronwy, Meg, and I arrived at Chepstow," Llywelyn said, not without a touch of pride at the memory. "We won't stand out because we'll be ten among hundreds. Also much like at Chepstow, the weather can only help because everybody's faces will be covered by hats and hoods."

Callum gave him a sour look. "Believe me, I remember."

"Do we really think they plan to grab us?" Cassie said.

"Tate didn't sound like that's what he wanted last night," Callum said, "but he's a politician and a professional liar."

"Nobody will question apprehending possible terrorists on the day of the prince's speech," Darren said. "If that is, in fact, his intent, it's a perfect set up for him."

"It also might mean that he doesn't believe what I told him about Lee. I am officially irked." Callum crumpled up a cloth that had been lying on the kitchen counter and threw it at Mark's head. "Wake up!"

Mark groaned, but he sat up and put his hand to his eyes to shield them from the light. "What?"

"Tate's up to something," Callum said. "We need you."

"Tate won't want to hear the plans have changed," Darren warned.

"Then he shouldn't have surrounded Abraham's clinic," Callum said. "He'll have to agree to what we want if he doesn't want us to disappear."

"Merry Christmas!"

Llywelyn turned to see Anna yawning as she pulled a sweater, what Bridget called a 'jumper', close around herself. She put her arms around Llywelyn's waist and squeezed. "What's happened to make everyone so unhappy? I'm guessing trouble."

Llywelyn hugged her back. "Yes indeed. It seems, yet again, that we can't go anywhere without it."

20

Anna

While the others continued to discuss strategy, Anna woke the rest of the house. She felt particularly bad about waking Mom and Aunt Elisa, who'd stayed up far too late talking. Then she had to practically jump on David to wake him. He sat up, bleary-eyed and with his hair stuck up on end. He ran his hand through it in a feeble and unsuccessful attempt to tame it.

"What's up?" David said.

Anna explained about the change in plans.

Ten minutes later, they were all back in the kitchen, where Callum told everyone, "Tate wasn't happy to hear from me, but he didn't argue either."

"Isn't that suspicious?" Anna said. "What excuse did you give him for changing the location of the meet?"

"The weather," Callum said.

David raised his eyebrows. "Did you tell him you knew the clinic was surrounded?"

"No," Callum said. "I'm holding those cards close to my chest, for now."

"Do you think he bought it?" Anna said.

"Are you asking if I trust him?" Callum said. "Of course I don't."

"Eat." Cassie came up behind Anna with a plate of food in her hand and prodded her towards the table.

Abraham had made a large breakfast, complete with Welsh bacon, which he and Rachel ate unapologetically along with their eggs and fried bread. It wasn't so different from the food she'd normally eat for breakfast in the medieval world. It was hard to go wrong with bacon and eggs, and everybody—medieval and modern—was satisfied. As they sat around the large table next to a fireplace that wouldn't have been out of place in a great hall, Anna could almost believe that they'd been miraculously transported home. But no, that was coming later.

It was only at the end of the meal that Abraham looked up and asked, "I'm sorry. Are there any vegans among you?"

Everyone laughed, though Anna had to explain the concept to Math before he got it. "Monks don't eat meat many days, but why would anyone else turn down good food when it's offered?"

"In this world, many people oppose the killing of animals for food," Anna said, and at Math's continued stare, she added, "Large farms keep animals in small cages or pens all their lives and stuff them full of chemicals. It's inhumane and unhealthy."

"But—

Anna smiled and put a hand on Math's arm. "This is one aspect of the modern world I really can explain later. Now—" she looked around the table, "—my guess is that it's time to go."

Christopher pushed away his plate. He'd kept pace with David's seconds and thirds, which given that he was seventeen, was no surprise. "I want to come with you when you go back to the Middle Ages."

Uncle Ted put out a hand to him. "Son—" while at the same time Aunt Elisa said, "Christopher!"

"I've been thinking a lot about this," Christopher said, not heeding his parents. "I know it isn't a decision to be made lightly, but it's one I've made."

"I know you want to go, sport." Uncle Ted's hand came down on his son's shoulder, though he met Anna's eyes and gave his own head a slight shake, which Anna took to mean *you're going over my dead body.* "I'd love to go too, but we just can't. Think of your mother and sister."

"It isn't their life." Christopher kept his attention entirely on David.

Aunt Elisa scoffed and rose to her feet. "You don't know what you're saying."

"I do too, Mom!"

Anna's mother put out a hand to her sister. "Elisa, may I?"

Aunt Elisa had been getting along well with Mom up until now, but color had flooded her face. She looked like she was going to protest again, but Uncle Ted drew her back to stop her from talking.

Mom rested her elbows on the table and studied Christopher over hands clasped in front of her chin. "You'd be leaving this world for another universe, one you might never come back from, and at seventeen, like it or not, you aren't a man yet. Not here. This isn't your decision to make."

Christopher opened his mouth, but Mom forestalled him with a raised finger.

"It's David's decision. He is the King of England, and in the medieval world, he would be your liege lord. You might not think you have to obey your father, but you do have to obey him."

"I know that," Christopher said. "I accept that."

"But David hasn't given you permission to come with us," Mom said.

All eyes turned to David, who studied Christopher for a moment before putting down his fork. "My mom is right."

Christopher's chin was wrinkled like a prune and his expression mutinous.

But then David canted his head. "Still, she might not always be. If I do come back, we will speak of this again. At that time, you can decide what is right for you."

Anna had seen David speak like this dozens of times, to many different people. It was as if he and Christopher were the alone in the room. It was David at his best.

Slowly Christopher eased back in his chair. "Okay. I will hold you to that."

Aunt Elisa let out a trembling breath, and Uncle Ted pulled her away from the table before she could ruin the moment. In another few seconds, everyone else was standing, clearing the table, and getting their things together to leave.

Except David and Christopher, who still sat looking at each other. "Do you mean it?" Christopher said.

"I don't say things I don't mean," David said. "If this is really something you want, you'd better do what you can to make yourself ready. I heard your grades weren't very good last quarter."

The mutinous look was back. David ignored it, getting to his feet and moving to where he'd left his laptop. Anna watched Christopher sit at the table for a few seconds, and then she pulled him up to give him a hug. When she let go, she said, "For now, we need you here, keeping this end of our lives safe, Christopher."

She put her hands on both sides of his face. He was nearly six feet tall, so she had to reach up. Seeing him like this made Anna miss her own boys even more. Cadell, at seven, was four years younger than Elen, but far more independent than many eleven-year-olds. Hardly a morning went by, however, when Bran didn't come in to her room, usually after Math was already up and gone, to snuggle with her. She could see both of them in Christopher, who in his disappointment was looking much younger than his seventeen years.

"How can I possibly help with that?" he said.

"You're a smart boy. You've had a taste of what it's like for us when we come here, running around Wales like we have. What do we need help with most?"

He scoffed. "It isn't like learning Welsh is going to do any good. You already speak it. But with those agents—" he broke off, his eyes widening with sudden realization. "I could join the FBI—"

Anna cut him off with a finger to his lips. "You should do what you want. It's your life—one which you must lead *here* because David might not come back for a long time—but if you really do want to make a difference for us when we return, having an ally in law enforcement, even in the United States, would be helpful. Alternatively, becoming an engineer or a doctor could be very useful too. We need educated people in the Middle Ages."

She had meant only to appease him and to make him less resentful of his mother and father, but she could see the gears turning in his head as he considered the possibilities.

"I know you're going to make good choices," she said.

The sun was just rising when they gathered in the oldest part of the house in preparation for their departure. It was snowing in earnest again, so it wasn't as if they could actually see the sun, but Papa, at least, had taken a walk outside and returned with a more contented look on his face. He knew this region of Wales like the back of his hand. Seven hundred years and the English conquest couldn't change that.

Callum called for everyone's attention. "We have multiple tasks before us. The first is to return Ted, Elisa, and the children to the Black Boar."

"I'm worried about what will happen to them when we do that," Mom said. "MI-5 might still want to question them. Tate might not honor our bargain."

"If that's what happens, it happens," Uncle Ted said.

"Under the circumstances, I find it likely that with our presence and the prince's speech, MI-5 have bigger fish to fry," Callum said.

"Tell them as much of the truth as you wish to," Cassie said to Uncle Ted. "You spent Christmas Eve with us, and then we went on our way."

"Unfortunately for her, Cassie needs to stay with the van, ready to leave at a moment's notice," Callum said. "I would prefer that at least Rachel, Abraham, and Meg stay with her while some of us escort Ted and the others into the city, and the rest scout the perimeter of the castle square."

David had confided to Anna that if he'd had his way, Abraham would have been left behind at the house, but Abraham was insistent that he come with them. He'd heard enough about the sudden nature of the appearances and disappearances between the Middle Ages and the twenty-first century to fear that a sudden event might take Rachel away from him again.

For her part, Anna liked Abraham very much and thought he could be a great addition to the family. He might be showing them only his good side, but since his good side had included accepting their origins in the Middle Ages, Mom's need for care, and housing them for the night at Aber—which Anna still could only just believe he owned—he would have to turn into an ogre pretty quickly for anyone to object strongly to his company.

"I don't like it," Mom frowned, "but I also know that I'm not trained for anything that will help you now."

"Nor am I." Rachel sighed. "I hate being left behind."

Cassie tsked through her teeth. "You and me both."

Abraham, however, raised a hand. "You might want to include me in the party that scouts the area around the bridge. At the very least, I have an invitation to sit in one of the VIP chairs during the prince's speech." Abraham looked sheepish as everyone gaped at him. "None of you are supposed to be here, so it might come in handy if we're stopped. I also know Caernarfon well."

David was chuckling quietly to himself. "I get it now. You're a Welshophile, aren't you?"

"I haven't ever heard that term before, but you're not wrong," Abraham said.

"If Abraham goes with David and Llywelyn—" Callum hesitated, and he actually turned a little red.

David smirked. "We aren't kings here, Callum. You can say our names."

Anna gave a sudden laugh, realizing as she thought back over all the interactions she'd witnessed between Callum and David and Papa over the last day, not once had he actually said their names. She was also kind of amazed that Callum wasn't trying to leave her behind too, but she supposed her black belt in karate, ancient history as it was, qualified her in his mind as a combatant.

"Mark and I will go with Math, Anna, and the Shepherds to the Black Boar, after which we'll make our way to the castle square. We'll keep in touch by mobile phone. These particular mobiles can conference all of us into one call, which means we can stay in constant communication."

"You're going to be inside the city walls, and there are only a few exits," David said. "You need to be careful—and Math should leave his sword in the van so as to be less conspicuous."

Math frowned, but he nodded.

"That leaves Abraham with David and Llywelyn," Callum said.

"I'll stick with David too," Darren said. "You never know when an MI-5 badge will come in handy."

"I expect security to be everywhere." Callum checked his phone. "We have an hour and a half before the meeting. I want to know how many men Tate brings and where they are."

Mark lifted his chin. "Only Math has never popped up on MI-5's radar. They may forgo men on the ground in favor of cameras."

"We should expect both," Callum said. "With the Prince of Wales—" he gestured to David, "—not you, of course, speaking in nine hours, all of Caernarfon will be crawling with security."

"That's why we will park again in the Tesco parking lot," Cassie said. "From there, I can monitor what all of you are doing and be on hand to pick any of you up if I need to."

"It's also is a quick drive from there to the other side of the swing bridge if Abraham's friend needs an assist," Callum said, "though the road is really narrow."

"I know my job, Callum."

Callum put out a hand to his wife. "I didn't mean—"

She stood on her toes and kissed his cheek. "I didn't either. It's okay. We should go."

They drove through the darkened village and entered the motorway heading west, driving past Bangor towards Caernarfon. Few people were on the move yet. Anna sat beside Elen, who grinned and said, "This was the best Christmas *ever!*"

Anna put an arm around her shoulders. "People are better than presents."

Behind her, Anna heard Aunt Elisa whisper to Mom, "If I were a better sister, I'd say that I want to come with you, but I don't."

"You don't have to explain," Mom said. "It's totally okay."

Meanwhile, Uncle Ted bent to Anna's ear. "What did you say to Christopher?"

Anna smiled. "You can thank me later." Then she laughed. "Or not."

Reaching Caernarfon, Cassie navigated the city with aplomb and stopped in the Tesco parking lot as planned.

Anna elbowed David in the ribs as he got out of the van, since he was eyeing the nearby McDonalds again. "You just ate."

He patted his stomach. "I could get something to go."

"After," Mom said, overhearing. "It's Christmas Day. They're not open anyway."

Callum laughed. "Since David isn't going to be allowed to eat again, we'd best get started."

21

Anna

Feeling pressed for time now that they'd arrived at the Tesco, the companions split up. David, Abraham, Darren, and Papa wended their way along the river that ran past the castle, heading for the swing bridge, while Anna's group walked through the neighborhood to the east of the castle square.

Within a few paces of entering the neighborhood beyond the main street, they saw that Mark hadn't been wrong about the high security. Men in black coats and yellow reflective gear were already setting up barriers everywhere, stopping all local traffic and waving only official vehicles through. The security men mistook them for tourists—one benefit of being with Aunt Elisa's family.

Once past the initial barricades, they turned north, heading for the walled city. Snow lay nearly half a foot deep on the ground in most places, and Anna tightened her parka around herself as she crunched through it. Math, having seen the wide-brimmed hat Papa had borrowed, now wore a floppy fishing hat pulled down low over his eyes. It kept the snow out of his face as well as hiding his features from cameras that might be pointed in his direction.

Callum was in his suit and trench coat, which made him look not only respectable and very handsome, but semi-official. Mark was far less so in a sweatshirt, jacket, and jeans.

"Once we get inside the walls, we might have trouble getting out," Anna said, as she watched two men in black winter parkas with striped reflective strips turn away three cars in a row that wanted to enter the walled part of the city. Fortunately, the guards weren't yet checking ID's. Callum could get them through any barrier, but Anna would rather he didn't have to show his badge and alert Tate to his whereabouts just yet.

Anna slipped her arm through Math's. "Act casual. We're simply visitors to Caernarfon out on a Christmas Day stroll."

They had initially thought to enter the walled part of Caernarfon near the entrance to the castle, but that entrance was blocked off even for pedestrians. Thus, they followed the wall around to the north to the next gate available. It turned out to be the one Cassie had tried to drive through the previous night, and the one which led directly to the Black Boar Inn.

A security guard manned the entrance, but other than a cursory look, he didn't pay them any attention and waved them through what had to have once been a formidable gatehouse.

"Just like at home," Math said.

Anna smirked. "Except at home you, in particular, can go anywhere you want and are recognized throughout Wales on sight."

Math moved his arm across her shoulders and squeezed. "I am much humbled by the experience of coming to your world, I assure you."

Mark laughed, and his laughter came at just the right moment, diffusing whatever suspicions might be directed at them, as one of the security guards had fixed him with a beady eye.

"This is where we leave you." Uncle Ted came to a halt outside the inn. "You should just keep walking."

Last night, Anna hadn't been sitting near the front of the van, so she hadn't had a clear view of what exactly had made Cassie avoid driving through this particular gate. Now she understood. While the road didn't end at the Black Boar, it became a pedestrian walkway. Three pillars in the middle of the road prevented all vehicle traffic from continuing past the inn into the city proper. If Cassie had driven through the hole in the wall, she would have had to enter the parking lot adjacent to the inn, turn around, and go back the way she'd come, all the while under the watchful eyes of whichever agents had been present at the time.

At the moment, Anna didn't see any men in suits watching the front of the inn, so she risked giving her family a last quick hug. "Be safe."

"I should be saying that to you," Uncle Ted said. "If you need *anything*, you call us. We aren't leaving Wales until the 27th."

"We fully intend to be back in the Middle Ages by then," Anna said.

Aunt Elisa had been holding her phone down at her side, but now she waved it at Anna, "Make sure your mother calls me at least once more. I need to know how this turns out."

"Absolutely," Anna said.

The family disappeared into the inn, and Callum pulled out his phone. "It's time to ring Tate."

As he prepared to dial, however, the phone rang. It was David.

Callum made a 'continue on' motion with his hand, indicating that they should keep walking, while David said, "Where are you?" His voice came tinnily out of the speaker.

"In the city," Callum said. "We've just dropped off your family, so I was about to ring Tate."

"What's the security like at the Black Boar?"

"Two men in a black SUV are watching the inn," Callum said.

At this unexpected bit of information, Anna turned to look, but Mark bumped her shoulder gently with his, blocking her view. "Don't look, and keep walking."

"Where are they?" Anna said.

"In the car park," Mark said.

"Did they spot you?" David said.

"I don't see how they could miss us, though they haven't made a move," Callum said.

"Keep talking to me," David said. "I want to know if they follow you."

Anna smiled down at her feet, hearing the authority of the King of England in her brother's voice.

"They'd have to come on foot," Mark said. "We're on a pedestrian-only street."

"Probably they're not supposed to leave their post, so they're calling ahead to someone else who will pick us up inside the city," Anna said, recalling the Christmas vacation in her former life where she'd mainlined spy thrillers for two solid weeks.

They hustled along through the unplowed snow, still without MI-5 in pursuit, and then turned left to follow the road that ran along the inside of the city wall. From here, Anna could see the castle looming above them a little over a hundred yards away.

By now Callum had conferenced in everyone else, including Mom and Cassie in the van, and Mark motioned that Anna should activate the earpiece that had come with the phone. By using it, she could leave the phone in her pocket but still talk and listen.

"I see more barriers the closer we get to the castle," Mark was saying when Anna came back on the line. It was weird to hear him talking as he walked beside her while at the same time having his voice echo in her ear.

"That shouldn't be surprising," David said.

"There's more people out and about too," Anna said, following Math and Callum as they cut down an alley to reach the next street over. "Believe it or not, people are starting to line up at the entrance to the castle. They must be going to wait all day!"

"It's because of the Prince of Wales," Callum said flatly. "Security is everywhere." He frowned. "I can't immediately identify what organizations we're looking at. Everyone's in black. It's snowing pretty hard."

David coughed and laughed at the same time. "Here too. What about you, Mom?"

Mom's voice resonated down the line. "I would agree that it is snowing."

"We're all clear here," Cassie said. "No security of any kind that I can see."

"I'm seeing mostly regular police wearing yellow reflective gear," David said. "They've taken over the booth where you pay for parking. Meanwhile, Abraham's friend is ready with his boat, as is the man in charge of the bridge."

"Not much to see here either," Anna said. "I feel like we're letting you d—" she broke off.

Math and Callum had stopped cold in front of her, and she almost ran into them.

Callum stepped into the shelter of the canopy over a nearby shop, and Math tugged on the fabric of her coat to pull her with him too. "This way."

Mark followed, swearing under his breath. The microphone picked up his cursing and broadcast it to everyone.

"What's going on?" David said sharply.

"Hold on," Callum said.

Callum peered around the corner and down the street.

Bracing herself with her hands on his back, Anna looked too. A hundred feet away, two men stood facing each other, talking intently. As Anna watched, they finished their conversation, and one darted across the street and disappeared down a side alley. The other, his hands deep into his pockets, started walking towards the line of people waiting to get into the castle. Just as he reached the gateway out of the old city, he glanced behind him, such that his gaze could have swept over Anna and Callum in the split second before they pulled back and out of sight.

"No." Anna spoke under her breath, not so much worried that her voice would carry, but because of her shock.

Math prodded her. "It is him, isn't it?"

Anna stared at her husband. She hadn't recognized the man who'd darted away, but Lee's face was burned into Anna's memory. She'd last seen him at Caerphilly Castle in a different world seven hundred years before today. Out of all the bus passengers, Lee had been most on everyone's minds since they'd arrived in Avalon.

"What is it?" David's voice came low and urgent.

"Lee is here," Callum said. "He's heading towards the castle now."

"Can you follow him without him knowing?" David's voice indicated a distinct lack of surprise.

Callum poked out his head and then stepped fully into the road. "He's disappeared."

Anna was still processing that Lee was *here* and up to no good, but she caught Math's hand and started after Callum and

Mark, both of whom had set off at a fast walk and were already halfway down the street. Callum's head swiveled this way and that as he searched for where Lee might have gone.

"Do your best," David said. "We've thought all along that Lee might be here. The Prince of Wales is his natural target."

"You need to call Tate right now, Callum," Cassie said.

Callum gave a grunt of disgust. "We've lost him, David."

Now it was David's turn to swear. "I don't want to ask if you're sure it was Lee, but I have to."

"We're sure," Anna said, not waiting for one of the men to answer.

"We're moving towards the castle," David said. "We'll try—"

Anna could hear the exertion in David's voice.

"You'll try what, David?" Anna said.

"—to get inside that castle," David said.

"No, David," Mom said. "Look what happened the last time you ran up against Lee. I don't want you anywhere near C-4 ever again."

"We are already near it. Give me a better option, and I'll consider it." As the King of England, David was used to making decisions that only he could make and was comfortable with the responsibility.

"Tate has a hundred men at his disposal," Callum said. "He can blanket the castle with security, and you won't have to fall into his clutches. I'm ringing him now."

Callum disappeared from Anna's ear, having disconnected from the call so he could telephone Tate, though she could still hear him as he strode beside her. Anna trotted beside Math as she tried to keep pace with the men's much longer legs. She was trying to listen with half an ear to Callum's one-sided conversation with Tate, while at the same time focusing on what was coming through her earpiece from the others.

"Could he have gotten inside the castle?" Cassie said.

"I can't tell," Anna said. "He was headed in that direction."

"There's really only one way to be sure," David said.

Anna took in a breath. "David's right, Mom."

"You're taking David's side, Anna?" Mom said. "He should not go into that castle."

"I'm not on any side," Anna said. "I'm just saying that except for us, nobody in all of Caernarfon knows more about medieval castles than Lee does, thanks to you and me."

"What Lee knows or does not know is not your fault, Anna," David said. "We've been over this."

"That's why you blame yourself for his actions, is it?" Anna retorted.

"Touché, sis," David said.

"We need to consider what he might be planning." Math had been listening this whole time on his own earpiece. "There are at least twice as many people in front of the castle as there were when we arrived, and Lee is not among them."

"The car park is almost full," David said. "We have to shut this down now before innocent people get hurt."

"How close are you to the castle, Cassie?" Darren said. "Can you get to the square to pick us up?"

"Earlier, I drove around a bit, just so as not to appear suspicious," Cassie said. "There are no spaces any closer to the castle than where we are now. The streets are closed off, and the police are only letting people leave, not enter."

"What about on the other side of the river from the swing bridge?" Darren said.

"It's a single lane road," Cassie said. "We could easily get boxed in."

"Not ideal, then," Darren said.

Callum came back on the line, having finished his conversation with Tate. "David, Tate wants to meet immediately."

"I bet he does," David said.

Callum ignored that, too intent on what needed to be done to respond to the sarcasm. "Meet us in the square."

"Did Tate bring what we asked for?" David said.

"He says he did," Callum said. "I've told him to forget the bridge. Too complicated, and too much can go wrong. We'll meet him in front of the NatWest as soon as an agent delivers the magnet and the power generators to the Tesco car park. Once Cassie says that she's collected them, Mark can come forward."

"What did he say about Lee?" David said. "They need to cancel the prince's speech."

"Tate is reluctant to do that," Callum said. "The royal family is all about standing firm and not giving in to terrorism."

"Goody for them." David's voice had risen to the point that he was almost shouting. "Standing firm isn't going to do them a whole lot of good if Lee has smuggled C-4 into Caernarfon Castle!"

"How far do you have to go to get to the square, David?" Callum said.

Muttered voices came across the line, and Anna could picture both Papa and Abraham talking David down. It appeared to have worked, because when he spoke next, David's voice was calmer, and he seemed to have gotten a grip on himself. "Not far."

They had reached the road that ran along the north side of the castle. "I'm seeing more activity in the square and at the castle entrance," Callum said. "I'm afraid if you don't come now, you'll be stopped from going past it."

"I'm not seeing that. It shouldn't be a problem on our end," David said. "What about you guys?"

"Give us a minute," Callum said, his eyes narrowed at the crowd and the security at either end of the narrow street. "We may have to go back the way we came."

"Fortunately, all the portcullises have been removed from the gatehouses," Math said. "We'll find a way out."

They wended their way through the lines of people waiting to enter through the front gate. The corner of the square was only a few yards away. Sawhorses blocked the street, as they had from the beginning, but only a single man stood guard. He was swathed from head to foot in all-weather gear, and from what Anna could see of his face, he was David's age or younger.

"Did you give Tate the what-for about the clinic yet?" Anna said.

"I did," Callum said. "He claims only to have been doing his due diligence. I decided, under the circumstances, that any more recriminations on my part would be unproductive."

"Huh," Anna said. "I don't trust him."

"If we get what we need from him and get back to the Middle Ages in one piece, it won't matter, Anna," David said.

Callum picked up the pace, loping down the sidewalk on the north side of the street, headed away from the castle entrance. As they approached the barriers, he reached into his breast pocket. The guard on duty lowered the walkie-talkie he'd been speaking into, tension in every line of his body, but then Callum pulled out his MI-5 badge. He left it open long enough for the guard to get a good look at it.

"Sir." The policeman stiffened to attention.

"As you were." Callum gestured to the others. "They're with me."

Anna gave the policeman her most sincere smile. "The line is too long."

"American, eh?" the guard said.

"Yup," Anna said, throwing in another Americanism for good measure.

With another nod at Callum, the guard waved them through the barrier. Callum slipped the badge back into his breast pocket. Anna had heard him speaking to Cassie earlier about how they wanted to keep a low profile and not wave their badges around if they didn't have to, but desperate times called for desperate measures.

"We're through the barrier, David," Callum said. "I chose to show my badge."

"Tate knows we're here, so I don't think it matters," David said. "I'm hoping Tate has warned the rank and file by now to be on the lookout for Lee."

"He told me he would," Callum said.

"The guard barely blinked at us," Anna said.

"Lee is an Irishman with an Irish accent," Callum said. "Clearly not you."

"Could be me or Mark," Math said. "He didn't even ask."

"You were with an MI-5 agent," Callum said. "He wouldn't see it as his place to ask."

Anna looked over her shoulder as a man ran up to the first guard and began talking and gesticulating, showing the sense of urgency they were hoping for.

"We're circling around the water side of the castle because it turned out we couldn't get to the square from the east or the south," David said. "The guard may have let you through, but it looks to me as if Tate is, in fact, moving quickly to tighten security. Too little too late if you ask me, but I hope I'm wrong."

"You're not going to be able to get here from there either, David," Anna said. "We've just come through there. They're ramping up the security even more on that side."

Callum looked down at his phone, where a text message had just appeared. "Tate says they've called out the canine unit to inspect the castle and the city, but they won't be here for at least an hour."

"What's the canine unit?" Math said.

"Dogs," Darren said. "They've been trained to sniff out bombs."

"It may be the only way to find Lee and his friend," Callum said.

"Again, too little too late," David said.

"Lee could be moving up his time table too," Anna said. "I couldn't swear that he didn't see me when he looked back, though his eyes didn't pause as they swept over me."

Math put a hand on her shoulder. "He would never expect you to be here today. In that wooly hat and coat, you look nothing like you do at home."

"I borrowed this coat from Cassie's aunt. I was wearing it when he first met me," Anna said.

Math frowned. "I'd forgotten that."

"What is he doing in the meantime to secure the castle?" David said. "Honestly, Tate ought to let you, me, and Darren in, Callum. We know what to look for. What do you bet the bombs are in the toilets?"

"I told Tate about that too," Callum said. "He appeared to take me seriously, but I also know that he also believes in his own methods and doesn't see how Lee could have circumvented them.

He's focusing on protecting the prince, which is fine as far as it goes—
"

"—but he doesn't really believe Lee could have set bombs in the toilets without being detected," David said. "Great."

"With Lee, you really need to think outside the box," Anna said.

"As we discovered to our loss." David released a breath that came out a hiss through the phone's receiver. "Wait where you are, guys. We're coming."

22

David

As it turned out, David should have listened to Anna. Though he, Abraham, Darren, and Dad were able to circle around the castle to the west, once they reached the north side past the sea wall, a line of barricades blocked their way into either the city or the square beyond, even though Anna's group had just passed through there. Their only choice was to go back, which would look suspicious, given the number of security men on guard staring straight at them, or stand in the line of people waiting to get into the castle.

They joined the line.

"This should be interesting," Dad said.

"Darren can get you out of this with his badge," Callum said into David's ear.

"No." David said. "This is what I wanted to do in the first place, and I'm not going to look a gift horse in the mouth." David felt a bit like Harry Potter on the day he drank the lucky serum. The whole of the last twenty-four hours had conspired to bring him to this point; he was meant to enter the castle, right here, right now.

"David." Mom's voice held a warning, and David could picture her in the van with Cassie and Rachel, all three of them with their eyes narrowed, openly opposing what he was about to do. "I don't like you going in there. Once you get inside, you may be stuck there all day, and Callum is going to have to come get you."

"Lee could be in here, and none of Tate's men knows what he looks like," David said. "They need us whether or not they know it."

"Remember too," Abraham said. "I'm *supposed* to be here. We'll be all right."

Even if it wasn't true, David was grateful for the support. Rachel's dad wore an old-fashioned fedora hat, currently covered with snow, and looked as confident and polished as he sounded.

"I agree. This is good," Dad said.

"We can check the toilets for bombs," David said. "Knowing that it has been done will make me feel a lot better about leaving Lee in Tate's hands."

Callum gave a low growl. "Abraham's invitation is for him alone, and Darren is the only one with a badge. They may not let David and Llywelyn inside."

"In which case, we'll know this was the wrong choice," David said.

"The line is moving pretty quickly," Dad said. "They're letting people in."

"Llywelyn—" Mom's voice echoed resignedly through the receiver in David's ear. "Take care of one another."

"Dafydd and I have always had each other's backs," Dad said. "This time will be no different."

They were only a few feet from the entrance. Men stood at the gate with dogs, though from what Tate had said, they weren't here to sniff out bombs. Then he saw why the line was moving so fast: anyone with a backpack or bag larger than a very basic purse was being turned away and shunted through another set of barricades into the square.

The tourists weren't being allowed to come back once they'd ditched their bags either, and David wondered if they should have known they couldn't bring in backpacks, or if it was a new rule based on the information Callum had given Tate about Lee. But even David, the non-MI-5 agent, could see that leaving so many tourists to their own devices on Christmas Day in Caernarfon created a security nightmare, which might be exactly what Lee was counting on.

"You're going to kill yourself if you can't learn to be more detached," Abraham said to David from a pace behind him.

"What?" David said, turning in surprise to look at him.

"I've seen many young doctors burn out because they can't separate themselves from their responsibilities," Abraham said. "You need to learn this too if you're going to survive."

"I've told you the same thing, son," Dad said.

"You have, and I'm trying," David said, resigned to having the conversation, even under these circumstances. "Years ago Mom talked to me about living more lightly, and I do mean to, but being King of England doesn't make that easy." He stopped talking as he saw in his mind's eye the enormous list of things he had to do and worry about each day. No wonder every American president, regardless of what party he belonged to or how poorly he managed the job, went gray within the first four years of office.

"I can only imagine what your life is like," Abraham said. "I don't suppose there's much in the way of self-help books in the Middle Ages?"

David laughed. "It's called the Bible, but sometimes it's a little short on specifics."

"Is it?" Abraham said. "I quote you the words of a different King David, 'The Lord is my light and my salvation; whom shall I fear?' That, to me, is the path to detachment."

"'I remain confident of this: I will see the goodness of the Lord in the land of the living'," David quoted back. "I know another Jewish doctor you're going to get along with really well. You can both harass me while trading verses from the Old Testament."

That got a laugh from Abraham, which carried them to the front of the line and made them seem innocuous—just four friends out for the once-in-a-lifetime experience of seeing the Prince of Wales. The irony of that was not lost on David.

The guards took them one at a time, directing each in turn to open their coats to show they had no weapons of any kind. Earlier, after a hurried conference with Callum, Darren had left his gun in the van for Cassie, who didn't have one. David wasn't even wearing a knife. He'd left his medieval gear in a bag in the van, ready to put on for the return journey. He was looking forward to showing up at home dressed right instead of in inappropriate modern clothing.

The guards waved them into the castle one at a time, David entering last. "You didn't show him your invitation," he said to Abraham once he reached the spot where he, Darren, and Dad were waiting.

"He didn't ask for it, and if I had done so, my name would have been recorded. So far, Tate doesn't know I'm here, and I don't see why we shouldn't keep it that way," Abraham said.

"That's why I didn't show my badge," Darren said. "I don't want Tate to know we distrust his security or we don't think he's doing a good enough job."

As they passed the gift shop, which was doing a thriving trade in water bottles and Welsh cakes, David reconnected to the conference call. "We're in."

Cassie came on the line at the same moment. "I have the supplies, Callum. Tate came through for us. It's a go."

"Good," Callum said.

As David listened, he followed the other tourists through the inner bailey of the castle. A pavilion had been set up on the west end, near the bathrooms, and despite the continued snowfall, castle officials were herding people onto the various wall-walks, of which there were many.

Caernarfon Castle, like many of Edward's castles, had corridors inside the stone curtain wall. Back in the Middle Ages, rooms, if they were small, had been built in the walls themselves or were meant to be accessed through doorways that led to the courtyard. By the twenty-first century, however, all of the buildings that would have existed back in 1284 were gone, destroyed by time. Many would have been built in wood in the first place, which never lasted.

"Where are you now, Anna?" David said.

The companions entered the first doorway straight ahead, which took them into a long corridor heading east. It was good to be out of the snow, and David wondered if the Prince of Wales was really going to deliver his speech in the middle of what was shaping up to be a blizzard. Probably that was what the pavilion was for.

"I'm still with Math, Callum, and Mark, near the NatWest bank on the opposite side of the square from the castle," Anna said, though the deeper they walked within the walls, the more broken up her voice became. "There are hundreds of people in the square, with more coming every second. Some of the shop owners have even opened their stores."

"How un-English of them," David said.

"Probably most of them aren't English," Darren said.

"Many tourists were turned away at the entrance to the castle, and they have nowhere to go," Anna said.

David had been very aware of the cameras above the entrance that had been trained on his face as he entered the castle. But, as Callum had assured them back on the bus when they'd first arrived, the guards hadn't asked for ID, not even for such an event as this, and David could see why they didn't bother—if someone was up to no good, he'd have a fake ID anyway, so there was no point in wasting the guards' time. The cameras were a much better preventive measure, since they could be linked to facial recognition software. If Lee had gone so far as to undergo plastic surgery to change his features, he deserved to win.

Static came over the earpiece, and Callum spoke words David interpreted to be 'you're breaking up'. Reception being what it was in Wales—sucky—and with the many feet of stone surrounding them on all sides, it wasn't surprising they'd lost contact. Hopefully the gap in service would be brief.

David put a hand up to his ear. "If you can hear this, we've started checking the toilets, beginning on the east side of the castle."

Callum didn't answer.

"There's one in here." Abraham, who to nobody's surprise knew Caernarfon Castle well, led the way up another staircase into one of the east towers of the castle. For all that security was incredibly tight getting into the castle, once inside, far fewer guards were visible. David supposed the security people felt everyone inside had been vetted—and certainly nobody had been able to smuggle in so much as a thimbleful of C-4, so they didn't need to be watched closely.

"Am I to understand that neither of you have ever been here before today?" Abraham said to David and his father.

"Caernarfon Castle was built by Edward to subdue the populace," David said.

"That would be after my death." Dad grinned. "Strange to think about, isn't it?"

Abraham shook his head. "I will never think about the Prince of Wales in the same way again."

"You'd better not if you're coming with us," David said.

Caernarfon Castle was the largest castle in north Wales and modern for its time. It had seven towers built into the curtain wall, not including the towers that guarded the two main gates. As a result, it had dozens of toilets on multiple levels. David ducked into a second one. He used his phone as a flashlight and shined it into the recesses of the toilet shaft. No C-4. He heaved a sigh of relief. The absolute best outcome would be to spend the day in the castle, hear the prince's speech, and go home.

"Why isn't anyone else in here?" Dad said.

"Because Tate didn't listen to Callum," David said. It made him kind of angry to be disbelieved. Again.

"Are you sure you want to return to the Middle Ages?" Dad said.

At first David thought his father was talking to Abraham or Darren, but Dad was looking at him when he spoke. David laughed. "We're really not going to go over this again, are we? People need to stop asking me that."

Dad held up his phone. "This is a miraculous world."

David scoffed and was about to make a sarcastic comment when they turned a corner, heading for the last of the toilets in the east wing.

Dad was slightly ahead of him—so he saw Lee first and stopped cold in the middle of the corridor.

Lee was coming straight at them from the other direction, dressed in a Caernarfon Castle maintenance uniform, with the little logo for CADW, the Welsh historical preservation society, on the breast pocket. The detached part of David's brain told him that it made sense for Lee to be wearing the uniform since that had to be how Lee could have gotten inside the castle without being stopped. He might have even come by the uniform legally, since he could have heard about the prince's speech as soon as it was announced, seen the implications, and applied at Caernarfon for a job.

They were still twenty feet apart, but Lee had noticed them too, so David didn't see much point in retreating. He put out a hand, trying to think of something appeasing to say to Lee while at the same time whispering a warning into his earpiece. As before, he got no response from Callum.

"You." A gun materialized in Lee's hand—maybe the same gun he'd brought to the Middle Ages and shot at David with last year—and he pointed it at them. "Put up your hands, David, or your father dies."

David obeyed, hoping that Lee hadn't seen Darren, who was still in the toilet corridor, or Abraham, who was shorter than either Llywelyn or David. Abraham had stopped in the shadow against the wall. David tried to make himself look bigger and more looming, even as he heard Abraham take a few quick steps backwards. David hoped he could bring help, or at the very least get to some place with better reception. David turned his head slightly sideways, tracking him out of the corner of his eye.

But before Abraham could get far, a second man moved out of the shadows further down the corridor. He held a gun in his right hand and shoved at Darren's back with his left. Darren edged forward until he reached Abraham's side. The man waggled the gun, urging Darren and Abraham to move past David towards Lee.

David would have told them to stall, but Abraham couldn't read minds and obeyed the terrorist instead of David's unvoiced thought. With a gun in his face, David couldn't blame him. Lee's accomplice came forward too until he was four feet away from David and Darren, with Abraham and David's father standing beyond them, closer to Lee. David had by now turned fully sideways, one arm outstretched towards Lee and the other towards his accomplice, keeping them both at bay.

Abraham, meanwhile, pressed his back against the corridor wall and faced David. He was very calm, as befitted his training as a doctor used to crisis situations, and his eyes kept flicking from one gun to the other.

"You don't want to do this," David said to Lee.

"I really think I do," Lee said. "I didn't exchange servitude to you for oppression here only to fail now."

Judging Lee to be the more dangerous of their two opponents, Darren edged towards Lee, taking a half-step to the right to end up in front of Abraham in order to act as his protector. Dad was closer to Lee than David, a matter of two feet from the gun, which Lee should have known wasn't a good idea. David sensed his father moving a split second before he did.

Dad grabbed the barrel of Lee's gun with his right hand, jerked the gun down and forward to pull Lee towards him, and then popped Lee's nose with the heel of his left hand.

A half second later, in a *what the hell* sort of way, David launched himself at Lee's accomplice.

Men with guns should be prepared to aim them, but Lee's accomplice either viewed the gun as a prop or simply didn't expect David make a move on him. As David rushed forward, the gun went off. David felt the bullet whistle by his left ear, but it didn't hit him, and then David was close enough to grasp the man's right wrist with his own right hand and twisted.

The accomplice released the gun, which David caught in his left hand. Still holding the terrorist's wrist at a brutal angle, David levered the man to the floor, kicking his left knee as he did so, and said, "Get down on the ground and put your hands behind your head."

David had never shot a gun in his life, but as Lee's accomplice fell forward on his face, he held it two-handed like he'd seen on television. David backed away too so there was a good five feet between him and the man on the ground. He wasn't going to make the mistake both these men had made, which was to get close enough to his victim to have the tables turned on him. David thought it would have been taught in Terrorist 101. Guns were uncommon in Britain, however, so maybe they really hadn't known—or their nervousness had overcome their training.

Once the man was on the ground, David glanced again at his father to see how he was faring. He had Lee on his knees, but instead of lying face down, Lee had both hands to his nose, which was pouring blood.

Dad held Lee's gun and was pointing it at him. His father had only seen a gun a few times in his life. He'd never held one and certainly never seen one fired, which was the only explanation David could think of as to why his father had taken the chance of getting shot and had moved as he had. He'd saved them, however, so David couldn't feel bad about it.

Before David could suggest Darren help out, the MI-5 agent moved swiftly to Dad's side, took the gun from him, and then kicked at the back of Lee's knee with his boot. "On the ground."

With that, David lifted his chin and tried to make his voice carry, though all the saliva in his mouth had suddenly dried up, and he found himself croaking, "Over here! We're over here!" He repeated the words in Welsh for good measure.

It would have been great if Callum had been able to hear him speak, but David wasn't counting on it. His own ears still rang from the sound of the gun going off in the enclosed space, so even if someone had replied, he might not have heard him.

He shouted one more time, and then answering calls came from outside the walls. A few seconds later, feet pounded along the stone passage.

"You okay, Dad?" David said.

Because of Darren, Dad had backed away from Lee, and now he stood guard over Abraham. "I am."

"Abraham?"

Abraham nodded but didn't speak. David turned the gun so the butt was towards the doctor. "I need a second."

Showing surprise for the first time, Abraham took the gun, his eyes a little wider than usual, and pointed it in the direction of Lee's accomplice.

David had to assume that the result of this encounter would be that all of them would spend the rest of the day being questioned by MI-5. He would have preferred to avoid that, and silently thanked Callum for insisting that Darren join his party. Even if it took a while to clear everything up, having an MI-5 agent among those subduing a terrorist had to put them all instantly on the side of the angels.

Still, it would mean no more toilet checking, and they hadn't even finished this tower, much less the six others. With that worry at the front of his mind, David ducked into the last toilet he hadn't checked, the one he'd been heading to when they'd been interrupted by Lee. In fact, it was through this doorway that Lee had entered the hallway a moment ago.

The small room was at the end of a zig-zagging corridor, and this toilet was more intact than some of the others. Looking down it, David couldn't see daylight. He stuck his hand into the chute, feeling around the stones, his mind more on Lee and his accomplice in the corridor than on what he was doing. Thus, it was a few seconds, as he felt around inside the toilet shaft, before he realized his hand was touching clay.

Not that it was really clay, of course, but C-4. David hadn't encountered explosives since that awful day at Dover Castle, but the experience of feeling around inside the toilet shaft at Canterbury Castle, touching the squishiness of the C-4 that felt more like modeling clay than anything else, wasn't something he'd ever forget.

David focused on his fingers, feeling around the edges of the block until they touched a cord, which ran downwards. He followed the cord it until it—and David's fingers—connected with another block of clay. He could just reach it if he bent over fully and stretched his arm as far as it would go down the chute. The awkwardness of the position meant there was no way David could pull the bomb out by himself—and it would be stupid to try anyway, in case the detonator went off when he moved it.

Fixing in his mind the particular details of what he'd found in order to convey them to the authorities as succinctly as possible, he pulled out his arm and darted down the passage towards the interior corridor. When he reached the doorway, Dad and Abraham were waiting for him, and Dad directed his attention to where two security guards were getting Lee and his accomplice to their feet while Darren talked to them urgently. His badge was closed, but still held in his hand.

"We need to get out of here right now," David said to his father and Abraham, and then raised the volume of his voice to add, "There's a bomb in the toilet shaft!"

David kept his eyes on Lee because—bloody nose or not, hands cuffed behind his back or not—he was going far more quietly than David thought he should be. Lee was violent and spiteful, and even with Darren's warnings, the two policemen had to be woefully unprepared for what he might do next.

At David's shout, Darren spun around, and as long as David lived, he would never forget the look of horror on his friend's face. While the two guards openly gaped behind him, and Lee's accomplice glared disdainfully, Darren ran back down the corridor towards David and the others. Meanwhile, the expression on Lee's face as he looked at David chilled him to the bone. It was a mocking smirk, which turned into an open smile as he turned his back in order to show David his hands cuffed behind his back—and the trigger he held in his hand.

"You get to be my ticket out of here," Lee said.

Fear coursed through David, but instead of freezing him, it gave him clarity and purpose. He didn't reply. He didn't protest. Instead, he grabbed Darren's hand and clapped it on Abraham's upper arm. "Don't let go whatever you do."

Then he hooked his arms through Abraham's and Dad's elbows, spun everyone around so they were facing away from Lee and the guards, and urged them forward. Instinctively, David tucked his arms closer to his body and clasped his hands across his chest so neither Abraham nor Dad had a chance to get loose. Darren by now had one hand on Abraham's arm and one arm around David's shoulders and was shoving them forward as he ran behind them, as if he was pushing a giant boulder up a hill.

Neither Dad nor Abraham protested at the treatment, though one of the policeman shouted, "Hey! You can't leave!"

Yes we can.

Ten feet ... twenty feet ... they were fifty feet away from the toilet, having made it almost all the way back down the corridor to the Black Tower, when the guard's echoing call was cut off by the percussive *boom* that resounded in the corridor almost at the same instant that the force of the explosion pressed Darren into David's back, and all of them were lifted off their feet and vaulted forward. David hit the wall in front of him full on.

And fell into utter darkness.

23

Math

The easternmost tower of Caernarfon Castle burst upwards and out, raining debris on the whole of the castle square. It was as if a giant fist had punched up through the snow that was falling from the sky, and then collapsed.

"Christ in heaven!" Math gazed up at the balloon of dust, which was already settling on the ground to be covered by a layer of snow from the swirling blizzard. He hadn't been with Dafydd when Canterbury Castle had been destroyed, but now he knew something of what it must have been like.

Horror was etched on Anna's face, and Math wished she hadn't been here to see this. Nobody had liked it when Llywelyn, Abraham, and Dafydd had entered the castle, and Math didn't have any doubt that whatever had made Lee set off the explosion before the Prince of England's speech, effectively half a day early, Dafydd had been in the thick of it.

In front of them, people ran every which way, crying and screaming. Security men appeared out of avenue and alley to converge on the castle. Sirens wailed in the distance, and the four of them—Callum, Mark, Anna, and Math—stood and watched from their vantage point over a hundred yards away.

"What just happened?" Meg's voice echoed in Math's ear.

"The east tower of the castle blew up," Mark said.

Math was glad Mark had chosen to talk, because he didn't know if he could have found the words to answer his mother-in-law. As he stared at the castle, he told himself that he believed with every fiber of his being that if anyone could survive such a blast, Dafydd could. It was whether or not he was close to Darren, Llywelyn, and Abraham when it happened that was the concern.

"David—" Meg said.

"They were in the castle when it went up. That's all we know." Callum spoke clearly and without emphasis or inflection. "We can't raise any of them on their mobiles."

"We couldn't earlier because of the stone walls, and now it's what you'd expect if they were caught in the middle of an explosion," Meg said reasonably. "They would have *traveled* home."

The lump in Math's throat was huge, but he managed to agree with Meg around it. "That's right. Of course they would. Dafydd would have seen to it."

Anna, who was white as a sheet, had her phone in her hand. She was dialing Dafydd's number alternately with Llywelyn's. Math slipped an arm around her waist and bent so that his chin was almost on her shoulder. He wanted to be able to hear if one of them answered.

When neither did after another round of tapping at the screen, he said, "You don't need to do that, Anna. Dafydd will either let us know he and Papa are fine, or he won't be able to let us know because they aren't here anymore."

"What should we do, Callum?" Cassie said.

Callum cleared his throat. "Stay where you are for now. I don't want you getting stuck some place you can't get out of. The only vehicles that are going to be able to get close any time soon are either security or emergency. I imagine Tate is going to want to speak to me sooner rather than later. I'm going to send Anna, Math, and Mark to you. Get some food. Try to rest. I will stay here to help."

"But—" Cassie started to protest again.

Callum gentled his voice. "Give me a chance to find out what's happening."

"Okay," Cassie said.

"I'm staying with you," Math said to Callum.

Anna looked up at him, her expression stricken, and she clung to his hand. He didn't like the idea of being separated from her either. Given the way the time traveling seemed to work, another explosion in Anna's vicinity could send her home. The last thing he wanted was to be stuck here without her while she took the others to the Middle Ages. But he needed to be the one to find Dafydd's body if it was in the rubble to be found.

He put a hand on Anna's shoulder. "Do you know how to get to the Tesco?"

"We do," Mark said.

Math wasn't sure that Anna was aware of anything but what was going on in her heart, but Mark had shown himself to be more than capable many times in the last year. And Callum was right that they couldn't be searching for signs of Dafydd and Llywelyn in the destroyed castle with Anna beside them. Beyond the personal loss, Math knew as well as Callum what a disaster it would be for Britain to lose the King of England and the King of Wales on the same day.

"Keep us apprised if you run into trouble," Callum said to Mark.

"Will do." Mark gestured for Anna to come with him.

Anna clung to Math, her arms around his neck, and he gave her a quick hug and kiss. "We'll take care of this," he said.

"What about Abraham and Darren?" Anna said. "What am I to tell Rachel?"

"That her father has reached the Middle Ages like he wanted, and she has only to join him," Callum said, "by the end of the day if we can manage it."

Then the pair set off east towards the Tesco.

Callum nudged Math as he watched them go. "They'll make it fine."

"I know," Math said. "If Dafydd and Llywelyn were in that tower when it blew up, however, Anna may never be fine again."

"You doubt they would have *traveled*?" Callum said.

Math took in a breath. "I have utter faith in Dafydd, but what if he wasn't holding onto his father at the time?"

The thin lines around Callum's mouth deepened. "I wasn't going to mention such a possibility out loud."

"We have always spoken the truth to each other," Math said. "Let's not start lying now."

"No," Callum said. "Especially not now."

Emergency vehicles had started arriving in the square, and a host of people were streaming into and out of the castle. Though only a short while had passed since the explosion, the chaos was coalescing into something slightly more organized. Caernarfon Castle had lost one tower, which was disastrous, but the bomb hadn't brought the whole thing down and couldn't have killed that many people. Math was almost more concerned for the people who'd been standing outside the castle in the square, who could have been felled by the flying debris.

Callum moved several yards along the walkway so he could see the northern castle entrance more clearly. He grunted his disapproval. "They should be stopping and questioning every person who was in the castle, but they aren't."

"Can you blame anyone for wanting to get out of there as quickly as possible?" Math said.

"No, but Tate should have been better prepared."

"He wasn't in charge of the Prince of Wales' security, was he?" Math said. "If he was only marginally interested in your toilet theory, he may not have passed it on immediately. Perhaps he was waiting to speak to you in person."

"I hope he's taking it seriously now because we don't want what happened when the twin towers fell to happen here," Callum said.

"What happened then?" Math said.

Callum turned to him. "In 2001, terrorists flew airplanes into two sky scrapers—which are enormously tall buildings—in New York City. Emergency personnel entered the building, in order to save people and put out the fires, and were subsequently killed because nobody was prepared for the towers to collapse in the aftermath of the crashes." Callum grimaced. "Though in this case, I'm more concerned about a second explosion."

"It would be good to know why this bomb went off," Math said. "If it was the only one, that would not correlate with Lee's previous methods."

Callum's phone sounded, and he looked at it. "Tate." He pressed talk and then another button, which Math knew by now meant he'd activated the speaker.

He and Callum huddled close to listen.

"Callum, I need you here. Now."

"Director Tate," Callum said. "It's good to hear your voice. I'm glad you weren't in the tower when it went up."

Tate tsked under his breath. "Where are you?"

"Outside the castle," Callum said. "We saw it happen. Where are you?"

"Inside. I was near the front gate."

"How can I be of service?" Callum said.

"A moment ago, I was informed that a security guard heard a gunshot in the Queen's Tower before the explosion and ran with his partner to the scene. He radioed in that he found one of our agents, Darren Jeffries, standing over a man he identified as Lee Delaney along with a second terrorist. Jeffries had subdued them both. The two guards were in the process of bringing everyone in for questioning when the tower exploded."

"You need to know that last I spoke to King David and King Llywelyn, they were heading towards that tower," Callum said. "Did the guard mention the presence of anyone else?"

"No."

"I hope you're searching all the toilets now," Callum said.

"We are." Tate paused before adding, "Most of the tower ended up in the square. We're looking for bodies now."

"That's pretty quick, isn't it?" Math said to Callum, as an aside. "Isn't everything on fire?"

"C-4 doesn't start fires," Callum said, "and the castle is only stone now. It doesn't have anything inside it that could burn."

"Who just spoke?" Tate said.

Math grimaced, silently apologizing to Callum.

"Lord Mathonwy ap Rhys, sir," Callum said.

Tate grunted, taking Math's presence in stride and not asking for clarification, which showed how far he'd come in his acceptance of the time traveling and everything associated with it.

"It looks like the bomb was PE-4, what the Americans call C-4, wouldn't you say?" Tate said.

"I agree, sir," Callum said. "That would be why there's no fire."

"What can you see from your side?" Tate said.

"The dust is starting to settle, what hasn't already blown away in the storm," Callum said. "We would like to offer our assistance in retrieving any bodies."

"One moment—" Tate left the line open as he spoke to someone else. Math had a hard time understanding conversations over phones. Although Tate had spoken clearly enough when talking to Callum directly, Math couldn't understand a word of the side conversation.

Callum frowned at Math. "Did he say *four* bodies have been found?"

Tate returned, having overheard Callum's question. "Yes. Four. We're combing through the rubble now for survivors."

"What about body parts?" Callum said.

"Not yet—and that would be unlikely unless someone was right on top of the bomb," Tate said.

"As in standing over a toilet, sir, checking it for a bomb?" Callum said.

Tate grunted his assent, his only acknowledgement that Callum had been right, and Tate should have listened to him an hour ago. "Such a person might have been vaporized, but even that is unlikely if the bomb was located in the toilet shaft on the outer wall of the castle. The wall of the castle collapsed, as you saw, but much of the bomb's energy was expended into the air."

"Have you identified the bodies?" Callum said.

"One moment." Tate gave some grunting breaths, implying that he was walking briskly or climbing stairs.

Math breathed shallowly, listening hard. It was several hundred heartbeats before Tate's voice returned to the line.

"We found two men in security gear and two men in Caernarfon Castle uniforms," Tate said.

"Are you there now?" Callum said.

"I'm standing over them."

"Can you send me images of their faces?" Callum said.

Mark reappeared at Callum's right shoulder. "You don't need to do that. I'll go to Tate. I was part of the deal."

Callum spun around to look at his friend. "Mark—

"I said I'd go." Mark's face was set into grim lines. "You need me to stay here with MI-5. I can testify that Lee was in Cardiff. Tate needs eyewitnesses, and you all need to go home."

Callum didn't speak, simply gazed at his friend.

Then Tate's voice came out of the phone. "Mark is right, Callum."

Callum appeared to shake himself. "Was anybody else injured?"

"The floors above and below the bomb were destroyed or partially collapsed, but not pulverized," Tate said. "So far, we have a woman with a broken leg, and a man with what might be a concussion. Nobody else was in that tower. The tourists were interested in saving places in the courtyard to watch the prince's speech."

"Good job the bomb went off early," Mark said.

"One of the handcuffed men was found with a trigger in his hand," Tate said. "We presume him to be Lee, though we're still working on facial recognition—though his face is badly damaged by flying stone and shrapnel."

"That's why I'm on my way to identify him for you," Mark said.

"I should come too," Callum said.

Tate cleared his throat. "I cannot believe I'm about to say this, but while I accept Mark's assistance and I realize that I am contradicting myself, you don't want to come in, Callum."

Callum glanced at the others and then said, "Why not?"

"Because you will be asked questions you cannot answer, or have answers to questions people do not want to hear. They're going to want to know what you were doing here, why you gave me advance warning about the toilet and, quite frankly, why I didn't follow up on your warning right away. It will imply that I had reason not to trust you."

"But the bomb was in the toilet," Callum said.

Tate paused before saying, "They are going to wonder, given that Lee was on the bus in Cardiff, and has reappeared here just as you did, if you didn't bring him. They will wonder about your advance knowledge of the bomb, and if you had a hand in it."

"What about Mark?" Callum said.

"He isn't the former director of the Project," Tate said. "He's been in Iceland this last year."

Mark's expression turned rueful, and he spoke to Callum in an undertone, "He's protecting himself."

Callum grimaced. "One moment, sir."

He turned the phone off speaker and pressed it against his thigh, looking at Mark as he did so. "Are you sure?"

"I'm sure."

Callum shook his head, but he held out his free hand to Mark anyway. "Good luck."

"I will keep the home fires burning." Mark shook hands with Math too, nodded once, and set off across the square towards the castle, his shoulders hunched against the blowing snow.

Callum turned the speaker back on. "Mark is on his way." Then he motioned that Math should start walking away from the castle square with him, which he did at a rapid clip, heading east towards the Tesco and plowing through six inches of new snow in some areas of the walkway where nobody had passed since the snow had started.

As they walked, Callum continued to talk to Tate. "Have you found any other bombs, sir? I find it hard to believe Lee would have planted only one."

"No, we haven't, and while even one bomb is unacceptable, I'm sure you are mistaken about there being more. Lee set the bomb off too early, dying in the process," Tate said. "The explosion was meant to go off during the prince's speech. With security focused on the east tower, terrorists could have abducted or even killed the prince in the chaos."

"That's quite an assumption," Math said in an undertone as he took long strides at Callum's side. "He sounds like he's already preparing his speech to his superiors." Math too had come a long way in a single day.

Callum chose not to express his disbelief. "Please ring me if you learn anything more that might pertain to King David and King Llywelyn."

"I will do that," Tate said. "Goodbye, Callum." He disconnected the call.

Callum instantly began to press more buttons, reaching Cassie immediately.

"Where are you?" she said.

"On our way to you," Callum said.

"What's going on?"

Callum skirted an unattended barrier, since the security guard appeared to have abandoned his post. "I think it's time we went home too."

24

David

D avid landed on his feet with a thud and rolled. The black abyss had come and gone, and even if he'd been screaming inside the whole time, he forced himself to stay alert to whatever situation they were falling into.

He came up from a full summersault into a runner's crouch in the grass, and as he caught his breath, the blades in the tuft directly in front of his nose came into focus. A drop of rain plopped onto it, and David shot a glance at the sky. It was raining instead of snowing, and low hanging clouds surrounded him.

He knew instantly where he was: the castle of Dinas Bran sat silhouetted against the sky to the southeast, meaning they had arrived approximately halfway up the mountain. The road from the village to the castle ran just to the northeast of their position, switching back and forth across the face of the mountain until finally climbing to the southern facing gatehouse. The gateway was new since Math had rebuilt the castle, moved from its original position on the eastern slope.

A moan came from behind him, and he spun around. A few feet away, his father and Abraham were getting to their feet, but beyond them, Darren lay in a heap in the grass, his coat shredded and his entire back covered in blood.

Abraham saw him in the same instant, and since he was closer, he crouched beside Darren before David could reach him. David's back was sore where he thought stones had hit him before they'd vanished, but it was nothing like what had become of Darren.

"Nobody has a knife, do they, to cut off his clothes?" Abraham said.

David knelt in the grass, wanting to touch Darren, but knowing that might not be a good idea. "No. I left everything in the van."

Abraham began to peel from his skin the remains of Darren's coat and shirt, both of which had been shredded by debris the bomb had thrown at them. David watched in silence for a few seconds and then moved to Darren's other side to help, giving thanks that the explosion hadn't been caused by a pipe bomb or one laced with gasoline, or else all their clothes might have caught fire too.

David gently peeled away the cloth. Darren's skin was shredded, and David's face twisted in sympathy at the pain Darren had to be feeling.

Abraham's brow was heavily furrowed. He glanced at David and said in an undertone, "It looks bad, but it could be worse."

"I've been in war," David said. "I have seen worse."

Darren groaned, "My shoulder."

"It's dislocated." Abraham looked at David. "If we don't fix his shoulder, the muscles will swell, and we'll be worse off than we are now." He studied David for a second. "I need you to hold him."

David didn't ask why Abraham needed help. Darren was six inches taller than Abraham and heavily muscled. The trick to popping a shoulder back in place was easy once you knew it, but Darren was in no condition to help in any way.

"Come on, Darren. Easy does it." As gently as he could, and with his father's help, David grasped Darren around the torso and raised him to his feet. Darren's flayed skin had to be screaming with every movement, but maybe not more than his shoulder.

"You ready?" Abraham had both of Darren's arms bent at a forty-five degree angle in front of him. Slowly, he moved the arms to the sides as if he were opening doors to a great hall and they were the doors. Darren seemed to be more awake now—and with all the pain he was feeling, how could he not be?—and realized what Abraham was attempting. Abraham raised both of Darren's arms together, and by the time he got to the point where Darren's hands were above his head, the dislocated shoulder slipped into place.

David hadn't realized he'd been holding his breath. Darren bent his head and sagged, as much as his shoulder would let him, in relief.

"My lord!" The call echoed from above them, and David turned his head at the shout. Even from this distance, he thought he recognized Justin's figure riding out of the gate, followed by six of David's men.

"Your mother is going to be very worried," Dad said, speaking for the first time.

"I know." David looked up at the sky, though there was nothing to see but clouds and rain. Somewhere above the ground was the hole in the universe they'd just come through, and on the other side of it was the rest of David's family.

David lowered Darren back to the ground. "Rachel," Darren said. "How is it that I am here, and Rachel is there?"

"Son, I don't know when, but I can tell you that she will be coming just as soon as she can," Dad said. "My wife will see to it."

Darren pressed his lips together and gave a sharp exhale through his nose.

"I shouldn't complain, since I would have been far worse off had I remained in Avalon. In fact, I'd be dead." Darren raised his head slightly to look at both Abraham and David at the same time. "Thank you."

"We need to get you to the castle." Abraham glanced at David. "Infection is the greatest worry—not for his shoulder, but for his back. I have nothing out here that will help me care for him."

David could see that. Many of Darren's wounds were deep, like he'd been flayed with a multi-thonged whip that had cut into the muscles of his back, some even down to his rib bones.

"None of you would have been there at all except for me," David said.

Abraham held up one finger. "Not true. I had tickets to the event. If you hadn't come, Lee would have set bombs throughout the whole castle. I could have died—the Prince of Wales would have died—if not for you." He canted his head. "The Prince of England, I mean."

Dad brushed at David's back. "Your coat is shredded too."

David's eyes had returned to the company that was coming to get them. The horses had slowed as they'd left the road, but there was no mistaking the urgency in Justin's tone and posture. "But not my skin."

Abraham smoothed his beard with one hand. "We really are in the Middle Ages."

Dad patted the smaller man's shoulder. "You are taking this very well. You should have heard Callum when he first arrived. All he could say was *my God!*"

"I confess I find that hard to believe," Abraham said.

Justin pulled up, breathing hard. "My lord. Lady Bronwen begs you to come to the castle. The queen—" Justin stopped, his expression stricken as he took in Darren's wounded body. Then his eyes returned to David's face.

"What's wrong?" David said.

"The baby is coming."

One of the guardsmen dismounted and gestured for David to take his horse. David glanced at Darren. "What about—"

But his father had taken charge of Darren. "You heard the doctor. Nothing more can be done for him out here. We'll get him to the castle, and then Abraham can help him when he's done helping Lili."

David shot a look at Abraham, who nodded. David mounted quickly, but when Abraham didn't mount a second horse, which another guardsman had vacated, David bent to him. "What's wrong?"

Abraham moved to David's stirrup and looked up at him. "I've never ridden a horse in my life."

"Come with me then." David held out his arm to Abraham while removing his own foot from the stirrup so Abraham could mount behind him. "I'm surprised, you being a Welshophile and all." It was a little joke, made reflexively and with a very small part of David's brain.

Abraham, for his part, didn't answer because he was too busy scrambling onto the horse behind David. Once settled, Abraham directed his next question at Justin. He spoke slowly because of their divergent versions of English. "Has something gone wrong?"

David repeated the question to make the words clearer to Justin. It probably wasn't necessary, since 'thing' and 'wrong' were ancient words that could be comprehensible to Justin, even with Abraham's modern accent.

"The baby is turned the wrong way around and comes too early—"

David didn't wait for more of an explanation. "Yah!" He spurred the horse towards the castle.

"What do we have for supplies?" Abraham had his hands clutched tightly around David's waist, holding on for dear life.

"The castle has an infirmary," David said, suppressing his impatience with his speed. Uphill and carrying two, the horse couldn't move as fast as if he'd been carrying only David. "It isn't as complete as the one down in Llangollen, but the village lies twelve hundred feet below the castle in the river valley. Rachel arranged for an infirmary to be stocked inside the castle because, in an emergency, the village was too far to bring a patient."

"Anesthetic?"

"Poppy juice and alcohol," David said.

"How far along is your wife?" Abraham said.

"Seven months," David said.

David didn't have to turn around to know what expression Abraham's face held. But while Abraham might not be a warrior, he was a good doctor, which meant keeping a clear head at all times was a way of life. David had already seen Abraham handle one crisis. He trusted that if anyone could handle this too, it was Abraham.

The longest ten minutes of David's life later, they surged up the ramp and through the gatehouse of the castle into the outer bailey. David swung his right leg over the horse's head, dropped to the ground, and then helped Abraham down.

Gwenllian was right beside him as he turned around. "She's in the infirmary."

All three took off in that direction at a run.

"How long has she been laboring?" Abraham said, showing his wisdom in using the medieval phrase rather than 'in labor' which would have made no sense to Gwenllian, even with her American English.

"Almost from the moment Dafydd left," Gwenllian said.

David found that he couldn't breathe around the fear in his throat. Lili had been suffering all night long, and he hadn't been here to help her. He'd thought that appearing on the wrong side of the motorway had cured him of whatever complacency he'd felt about time traveling, but it hadn't been true. When he'd grasped Dad's and Abraham's arms, he'd known with utter certainty that he would live through the blast that was coming. What had happened to Darren, however, showed how terrifyingly erroneous that assumption had been. With Abraham's help, Darren should live, but the close shave showed him he had no reason to think that Lili would be equally favored.

Abraham jogged calmly beside him and entered the infirmary with a firm stride. Aaron and Catriona stood talking, deep in conversation with Bronwen, who had Rachel's stethoscope around her neck. All three looked over as Abraham entered. Birth in the Middle Ages was an obsessively female endeavor. All the midwives and ladies had been horrified by David's attendance at Arthur's birth, but he'd overridden them then, and he was well past the point of caring about medieval sensibilities now.

Thus, without more than a *thank God you're here,* Bronwen directed David to the side room where Lili sat on a stool. She held her head in her hands. Branwen, her maid, a no-nonsense woman if there ever was one, folded spare linens a few feet away.

She looked up as David entered and said before David could ask, "She didn't want me touching her."

David crouched in front of his wife. Not sure if it was okay for him to touch her either, David put his hands on either side of Lili's thighs. "I'm here, Lili. I've brought Abraham, Rachel's father. He's a doctor."

David had expected to find his wife limp and exhausted, but Lili's head came up, and her expression was fierce—though dried tear tracks showed on her face. "I am not going to die like my mother did. I'm not going to leave my children without a mother."

"Lili." David's voice caught in his throat, but he managed to speak around it. "You are the strongest woman I know. There is nothing you can't do, including this."

Abraham stepped into David's line of sight and made a gesture with his chin. "Can you help her up onto the table?"

Between David and Branwen, they lifted Lili, who even pregnant weighed only two-thirds of David's weight, and settled her onto the examining table. It wasn't the same kind as in the modern world, obviously, but it was clean, covered by a long cushion and a sheet with a pillow at the far end. They lowered Lili so she lay on her left side. David moved to her head to hold her hand and kiss her forehead.

"David said you're seven months along?" Abraham hands moved along Lili's belly.

"Maybe more," Bronwen said, from the doorway.

David looked up, startled. "More?"

"Lili told me after you left that her dates could be very off," Bronwen said.

Abraham straightened. "By two months?"

"Possibly a month and a half," Bronwen said.

Abraham nodded. "That's good news for both of them."

David kept his head close to Lili's, unable to speak. Now was not the time for recriminations, but then Lili opened her eyes to look into his face. "I'm sorry I didn't tell you ages ago."

He shook his head. "*Cariad,* you have nothing to be sorry for. If anything, I should apologize to you. If I'd been paying better attention, I wouldn't have left you to carry this burden on your own."

Abraham broke in. "Lili, I'm going to lift your gown and examine you. Has Rachel done this?"

Lili gave a slight nod, which David confirmed. "Once or twice."

"But her water hasn't broken?"

Bronwen shook her head. "No."

"More good news." Abraham went to a nearby basin of hot water from which steam rose. He used the soap and scrubbed at his hands.

Lili breathed through another contraction. Her tears hadn't returned, and David could hear her whispering a psalm over and over again. He bent to her and chanted it with her.

Abraham pulled out a stethoscope from the inside pocket of his coat and put the ends into his ears. David wouldn't have been surprised to discover that he had an entire array of medical tools secreted in various pockets about his person. The man was nothing if not prepared.

Abraham put the end of the stethoscope to Lili's stomach and, after a moment, he nodded. "The baby's heart is strong."

David let out the breath he'd been holding.

"I need everyone in this room to wash their hands, even if you have already," Abraham said.

David obeyed, followed by the women. Abraham eyed them for a second. "Bronwen, Branwen, is that right?" He pointed from one to the other.

Bronwen smiled. "I know. It's confusing. Wait until you realize that every man in Wales is either Dafydd, Gruffydd, or Rhys. You won't find any Toms, Dicks, or Harrys here."

Abraham looked to Branwen. "I need fresh hot water and warm cloths. Can you get those for me?"

Bronwen translated into Welsh, and Branwen said, "Yes, sir." She left the room with the now dirty basin.

Abraham turned to David. "I have medical gloves, but I fear a greater need for them in the future, so with your permission, I'll examine her barehanded."

"Do what you have to do," David said.

Lili nodded too, and Abraham lifted Lili's gown.

While Abraham examined Lili, David put his forehead to hers, both of them breathing slowly through another contraction. At one point, Lili moaned and, without opening her eyes, said, "I can't do this anymore."

"You can," David said, with absolutely no evidence to support his claim except that he knew his wife. "You can be strong and still allow other people to take care of you. You don't have to hold on so tightly. Let go. Let your fear go." David had a moment of insanity where he thought about quoting the Litany of Fear from *Dune*, but immediately thought better of it, instead quoting King David as Abraham had done a lifetime ago at the entrance to Caernarfon Castle: "The Lord is my light and my salvation; whom shall I fear?"

Abraham straightened. "She's only nine centimeters dilated, but the baby is, in fact, turned the right way. I believe the problem to be that the head hasn't been centered properly on her cervix, and I can feel that the baby's hand is up to his head." He looked over at Bronwen. "It isn't surprising, given how long the labor is taking, that the midwife thought the baby was turned wrong."

"None of the usual birthing positions were working," Bronwen said. "Once we understood that the baby was coming whether or not we were ready, Lili paced around the castle all night."

"I'm sure your midwives are very knowledgeable," Abraham said. "I don't want to interfere, but this is one instance where keeping Lili upright hasn't been helping. Just as I examined her, I felt the baby's head shift slightly and settle more fully onto the cervix."

"Can you do something for Lili?" David said.

"At the moment, she doesn't need me to do anything for her. What she needs is a little sugar and protein for energy for what's to come."

Branwen had returned with the fresh water, and at a quick word from Bronwen, she immediately left again. "She'll see to it," Bronwen said.

"David, will you come with me to talk to the midwife?" Abraham said. "You need to be part of the consultation and probably translate for me."

Bronwen moved to take David's place at Lili's head, though not before David kissed Lili's temple. "I'll be right back. You and the baby are going to be okay."

He and Abraham returned to the central room where Aaron and Catriona were standing. Neither of them had been talking, and both started towards him when David appeared, speaking in unison, though saying different things in two different languages.

David made a slashing motion with his hand, cutting them off, and then held out his hand to Abraham. "This is Abraham, Rachel's father and a doctor from Avalon. Abraham, this is Aaron and Catriona."

Catriona curtseyed, and Aaron and Abraham greeted each other, one Jewish man to another. Then Abraham went straight to the point. "What have you given her, and what do you see as the problem?"

Both Aaron and Catriona looked blank until David translated, first into Welsh, which was the only language Catriona spoke, and then into medieval English.

Aaron responded by gesturing to Catriona. "Birth is not my area, though I have been learning."

"For a second baby, the birth is taking a very long time," Catriona said. "I have given her raspberry tea, rubbed her with rose oil, and she's taken a tincture of vinegar and honey."

"She couldn't keep the latter down," Aaron added.

David translated for Abraham, who grimaced at David. "Most of the herbs I know that are helpful in birth are native to North America."

"Can you do a c-section?" David blurted the words out before he could stop them, glad that neither Aaron nor Catriona could understand American English.

Abraham turned to face him fully. "I will if I have to, but as long as the baby's heart is beating strongly, I will do everything in my power to help her deliver the child naturally." He gestured to Aaron and Catriona. "In the modern UK, the vast majority of babies are born with midwives, and Lili has been in good hands up until now. It may be that what she needed was you, not me, and only you could say to her what she needed to hear."

David opened his mouth to reply, but was interrupted by Bronwen skittering through the doorway. "She says she has to push!"

David took off at a run for Lili's room, and as soon as he reached the head of the table, Lili wrapped an arm around his neck and held on. Abraham and Catriona followed, Catriona carrying a birthing chair, which she set on the floor at the end of the table.

"Do you want to sit on that?" David asked Lili when the contraction passed.

"I want the baby OUT!" Lili still hadn't let go of his neck, so without asking for permission, David picked her up in his arms and carried her to the stool. As she sat another contraction took her. She gripped the sides of the chair, screaming bloody murder but also pushing as hard as she could.

Catriona crouched in front of her, while Abraham stood to one side, counting through the contraction. Abraham indicated that David should take over the counting, in groups of ten as Lili pushed, while he and Catriona washed their hands one more time.

By the time they crouched in front of Lili again, she was bent double, pushing for dear life, and then as the contraction ended, in a wave of frustration, she pulled her loose-fitting birthing gown off over the top of her head and threw it in a corner, revealing a short t-shirt-like shift which was all she had on underneath. Bronwen crouched nearby with a fresh linen cloth to wrap the baby in when it came. David knelt beside Lili as another contraction took her, counting out to ten in a calm monotone.

Catriona gasped as Lili's water broke in a rush. "It's coming! It's coming!" She looked up at Lili. "The head is right there, Lili. Do you want to feel it?"

Through streaming tears, Lili nodded. Then a fifth contraction rose in her.

"Yes! Yes! You're doing it, my dear," Catriona said, her affectionate tone an indication of how birth was an equalizer, and there were no kings and queens in the room, just parents. "One more. Dafydd's going to count it out again, and by the time he gets to ten, you're going to have your child."

Lili nodded, pushed harder than ever, and then the head was out, followed by the rest of the baby, with no worries about a cord, though the baby's hand was up to the side of its head as Abraham had predicted.

Lili rested against David as Bronwen placed their newborn baby boy in Lili's arms.

25

Rupert

Rupert had decided that the best defense was a good offense, and if he was going to get to the truth, he needed to be more aggressive in his pursuit of it. Was time travel real? The people in the Black Boar swore up and down that it was. So far, he'd been chasing after leads but hadn't been able to find any independent confirmation. These bus passengers were like UFO abductees—all talk and no substance. Though admittedly, they had been gone for a year, and he recognized many of the names from the list of the missing after the Cardiff bombing.

It was time to dig into the heart of the matter. If that meant not milling about in the castle square until someone from the security forces deigned to talk to him, so be it. There was a larger story here, and he had bigger fish to fry.

He had hardly dared to believe his luck at first when he caught a brief glimpse of the girl in the purple parka, Anna, whom he'd talked to at that clinic in Bangor. She was walking away from the square with another man, one he didn't recognize. But as they hustled through the snow with barely a look backwards, he made the instant decision to leave his vigil at the barricade at the northeast corner of the city and follow. He tailed them to the Tesco, to a black van that sat immobile in the middle of the car park.

He warred with himself then as to whether to follow the man back to the castle once he dropped off the girl in the purple coat, or to wait in the car park. Because it just so happened that he'd left his own car nearby, he decided the coincidence was too great to ignore. He was hot on the scent now, and he could feel the back of his prey's neck between his jaws. If he hung on, soon he'd have the story of a lifetime. A thrilling shiver went through him that his quest might finally be at an end.

He thought he might have a long wait, but within a half hour, two men turned into the car park, walking from the direction of the castle. The initial bloke wasn't with them, but he recognized one of the men—the one who'd worn a sword back at the medical clinic—and the trench coat the other wore indicated government service.

Grinning, Rupert started his engine. He watched as one of the men sat in the front seat of the black van beside the driver—a woman—and the other climbed into the back. Rupert was too far away to hear what they were saying, beyond a single echoing, "Let's go."

The van pulled out of the car park, and Rupert settled into what he hoped was the right distance for a tail. He couldn't get so close that they'd notice him, but he couldn't stay so far back he'd lose them. He realized as he went along that he was out of practice.

As a result, as they neared Bangor, he fell back, the Christmas Day traffic being thin to say the least, with few trucks to hide behind.

He was also focusing on the snow and the slick roads, so when the van switched lanes at the last second to exit before Y Felinheli, he was already past the exit before he realized it had gone.

In a panic, he swore and slammed the butt of his hand into the wheel. Then he pressed the pedal to the floor, hoping no police were patrolling this particular stretch of road. He sped all the way to the next exit, praying the whole time to a god he didn't believe in that he hadn't lost them for good.

He decided the fact that no police stopped him was a good sign, and he followed his gut where it led him, circling the roundabout until he was heading the other way, west towards the village.

He had driven no more than a quarter of a mile when—

"Bloody hell!" Rupert's words echoed in the silence of the car as the van and then the Cardiff bus—the goddamned Cardiff bus—blew by him going the other way. His heart pounding a million miles an hour, he felt almost lightheaded as he spun the wheel and performed a U-turn for which there was barely room on the narrow road. He managed it without bottoming out the undercarriage on the grassy verge of the road.

Hardly worried now about secrecy, he sped after the bus. That they'd chosen to drive it in broad daylight told Rupert that something was up, and he wasn't going to lose them again—despite the fact that he didn't actually know who 'them' was.

With pound signs flashing before his eyes—and, dare he even think it, a British Journalism Award—he coasted to a stop against the curb on the wrong side of the road just before the entrance to the car park of a car hire firm, which both the van and the bus had entered. There wasn't really room for the bus to park in front of the building, so the driver backed it up until its tail was parallel with his car, except that it was in the car park on the other side of the sidewalk while Rupert was parked in the street.

He sank down low in his seat, hoping the driver wouldn't notice him, and as she opened the front door in order to exit the bus, the back door opened too. It stayed open as she disappeared around the front of the bus, heading towards where the van had parked. Maybe she didn't know to press the button by the front door that would close both front and back doors.

Spurred by an impulse he didn't choose to examine closely, Rupert pushed open his car door and ran at a crouch across the three feet of sidewalk between his car and the back door of the bus. He hit the bottom step with a thud and went up the stair to the interior of the bus, and then up the stairway to the upper level. Once in the aisle, he bent more than double so that his head remained below the level of the seats and the windows, and cat-walked towards the front of the bus. It was in his head that if he could find a seat at the very front and keep down, they wouldn't see him even if someone checked upstairs.

He really had no plan at this point other than a desire to find out what in the hell was going on. The Cardiff bombings had haunted him from the first he heard about the disappearance of the bus. He'd spent more time in this god-forsaken country in the last year pursuing this story than in his previous thirty-nine. When his editor had taken him off it for lack of new information, he'd used his weekends and holidays to return to Wales in a quest to find one more person to interview, one last piece of evidence that would make the whole puzzle complete.

Something about what was happening here wouldn't let him go.

So when he heard people boarding the bus, he didn't move. His thought was that he would cadge a ride to wherever they were going, and decide at that point whether or not to reveal himself. He had his mobile with him, and this morning he'd made sure that it was fully charged, so it would be a simple matter to telephone for a ride if it became necessary.

A murmur of voices reached him, but he couldn't make out what they were saying. The driver—probably the woman with the dark hair who'd driven it earlier—started the bus again, and he held onto the metal rail that ran across the front of the bus. He risked putting his head above it so he could see out the front window. Snow had fallen so thickly on the windscreen in the few minutes the bus had been stopped that it was building up on the wipers. Then they activated and flicked the snow away. He'd noticed when the bus came in that they operated in tandem with the wipers on the main windscreen downstairs.

He saw now why the driver had parked as she had, because it was a simple matter to leave the car park by pulling forward and turning onto the side street they'd come down initially. On his knees, he watched the road ahead, feeling a bit like the kid he'd once been when his father had taken him for a Sunday tour of London on one of the red double-decker buses. The Cardiff bus entered the main road again, navigated through a series of turns that took it into Bangor proper, and then headed towards the Menai Bridge, the easternmost and smaller of the two bridges across the Menai Strait.

The bus picked up speed, the windscreen wipers struggling to keep up with the snow, and because he was watching the wipers instead of the road, Rupert failed to notice at first not only the speed at which they were driving, but the fact that they were driving down the center of the road, rather than in their designated lane. Worse, they were approaching one of the more hazardous features of this bridge, which was a double archway with a central pillar centered in the middle of the span.

Rupert had seen buses attempt to navigate through the archway many times, and the drivers of some of the larger buses, of which the Cardiff bus was one, had to go so far as to pull in the bus's side mirrors in order to get through it.

Nobody on this bus was making any attempt to pull in the mirrors, to slow down, or in any way to prevent the catastrophe that was bearing down upon them at a hundred kilometers an hour. Open-mouthed with horror, Rupert watched the bus careen down the roadway towards it.

He screamed. "Stop! Stop!"

When his cry made no appreciable difference to the speed of the bus, he clenched the bar in front of him and closed his eyes, too frightened and overcome to even make a pledge about how he was going to change his life—at a minimum to drink and smoke less—if someone would only get him off this bus in one piece.

Rupert opened his eyes. The hundred yards from the barrier had turned into fifty—to twenty. His eyes bugged out as death rose up to meet him.

And to his surprise, not only was there life after death, but it turned out to be something other than an endless black abyss.

26

Bridget

"**I** don't know if coming here was, in fact, a good idea," Bridget said.

They'd left their somewhat cramped quarters at Chirk at dawn, saying goodbye to the steward and thanking him for his hospitality, and ridden the five miles to Whittington castle. It was Christmas Day, so George had thought them odd to be leaving so early, but he was also a medieval man, so he hadn't taken it upon himself to question the decisions of a knight in the Earl of Shrewsbury's company.

"Might not have been." Peter had borrowed the binoculars that Ieuan had been looking through back at Llangollen. He was using them to study the ramparts of Whittington Castle, which lay to the west of their position. They had taken up a post in the tavern across the road from the castle, and since there were no other customers in the main room this morning, nobody had so far objected to the open shutter.

The rain had abated for the time being, but Bridget couldn't decide if that was good or bad. December rain made men miserable and less likely to go out, ask questions, or wonder about anything other than when they would next be able to put their feet to a fire. She and Peter had already spent the hour since they'd arrived watching the castle entrance and the traffic in and out of the main gate. A hay cart had entered while one hauling waste from the stable had left. Local men and women, perhaps hired as extra workers to deal with all the guests, lifted their hands to the guards as they passed through.

No riders or Scots made themselves known. James Stewart hadn't put in an appearance.

"What if we were to walk up to the castle and ask for hospitality like we talked about last night?" Bridget said. "You are one of Callum's men, and it's Christmas Day."

"We could," Peter said.

Bridget pursed her lips. "If we were to do that, it would probably be better if it appeared as if we've just arrived—except that the gossip from the tavern could reach the steward's ears that you and I spent an hour in here before we showed up over there."

"Maybe," Peter said.

"Definitely," Bridget said. "How do you think I get my information to pass on to you and Callum in the first place?"

Peter smiled.

The castle plan bore some resemblance to Caerphilly Castle, where Bridget had spent just a little bit of time before finding her feet in Shrewsbury. The keep sat in the middle of a moat such that water surrounded it on all sides. A bridge led from the keep's inner gatehouse over the moat to the outer bailey, which was also surrounded by water. Its gatehouse, in turn, protected the entrance and was guarded by two giant D-shaped towers. A system of dikes and ditches also surrounded the whole site.

"My lord." Simon appeared in the doorway that led to the tavern's kitchen, which was located in the back of the main building. "Over here!"

Bridget and Peter left their station by the window and followed Simon out the back door; across the courtyard where hens pecked at the ground, looking for bits of grain; and then out the rear gate into the field beyond.

A few paces further on, to the north of the tavern, Simon stopped. The short walk in the grass had Bridget's dress soaked to mid-calf, a natural consequence of wearing medieval clothing, but she was warm enough in her leather boots, wool socks, and leggings. Women might not wear pants as the outer layer in the Middle Ages, but they weren't such fools that they couldn't figure out a way to keep warm by wearing them underneath.

"What is it?" Peter said as he stopped near a row of bushes that marked the end of the tavern's land and behind which Simon appeared to be hiding.

"Look." Simon canted his head to indicate a gap in the vegetation.

A dozen men had gathered on the road to the north of the castle, in an area Bridget and Peter hadn't been able to see from the inn itself. The men seemed to be having a conference. One man spoke heatedly, and another responded in kind.

"It looks like a disagreement," Bridget said. "Where did they come from?"

"Either they left the castle before dawn, or they've been out all night," Simon said.

"It would be good to know if they're coming from the castle or going," Bridget said.

"Can you tell if they're Scottish?" Peter said.

"It isn't like anybody's wearing a kilt," Bridget said.

"I know, but—"

"My red hair isn't some kind of radar for Scottishness. I don't even speak Gaelic!" Bridget had been very disappointed to learn from Callum that the kilt, as popularized by films and time travel romances, hadn't come into being by the thirteenth century. The Scots still wore their kilts as cloaks, just like the rest of medieval Britons.

Peter reached over and twirled a strand of her hair around his finger. Coming from him, it was far more intimate act than sleeping in the same room with him at Chirk had been—fully clothed with her on the bed and him on the floor. Somehow Bridget had never responded to his question regarding how she felt about pretending to be his wife.

Last night, when he'd confirmed the steward's misunderstanding as fact, at first Bridget had been so surprised, she hadn't known what to say. Then they'd been interrupted by the needs of the investigation—and after they'd talked about other things, it was hard to come back to the topic of their relationship, especially amidst all the people in the hall.

Once they reached their room, Peter had dropped her off to inspect the security of the castle and confer with Simon. She'd lain awake for a long time waiting for him, but she'd eventually fallen asleep and then awoken in the darkness with him lying on the floor a few feet away, breathing as if he was asleep.

It wasn't as if she'd planned to sleep with him—not with the paper thin walls of the room and the narrow lumpy bed. Even as twenty-firsters, there was something to be said for not sleeping together straight away, but she would have liked to at least *talk*. Somehow, she was going to have to say something about his question, regardless of how inconvenient or weird the timing was. By now, he probably thought she was having second thoughts about kissing him, when the opposite couldn't be more true.

"From this far away, I can't hear what they're saying," Simon said, and then set off at a half-crouch to get closer to the road. Bridget lost sight of him in the shrubbery. Peter took her hand so they could creep forward together.

"If these men are responsible for the attack on the emissary, we'd need an army to get into that castle," she said. "What are we hoping to accomplish here?"

"I'd like *something* to report back to Ieaun and Samuel for our efforts," Peter said. "I'm supposed to be an investigator, so I'm investigating. Whittington Castle with Scots in attendance is currently our only clue as to the whereabouts of James Stewart."

Then the men in the road seemed to decide something because as Bridget, Peter, and Simon watched, half led their horses across the forty-foot drawbridge to the gatehouse, and the other half pointed their horses north and rode away. Bridget expected them to take the road that led northwest back to Chirk, some five miles away, or towards the turnoff a hundred yards north of the castle which would take them northeast, back to Scotland.

Instead, they circled around the moat and dismounted before the most distant watchtower that lay to the northwest of the castle. It was reachable only by this external road, or by boat from the outer bailey, were someone to row across the moat to a narrow landing at the back.

"I don't suppose we need to wonder what—or who—might be in that watchtower," Simon said.

"I still can't believe King Philip would attack his own emissary," Bridget said.

"We have no evidence against anyone one way or the other," Peter said. "Just because these men are Scots doesn't make them villains."

Typically English, Simon didn't look convinced.

Peter backed away. "There's only one way to find out."

They loped back to the inn where they'd left the horses. As they had come into Whittington from the west and north earlier that morning, it was unreasonable to think that none of the watchers on the walls had noticed. Thus, they abandoned any notion of making it appear as if they'd just arrived and mounted their horses in order to walk them the few dozen yards down the road to the gatehouse of the castle.

This same road, if they stayed on it, could take them all the way home to Shrewsbury. Despite her nervousness about entering Whittington Castle, Bridget wasn't ready to go home just yet. She'd never been on this end of an investigation before, and she was extremely curious about what would happen next.

The drawbridge remained down. Bridget didn't know if the sentries normally left it down all day, or if they were leaving it down because so many people were coming and going, and it would be silly to pull it up when they'd only have to put it down again five minutes later.

Peter dismounted before the portcullis, which was also up. Unlike the local visitors, it would have been impolite of him, especially as an officer of the law from Shrewsbury, to walk right in. A guard stood just inside the gate, and Peter said, "Greetings! We seek admittance,"

A second guard hurried towards them, gesturing with one hand that they should cross the drawbridge and approach the gate. Bridget was glad because she felt the first drops of rain on her head and preferred not to get soaked again when her clothes had barely dried from yesterday.

"I am Peter Cobb, liege man of Lord Callum, the Earl of Shrewsbury. I would speak to your lord."

The guardsman bobbed his head. "You are welcome to enter. Please wait here beneath the tower while I send a man to find the steward."

"Thank you." Peter gestured to Bridget. "I would prefer my lady wife doesn't become chilled."

"Of course, my lord." He smiled ingratiatingly and pointed at another one of the guardsman, who took off at a run, his feet pounding on the slate walkway of the courtyard towards the bridge that crossed the moat to the inner gatehouse.

Bridget shifted on her feet, impatient with the wait.

Peter caught her hand, and she stilled, his message coming through loud and clear. It was important that they didn't do anything that would call attention to themselves or arouse suspicion. Peter would talk briefly to Fitzwarin, they would gather as much information as they could about the inhabitants of the castle, and they would leave. That was all.

They had to wait only a few minutes, during which time the rain began to fall in earnest, before the guardsman reappeared with the steward, who, heedless of the rain, maintained a steady, unhurried pace towards them. He came to a halt in front of Peter and bowed.

"My lord, I'm sorry for the delay. How may I be of service?"

"I am Peter Cobb, undersheriff in Shrewsbury, traveling to Chirk with my lady wife. Is Lord Fitzwarin in residence?"

"Yes, he is." The steward frowned and lowered his voice. "But he has visitors already, and they have been much in conference. I do not know that he has a moment to receive you."

"I am here with Christmas greetings from the Earl of Shrewsbury," Peter said, blithely dropping Callum's title again.

The steward's face blanched. "Of course, my lord. I will let Lord Fitzwarin know you are here."

Bridget placed a hand on her belly. "I am really feeling quite faint."

The steward's eyes widened, getting the message Bridget intended to send—that she was in the early stages of pregnancy. "My lady, this way."

The steward jerked his head at the guard, who directed Simon to lead the horses towards the adjacent stable. Meanwhile, Peter and Bridget followed the steward towards the inner gate. It was a hundred feet from the gatehouse to the bridge across the moat, and then another hundred feet across the bridge in order to reach the shelter of the inner gatehouse. The castle hadn't looked very large from inside the tavern, but it seemed much bigger now that they were inside, and, despite the rain, the bailey bustled with people and animals.

Passing beneath the second gatehouse, Bridget and Peter entered the inner ward, the heart of the castle. With both hands, Bridget gripped Peter's arm, which he'd bent at the elbow to escort her. "This may have been a very bad idea."

"Breathe," he said. "It's going to be fine."

She had no choice but to believe him, and she worked to steady her breathing and ignore the fact that the hairs on the back of her neck were standing straight up. The great hall crouched at the eastern end of the castle, having been built into the curtain wall, and was accessible by a set of wooden stairs.

Bridget and Peter followed the steward up them and entered through the narrow doorway. Like many Norman castles, where security was the primary focus, the door was meant to be the last defense in case an enemy breached the inner and outer walls.

Only seventy feet by twenty-five feet, the hall wasn't even as large as the one at Dinas Bran, but it was warm and well-appointed, with tapestries on all the walls and a raised dais at one end upon which the high table sat. The hall was full too, with at least sixty people in it, mostly armed men. A fire burned hot in the fireplace. Bridget half-expected to see Christmas stockings hanging from the mantle but, of course, that custom wouldn't arise for hundreds of years.

As they entered, the people closest to the door looked over but returned their attentions to their meals when they didn't recognize either Peter or Bridget. At the far end of the hall, a dozen men ranged around the high table, eating and talking jovially. It was Christmas Day, mass had probably already been said, and the rest of the day would be spent in revelry. A few men stood in a circle on the near side of the table, opposite the lord's seat, but Bridget could see through the moving figures to the central trio.

Peter bent to Bridget's ear. "That's Fulk Fitzwarin, there, in the center."

Fulk was a middle-aged baron with a full head of salt and pepper hair and a dark brown beard also shot with gray. She couldn't make out his expression well from the distance, but his head was turned to the man beside him, who was hidden from her view by someone standing across from him.

"Who does Lord Fitzwarin entertain?" Bridget asked the steward.

She would have liked to have asked that question earlier, but she hadn't wanted to appear nosy and blow their cover.

"Foreign relatives," the steward said, and Bridget didn't think she mistook the disapproving *sniff* that accompanied the words.

"Who might they be?" Peter said.

Even as the steward answered, Bridget cursed herself for not thinking more deeply about Fulk Fitzwarin's Scottish ties a bit sooner and realizing that this branch of the Warenne family might have other ties to Scotland beyond King John Balliol. She hit upon the name of one of the men only a half-second before the steward said it.

"That would be Red Comyn, nephew to the King of Scotland. And on the other side of Lord Fulk is Comyn's brother-in-law, Aymer de Valence."

27

Peter

Bridget stood frozen next to Peter, her hand clutched around his arm in a tight grip. She needn't have worried that Peter would give away her shock. The message she was sending was getting through loud and clear, and Peter already regretted walking into this castle without a plan for getting out. Fortunately, the steward seemed oblivious to the tension emanating from his guests, though if Bridget gripped Peter's arm any tighter, he might lose all feeling in his hand.

Peter cleared his throat. "I didn't realize Fitzwarin was related to the Comyns."

"Lady Isabella de Warenne is John Balliol's wife, of course. It's through her connection that my lord Fulk is related to Comyn and Valence. If you give me a moment, I will tell Lord Fulk you are here."

Peter was trying hard not to choke on his own breath. "Thank you."

The steward gestured to a vacant spot at the end of one of the long tables, and then he glided, head held high, towards the dais.

"You'd better tell me everything that you can remember about these family ties before the steward gets back," Peter said.

"Okay. So William de Valence had several children who—"

Peter grasped her hand as it lay on the table. "William de Valence? I never met him, but I heard about him. You're telling me that this is his hand reaching out to us from beyond the grave?"

"I don't like it either. But Aymer is his only surviving son and heir and, given what happened to his father, he bears no love for England or David. He would stab David in the back and never blink an eye."

"Does David know?" Peter said.

"He knows," Bridget said. "Since David confiscated Valence's lands in England, the only estate Aymer de Valence inherited from his father is a small tract of land in Angoulême, which has been taken over by King Philip. Although Aymer's grandmother was once Queen of England, after King John's death, she married the Count of Angoulême and had William, Aymer's father. Thus, they aren't royal, but they have always felt they should be, and have deeply resented being continually snubbed by the French court. In fact, it might be a contest between David and Philip as to who Aymer hates more."

"How is Aymer related to Red Comyn?"

"One of Aymer's sisters is married to Red, so they're brothers-in-law as the steward said. In addition, another one of Aymer's sisters married John Balliol's older brother, Hugh, who died twenty years ago—and, for added flavor, Red Comyn's mother is King John Balliol of Scotland's sister."

"Christ." Peter's stomach sank into his boots.

"That's how we get a connection to James Stewart," Bridget said. "The Stewarts supported the Bruces during the conflict over the throne three years ago, to the point that when Callum met James Stewart, Robbie Bruce was his squire. As you may recall, that was during the time when Black Comyn colluded with William de Valence in an attempt to wrest the throne from his own brother-in-law, John Balliol. While one of Balliol's first acts as King of Scotland was to re-lease both Comyns, father and son, after they paid a sizable ransom to the Scottish crown, bad blood remains between the Comyns and the Bruces."

Peter gave a low laugh. "You're telling me we should be glad Robbie Bruce wasn't among the emissary's party, because Comyn wouldn't have hesitated to murder him?"

Bridget smiled. "So you do know something of what I'm talking about."

"I listen," Peter said lightly, "and I find it hard to believe that Balliol would approve such a move."

"Balliol might not be involved at all," Bridget said. "Red Comyn and Aymer de Valence could be making their own plans without consulting him."

"That, of everything you've said so far, would surprise me the least. Any more bad news, Bridget?" Peter said.

"It's also possible that Red and Aymer hope for the chance to bolster Aymer's lands in Angouleme while Philip is distracted by war with England."

Peter's eyes crossed. "That's mad."

"You're not a Valence. David did see to the death of Aymer's father. Anyway," she waved a hand, "the only thing you have to know is that Aymer de Valence, Red Comyn, and John Balliol are allies, and that it is perfectly credible that these two here are seeking to expand their lands, destroy the Bruces, and cause trouble for David and Philip."

"I can see why they viewed James Stewart's journey with the ambassador from the French court with dismay," Peter said.

Bridget laughed under her breath. "And now, if he isn't dead, they may have no idea what to do with him." She glanced towards the high table. The steward was turning away from Fulk and coming towards them. "Do you think he knows what Fulk's guests have done?"

"You heard him talk about the Scots," Peter said. "I find it likely he doesn't."

Peter watched the steward's approach with some trepidation. He wasn't comfortable speaking to Fulk on Callum's behalf, though it had seemed like a good excuse to be here when they were at the entrance to the castle. He kept his eyes fixed on the high table, trying to imprint the faces of the various Scots and Normans on his memory. He wasn't any more of an artist than he was a conversationalist, but he was pretty good at remembering faces. Mostly, he just wanted to get Bridget out of there as quickly as possible without having it seem hasty and rude.

"Sir." The steward had arrived at their table again. "My lord Fulk would be happy to greet you now."

"Thank you." Peter stood and held out his arm to Bridget, who took it, and they processed towards the high table behind the steward. This time Bridget's hand rested gently in his elbow. She was doing a better job about faking a calmness she didn't feel. Peter's breakfast, which he'd eaten back in Chirk, was doing a dance inside his stomach.

"My lord." The steward bent his head to Fulk. "May I present Sir Peter Cobb and his lady wife."

"Cobb." Fulk canted his head. "My lady."

"Bridget," Bridget said, with a dipping curtsey. "I am honored to meet you, sir."

Fulk fixed his eyes on Peter's face. "You have news for me from Earl Callum?"

"He simply asked me to give to you his Christmas Day greetings," Peter said.

"He is in Shrewsbury?" Fulk's eyes had narrowed.

Aymer and Comyn were whispering to each other, both leaning back in their chairs as Fulk leaned forward. He gave them an annoyed glance, and then returned his gaze to Peter.

"He celebrates Christmas with the king." Peter opted not to mention that the celebration would be occurring—if at all—in Avalon.

Comyn was listening closely now. Peter didn't know if he had met Callum several years ago when Callum brokered the deal for Balliol to become king, but he thought it likely. "The earl is here?"

"At Dinas Bran." Peter wished he could have avoided saying that, but he didn't feel like he could lie outright. Politics were not his thing.

However, Bridget smiled. "He commemorates the birth of our lord with the ambassador from the French court and James Stewart. We are honored to have been invited to share the day with him."

Peter gave a short bow in Comyn's direction. It was obvious why he was called 'Red', given the color of his hair and the millions of freckles covering his face. "I'm sure, my lord, that you would be welcome if you cared to travel the last few miles to Dinas Bran with us."

Comyn gave what had to be an involuntary shake of his head, and Aymer just managed to arrest the sneer that had formed on his lips.

"Please give my regards to your lady wife, my lord Fulk," Bridget said. "We should be on our way. We wouldn't want to be late for the Christmas feast."

Fulk gave her a sickly smile. "I won't keep you. Godspeed."

With a last nod, Peter spun Bridget around and directed her towards the door of the hall.

"That went well," she said.

"Let's not count our chickens until we are free," he said. "You took a risk mentioning Stewart."

"What good is it to be here if we don't learn what they did with him?" Bridget put out a hand to the door and pushed through it. "Did you see Comyn's face pale when I said James's name?"

"You could hardly miss it." Peter glanced back before he followed her. No alarm had been raised.

Bridget hesitated on the top step. "Are you sure we should just leave? What if James is locked in one of the towers?"

"We are only two, three with Simon," Peter said. "We have what we came for. If Aymer de Valence has truly conspired with Red Comyn to murder the ambassador from France and abduct James Stewart, then the sooner we tell Samuel and Lili about it, the better."

"And if Fulk is completely innocent of the attack on the emissary?" Bridget said.

"When has Callum ever condemned an innocent man?"

Bridget nodded and preceded Peter down the stairs. A dozen men moved about the courtyard, many speaking Gaelic or English with a thick Scottish accent. That the men in Fulk's garrison or their Scottish visitors had left Molier and Geoffrey for dead and killed everyone else in their party wasn't a good sign as to what would happen to them if they were found to be spies. Peter urged Bridget towards the gatehouse and the bridge.

"If he is not innocent," Peter took her arm again, "then I am quite worried about what he might do to us if he learns that we aren't really passing through or that you are not yet my wife." Peter said the last few words with some hesitation. He hadn't mentioned the wife issue since last night and hadn't really meant to say anything about it again unless Bridget did, but the situation seemed to call for it.

"I don't mind, by the way," Bridget said.

Peter glanced over at her. "You don't mind what?"

Bridget tipped her head back to look up at the sky, laughing silently. "All this time I've been stressing about not replying, and you forgot within moments of asking me, didn't you?"

Peter stared at her for a second, the rain dripping off his forehead. He wiped at it with the back of his sleeve and then swallowed hastily.

"I hadn't forgotten. I was just distracted by the case. Do you mean it?"

"I mean it," she said.

"When?"

"When what?"

"When will you marry me?"

"You want to decide that now?" Bridget was laughing at him, but Peter didn't care.

Once he'd decided she was the girl for him, it was as if the words were just waiting on the tip of his tongue for him to say them. "I love you. I've loved you from the moment you stuck that first wool hat on my head."

The time travelers had been given a true taste of medieval Wales on their long journey from the battlefield, where they'd arrived, to Llangollen. Bridget, whose backpack had been full of yarn, had spent the whole journey knitting hats for everyone. She'd made a gray one for him, and practically his first words to her had been *thank you*.

"I'd marry you tomorrow if you'd have me. Once we've decided, what's the point in waiting?" He gestured to the moat. "This is the

Middle Ages. Life is short, and it isn't like we can move in together, is it?"

"You don't think we need more time to get to know each other?" she said.

"You're smart, honest, adventurous, patient, and kind. Are you saying you've been keeping a dark side of your personality from me all this time that's going manifest on our wedding night?"

Bridget had the back of her hand to her mouth. "All right, then." And then she laughed and dropped her hand. "For someone who's a terrible communicator, you do all right. Better than some."

Peter smiled down at her. Maybe he would never stop smiling. He guided her across the bridge in double time, and they had almost reached the outer bailey on the other side when—

"My lord! My lord!" Peter looked back to see the steward with his hand up to gain their attention. There was no mistaking that he wanted them.

"Damn," Peter said under his breath.

The steward started across the bridge, and Peter felt he had no choice but to wait for him. By the time the steward reached them, he was breathing hard. "Lord Valence begs you to return to the hall. He has a gift for you to bring to the king."

"That really isn't necessary," Bridget said.

"He acknowledges that the king's invitation should not be lightly discarded, and he pledges not to inconvenience you unduly," the steward said.

Bridget and Peter looked at each other. Peter had to accept that there was no real way to deny the request, but his feet itched to be on the other side of the moat. He took a step towards the outer bailey. "We really should go."

The steward made a move to tug on the fabric of Peter's cloak. "I must insist—"

And then with a *whuff* as if all the air had suddenly been sucked out of the atmosphere, the Cardiff bus burst from a gash in the sky, just like it had a year ago. Except this time, instead of driving through the middle of a battlefield, it soared through the air for a half-second before settling with a jaw-rattling thud on the road to the north of the castle and then its momentum carried it headfirst into the northeastern watchtower itself.

The tower shuddered, and the unmortared stones that made up the top floor crumbled onto the roof of the bus. The steward gaped in shock and astonishment. But Peter grabbed Bridget's hand and took off at a run towards the outer bailey. While Simon may have warmed the horses and even unsaddled them in their absence, he'd known enough to be ready at a moment's notice because he had all three horses out of the stable and waiting as Peter and Bridget ran up. From his position, he couldn't have seen the bus come in, but there was no mistaking the hurry Peter and Bridget were in.

With a quick boost, Peter settled Bridget into her saddle and then mounted his own horse. With Simon, they spurred their horses towards the gatehouse. The portcullis was still up—probably because the two guards who were supposed to be attending it were staring towards the moat, mouths open at the arrival of the modern bus. Peter had a better understanding now of what the shock of his own arrival a year ago must have been like for the medieval onlookers. For his part, he felt only satisfaction as he led the way out of the gatehouse and onto the road.

While Peter could honestly say he would have been happy never to see the bus again, there was a certain satisfaction in knowing that he and Bridget were free of Whittington—and that Callum and David had returned.

28

Anna

Cassie killed the bus's engine and turned to look at her friends. "Who's screaming?"

Anna swept her gaze around the few friends who'd returned with them, all of them sitting frozen in their seats, hearts pounding at the suddenness of the transition from the twenty-first century to the thirteenth. They were all accounted for, which meant they had a stowaway. When he found out, David was not going to be pleased, and none of them had thought to give the bus the once-over to make sure they were alone.

She stood. "The noise is coming from upstairs. I'll check it out."

Without waiting for anyone else's thoughts, she trotted down the aisle towards the stairs at the rear of the bus, which projected all the way across the road, blocking it completely. Footsteps behind her told her that someone was following, and she was in no way surprised to find that it was her husband.

"We appear to be home," Math said, with that dry wit he often brought out in times of crisis.

"It seems so." Anna ducked her head slightly so she could see out the windows. "But I'm not sure where we are."

"England?" The word came out of Math's mouth with something of a sneer, the automatic reaction of a Welshman to finding himself in the wrong country. "I believe we have driven into a watchtower."

Anna gestured with her head to the stones that were hitting the top of the bus before falling past the windows to the ground. "I have never been to this castle before."

"Nor I," Math said.

They took the stairs to the upper level two at a time, Anna already wishing she was back in her jeans instead of the medieval dress she'd changed into so she would fit into the Middle Ages once they'd time traveled again. Though Math had showered at Abraham's house—every medieval man needed to try it once—he was wearing the same clothes he'd come to Avalon in yesterday.

Anna and Math popped out of the stairwell to find the source of the screaming. A man stood before them, blood streaming down his face from a giant contusion on his forehead. That they had a stowaway, that it was Rupert, and that the accident had injured him was just bizarre enough to prompt sudden laughter from Anna. "You've got to be kidding me."

Rachel appeared at Anna's shoulder, took in the situation with an assessing glance, and walked down the aisle towards the front of the bus.

Rupert staggered backwards towards the windshield, his hands reaching for the metal bar beneath the window. "Stay away from me!"

"I'm a doctor," Rachel said.

Rupert's panic didn't abate. "What have you done?"

"Time traveled. What did you expect?" Math edged his way past Anna and strode down the aisle too.

Though Rupert was still shrinking back against the windshield, he didn't turn away from Rachel, who reached out a hand to him. "What-what are you going to do to me?"

"Help you," Rachel said at the same time Math clicked his teeth and said, "Nothing." He stopped halfway along the aisle and reached up to the ceiling.

Anna frowned and moved towards to her husband. "What are *you* doing?"

"Someone in the tower is shouting 'help!' Can't you hear him?"

Anna held her breath and listened. The insulation in the bus was good, which was why the faint sounds hadn't come more clearly sooner. Math pulled a lever and a trapdoor in the ceiling lifted up with a hydraulic hiss. Then, putting a booted foot on the back of one of the adjacent seats, he hoisted himself through the opening.

A moment later, he stuck his head back through the hole, followed by his arm, which he stretched out towards Anna. "You coming? It looks like the stones have stopped falling."

"Of course I'm coming!" Anna grasped Math's hand and stepped onto the back of the seat as he had.

She wasn't as tall as Math, nor as strong, but as he pulled her through the opening, she got her elbows out on the roof of the bus and then, with another assist from Math, was able to scramble upright. It was raining, which was no more than Anna would have expected, and about thirty degrees warmer than it had been in Bangor. Whatever snow had come with them on the exterior of the bus to the Middle Ages had already melted.

She found herself twenty feet in the air with a spectacular view of the surrounding countryside. Anna turned around and saw that her head was nearly level with all that was left of the top floor of the collapsing tower, over the stones of which leaned a dark-haired, dark-eyed man with a slender, patrician face. His eye had been blackened, and the knuckles of both hands that clutched the stones in front of him were scraped and bruised.

Math gazed up at him and spoke in English. "I am Mathonwy ap Rhys, Lord of Dinas Bran. Who are you?"

"James Stewart, High Steward of Scotland," came the reply—in English but with a distinct Scottish accent.

Anna clutched Math's arm for balance as she moved closer to the window. "I am Anna, King David's sister. I'd ask what you're doing here, but maybe questions can wait, and you should just come with us. I don't know how much longer that tower is going to be standing."

"Excellent idea." James perched a hip on what Anna hoped was a somewhat stable stone and swung his right leg over the wall, followed by his left. Math held out a hand for James to grasp, and James jumped down onto the roof of the bus, landing with a thunk. Math caught his arm to steady him, not wanting him to slip on the wet surface.

"James!" Callum poked his head through the trap door. "What are you doing here?"

James's mouth fell open, but then he laughed. "Is this your doing? Would it be possible for me to find myself in captivity without you affecting a rescue? Especially one as dramatic as this." He stomped a foot on the roof of the bus, and the sound echoed metallically. Unfortunately, since the bus abutted the tower, it also caused a few more stones to fall, and everyone moved away from it towards the rear of the bus.

"If you would prefer not to be rescued, you're free to climb back into your disintegrating cell." Callum grunted as he pulled himself through the trapdoor and sat on the edge, his feet dangling into the interior of the bus. He'd put on his medieval garb in the time it had taken to drive to the bridge, and his sword was belted at his waist.

"That is quite all right." James bent and held out his hand to Callum, who smirked and allowed his friend to pull him to his feet. Then the two men grasped each other's shoulders in an affectionate way.

Callum released James in order to gesture to Math and Anna. "I see you've met Lord Math and Princess Anna."

James bowed at the waist. "It is an honor."

"My lord!" The shout came from the ground outside the tower.

They all turned to see Bridget, Peter, and a man Anna didn't know grinning at them from the ground on the east side of the bus. The bus had been driven into the tower at the front, such that it was oriented north/south and blocked the whole of the road. Until they moved it—if moving it was possible—no horseman could get by without riding into the adjacent field or swimming in the moat.

Callum bent forward, his hands on his knees. "I don't suppose there's any point in asking what you're doing here?"

Peter gestured to James Stewart. "We were on his trail."

James shook his head with something that looked like rueful dismay. "How many lives do I owe you now?"

"Ach." Callum straightened and clapped a hand on James's shoulder again. "You would do the same for me. But now—" He turned around and gazed towards the castle.

Anna looked too: a crowd of people—perhaps as many as a hundred—had come to stand on the bridge across the castle's moat, on the battlements of the castle, and in the outer bailey, which was effectively an island in the middle of an extensive moat. She couldn't see anyone's expression from this far away, but nobody seemed to be moving or speaking.

That they were feeling shock wasn't surprising. By now, many people had heard of the giant orange and turquoise bus that had appeared out of nowhere in the midst of a battlefield a year ago, but seeing it with one's own eyes was something else entirely.

"Whose castle is this?" Callum asked.

"Fulk Fitzwarin's," Peter said.

"Ah yes," Callum said. "This is Whittington. And how, exactly, did James Stewart end up a prisoner in his tower?"

James cleared his throat. "I was riding to Dinas Bran in the company of Geoffrey de Geneville and Jacques de Molier, an emissary from the French Court, when a band of ruffians ambushed us. They brought me here. I didn't know where I was until this moment for they blindfolded me, and my room had no windows until this—" he paused, searching for the word, "—vehicle created one."

Callum ran a hand through his hair, in what looked to Anna like disbelief. "Why would Fitzwarin abduct you?"

"My lord," Peter said from the ground, "it isn't Fitzwarin's doing, or not in the main. Red Comyn and Aymer de Valence are at the root of this."

Anna had never concerned herself much with Scottish politics, but even she knew that marriage had allied these two, and David had worried about it from the first he'd heard of it. "Where are they now?"

"Here!" A voice bellowed as a host of horsemen materialized on the other side of the bus—the west side—from Peter and Bridget. Every man in the company wore armor and held a sword or axe bare in his hand. Horses filled the road that ran beside the moat and intersected with the road that ran in front of the tower, to which the bus was currently semi-attached.

The lead man, whom Anna didn't recognize, bared his teeth at Callum. "And who might you be, sir?"

Callum pulled his sword from his sheath, though he kept it pointed at the roof of the bus. "I am Alexander Callum, Earl of Shrewsbury, which the man beside you could have told you if he'd had a mind to do so, Aymer."

Anna looked to the man on Aymer's left, noting his shockingly red hair and understanding that this was Red Comyn.

Aymer's eyes didn't quite skate to the left, but his horse shifted, and he had to tug the reins in order to keep him under control. The men around him were murmuring too. Callum had been central to the negotiations in Scotland that had put John Balliol, their king, on the throne. Even if David would have preferred Robert Bruce as King of Scotland, he hadn't forced the issue, and Callum was well-known and well-respected for the role he'd played in averting war.

"You should go, Aymer," Red Comyn said, his eyes on Callum instead of his brother-in-law, "right now, while you still can."

"What? Why?" Aymer jerked his chin to indicate Callum and—as it turned out—the rest of Anna's family, including Mom, who had climbed onto the roof of the bus too without Anna noticing. "They're outnumbered. We have the advantage."

"I wouldn't be too sure about that. I imagine cousin Fulk is reconsidering his position right about now," Red said.

Aymer's face twisted in fury. "Coward! This jumped-up earl holds no power over you."

David had been called an 'upstart prince' more than once by angry Norman lords, but Anna had never heard Callum referred to in such a derogatory way. Medieval people, familiar with nobility, could tell at a glance that he had been born with a silver spoon in his mouth, and the mantle of authority rested naturally on his shoulders.

Red kept his expression serene. "I'm cutting my losses, Aymer. I should never have listened to you."

"This is as much your doing as mine, Scotsman."

The murmuring rose in volume among Red's men, not liking the tone of Aymer's voice.

"I say otherwise," Red said, "and I can muster witnesses to prove it."

Aymer scoffed, while at the same time raising his sword above his head and speaking to the Frenchmen among the soldiers behind him. "We're leaving!"

"I don't think so," Callum said.

Aymer threw a glance up at him. "You can't stop me."

"I can."

"You have no army."

Callum pointed to the road behind them.

A swell of relief filled Anna's chest. Whether or not Aymer escaped, none of them were in danger anymore: the road behind Aymer was filling with soldiers from the garrison of Whittington, which had filed out of the castle while Callum had been talking to Aymer—

perhaps even stalling him. They'd followed the same route from the castle entrance Aymer had taken, circling around the moat to the south and west before turning north to make up three sides of the square. At the same time, thundering hooves sounded, coming down the western road. Thirty seconds later, Samuel, with Callum's entire guard behind him, appeared out of the rain.

Even better, Aymer wasn't going anywhere because the Scottish guard that surrounded him chose that moment to close ranks. Their loyalty, it seemed, was to Red Comyn, not Aymer.

Callum sheathed his sword. "We done here?"

He glanced at James Stewart, who shrugged. "I am at your service, my lord."

"What I want to know," Anna said, "is if there's any way I can get home to Dinas Bran in the next few hours in order to celebrate Christmas with my sons?"

29

Meg

From the moment the bomb had gone off at Caernarfon Castle, Meg hadn't been able to think about anything but the whereabouts of David and Llywelyn. Throughout the discussions of how to get themselves back to the Middle Ages, she'd sat unspeaking, in kind of a comatose state.

No matter how many times she'd told herself that David would have contacted them if he'd been in the modern world, and that Director Tate had reported only four bodies in the ruins of the tower, her heart had been beating too fast, while at the same time her whole body felt stiff, even frozen.

She'd played no part in the decision to return the rental van—if only because Cassie and Callum would have had to pay for it if they didn't—and return to the Middle Ages in the Cardiff bus. She wouldn't have seen Rupert enter the bus because she hadn't been looking. All she could see was the empty seat beside her where Llywelyn should have been sitting.

There had been times before when she'd thought she'd lost him. He was twenty years older than she and the King of Wales, which meant that war and warfare had been a way of life since the day he'd walked away from his family at sixteen and joined his uncle's court. Though Meg hadn't seen the explosion at the castle, she'd seen Anna's white face, and that was all she needed to know about what had happened.

And yet, she hadn't felt his death in her heart. Love for Llywelyn wouldn't let her go, wouldn't let her rest, and was the only thing keeping despair at bay. That and the knowledge that David might have known what was coming and would have known to hold onto his father with all his strength. She found some comfort in the knowledge that wherever they were, they were together.

She didn't know who had come up with the idea to drive headfirst into the center stem of the archway on the Menai Bridge, but even she had to admit, in the moments she was capable of rational thought, that to do so was a genius way to get home. The consequences of hitting it, had the time traveling not worked, would have been irretrievable.

Meg had believed in the moment of impact that she would survive, for her four children's sake if not her own. And thus, she was in no way surprised when the bus dropped onto the road in time to rescue Bridget, Peter, and James Stewart, of all people, from the malicious hands of Aymer de Valence.

Honestly, Meg was good with that.

She was even better with Fulk Fitzwarin's offer, seemingly worked out with Callum as part of his penance—Meg hadn't bothered with the details—to give them horses to ride home to Dinas Bran and carts to haul all their stuff with them, which thankfully had been well packed into the bus's storage compartment and hadn't been damaged in the collision with the tower.

It was obvious to anyone looking that the bus wasn't going anywhere any time soon. They had only seven miles as the crow flies to ride, though of course a bit longer by road. No journey she had ever taken had ever felt as long.

Riding, she was surrounded by friends and family—as well as Red Comyn and his Scots. Testimony by the various witnesses had revealed that James's abduction had been a mistake from start to finish—in that Red and Aymer had meant to disrupt the emissary's journey but then found they had more than they bargained for in James Stewart. Faced with the decision to either kill him, which had been Aymer's choice, or grab him, Red had insisted on the latter.

His protection hardly made up for the death of the French emissary's entire guard, and it wasn't as if Comyn was forgiven his actions. But arresting a nobleman was a different matter entirely than arresting a commoner, and Red Comyn knew he was far better off surrendering, apologizing, and admitting fault than running. He had lands and status, which, if he fled to another country, he abandoned. In the Middle Ages, starting over wasn't quite the same as in the twenty-first century. It wasn't as if he could just go get a job.

Thus, Callum—and James Stewart, in fact—believed rehabilitation was the better path to follow in this instance; and that furthermore, it was possible.

Callum was known for making those kinds of decisions.

As, in fact, was David.

"We're almost there, Mom. Hang on," Anna said.

"There's no guarantee they're even here," Meg said. "What if they ended up in Scotland?"

"Then that's where they needed to be," Anna said matter-of-factly.

Neither of them had mentioned—nor would they—the possibility that David and Llywelyn could be dead. If they weren't at Dinas Bran, Meg would wait. Painfully and dying a little herself each day perhaps, but she would wait.

"How can you be so calm?" Meg knew the question had come out a wail, but she couldn't help it.

"In a few more minutes we'll know, and knowing will be better than not knowing," Anna said.

The sky was darkening as clouds formed on the western horizon, and the sun, never high to begin with, sank behind them, shrouding in semi-darkness the mountain they were climbing. Meg kept glancing towards where she hoped to see the battlements, but trees hid her view of them until they reached the final switchback.

Turning, they crested a rise, and Anna gasped and pointed. "Mom! Look!"

The towers above the gatehouse were clearly visible, and each flew a flag. On one tower flapped the three lions that were Llywelyn's personal crest, and on the adjacent tower flew the red dragon of Wales. Neither flag would have been flown had David or Llywelyn not been in residence.

A company of riders burst from the gatehouse. It was a scene Meg would play over and over again in her mind, seeing Llywelyn riding towards her, his face split by a glorious smile. Meg dismounted without waiting for help from Math and ran to him. As Llywelyn approached, he reached down and, with a strength that denied his sixty-plus years, scooped her up and pulled her in front of him like he might have twenty years ago when she'd been a girl and life had held nothing but possibility.

Meg flung her arms around his neck and sobbed. She couldn't find the words to tell him that she'd feared she'd lost him, but he didn't need to hear her speak to know how she'd felt.

"I am well, *cariad,* and so is Dafdd. And ... you and I have another grandson."

Of all the things he could have said, Meg had never expected that. She pulled back slightly, eyes streaming tears, though she was starting to recover. "When?"

"Just now. We arrived in time for Dafydd to be here for the birth."

With that, as had been the case so often in the past when emotion overwhelmed her, Meg began to laugh—and the tears that flowed now were joyous.

30

David

By the time six in the evening rolled around—which David knew because of the cell phone he still had in his pocket—word had spread throughout Llangollen that not only had he and his father gone to Avalon and returned, but that David had a second son. By eight o'clock, the hall at Dinas Bran was full to bursting for Bridget's and Peter's wedding, which, while impromptu, was an appropriate finale to an incredible day.

Then the whole family, except for Lili and the baby, who were sleeping, and Darren, who was drugged up on poppy juice, shared a meal with the people of Llangollen.

Math munched away happily from beside David. "Finally, real food."

"Abraham fed us real food." David glanced towards the end of one of the long tables that ran down the hall.

Their friends who weren't royal or noble sat there, and even though eating with Gentiles was forbidden among observant Jews, tonight Aaron remained among them, sitting next to Abraham.

Aaron had taken Rachel's father under his wing, though it might not be long before he discovered, as David had, that it was really the other way around. Rupert sat with them too, morosely eating his roast pheasant and onions. So far David hadn't heard him speak a single word, which seemed to be due less to the concussion he'd received than his anger at finding himself in the Middle Ages. David would have thought he'd have been happy that his underlying suspicions had proved true.

Of course, as long as Rupert was here, he wasn't going to have the chance to write his story, and David certainly wasn't taking him back to Avalon so he could.

While time travel wasn't a get out of jail free card, and David still didn't think he'd ever used it as such, God help him, he wasn't sorry for the gift either.

David gazed down the table at his family, relieved beyond measure that he hadn't screwed up so badly that anyone had actually died. If things had gone even a tiny bit more sideways, they could have been mourning on Christmas Day in the years to come rather than celebrating. That was a legacy he didn't want to leave his children.

David had the sense that his family and friends were feeling similarly—that the brush with death was only adding to the already festive mood, since Christmas was as huge a holiday in the Middle Ages as in the twenty-first century. Children raced about the hall, led by Cadell, who was amped up on sweets and the return of his parents. They played tag among the tables, looked upon indulgently by all and sundry.

The bus remained at Whittington Castle, guarded by Samuel and his men. Eventually, someone would need to figure out how to move it. The front axle had broken so it was no longer drivable. Despite the damage, the bus had exceeded its design specifications in more ways than one. David wished he could send the company that built it a letter of commendation.

The repentant Fulk Fitzwarin had imprisoned Aymer de Valence in his tower—inside the castle, rather than in the one next to the bus—until such a time as Callum and David figured out his punishment. Callum had allowed Red Comyn and his men to form part of the escort for Mom, Anna, and the others to Dinas Bran. The Scots had one of the long tables to themselves, and David was in something of a quandary to know what he and Callum were going to do with any of them either.

That, however, along with David's relationship with the pope, John Balliol, and King Philip of France, was a problem he was going to kick down the road until tomorrow—or maybe January. Thankfully, Jacques de Molier had woken, and it appeared now that he would live. He lay in the infirmary in a room next to Darren.

"I want to know more about what Lee's been doing the last three months," Mom said. "What was his overall goal? Why did he set off that bomb?"

"I've been wondering that myself," Dad said.

David had been avoiding thinking about Lee, and with all that had happened, it hadn't been hard to do. But now he sighed. "In regards to your first question, Mom, I don't know any more than you. I suspect that MI-5 will be doing quite a bit of backtracking in the coming weeks. But as to why he set off the bomb—did you hear what he said, Dad, there at the end?"

Dad frowned. "Something about you being his ticket? I didn't understand what he meant."

"I think Lee misunderstood the nature of our time traveling." Something oily and unpleasant twisted in David's stomach, counteracting the very good meal he'd eaten. "He was right that I would time travel if my life was endangered in the explosion, but I'm pretty sure he thought he would travel with me."

"I can't be sorry," Mom said. "I know that's wrong of me."

"Lee killed people." David sighed. "He was mistaken if he thought he wouldn't have paid for his crimes here too."

"He thought you were soft," Dad said. "People should stop underestimating you."

David shrugged. "I won't always be a punk kid."

Mom laughed into her drink. "You weren't ever a punk kid."

"That reminds me—" Dad rose to his feet, holding out his goblet before him. "If Lord Math would allow me to impose on his hospitality for a moment, I'd like to propose a toast."

Math nodded at Hywel, who tinged the little bell that rested on the side table for just this purpose. Anna shot a warning look at Cadell, who stopped running and straightened up. As a child growing up in a medieval hall, he had learned when he was supposed to sit quietly while his elders spoke. With a few snaps of his fingers, he had the rest of the children finding their way to a bench or a friendly lap. Arthur crawled into David's. At three and a half, he was thrilled to have a younger brother and had already begged his Uncle Math to make the baby a wooden sword so they could play together.

Dad waited until the hall was silent, and then he lifted his glass again. "To my newest grandson and prince of Wales, Alexander Rhodri."

"Alexander Rhodri ," murmured everyone in the hall. In solemn silence, they drank, and then Dad sat down and the buzz of talk and laughter started again.

Callum, who was sitting on the other side of David from Dad, put down his glass. "Sire—"

David forestalled him, smiling. "Rhodri Mawr was a great king of Gwynedd, and King Alexander II of Scotland was my supposed great-grandfather. But really, you should know that I've named my son for you."

"But—"

Cassie, who was sitting on the other side of Callum, put her hand on Callum's arm. "It's a perfectly good name, and somebody should use it if you won't."

David had told Cassie what he planned, wanting to make sure in advance that Callum would accept his choice for the honor it was.

Callum was still looking stunned. "You should not be naming your son after me, my lord. Mathonwy or Ieuan—"

"—are both completely unpronounceable to the English. I'm the King of England. In this, I can do as I like." David lowered his voice. "Besides, I can't give him a name that is shared by any of my Welsh or Norman lords. The ones left out would view it as a slight on them—not that I could possibly tolerate a 'Prince Gilbert' or 'Prince Humphrey' anyway." David shuddered theatrically.

Callum smiled, and David could tell he was truly touched. David could think of few things that could do more to show Callum how much he meant to him than the naming of his son.

Then Callum's brow furrowed, and he said with an air of suspicion, "Naming your son after a king of Scotland couldn't have anything to do with the little altercation we witnessed today in Whittington, could it?"

"I'd named him before you arrived, and besides, I mentioned to Cassie before we went to Avalon that I wanted to name my son Alexander. Isn't that right, Cassie?"

She held up three fingers. "Scout's honor."

"But now that you mention it—" David sat back in his chair with a smile of satisfaction on his face, "—I like the message it sends."

"Everyone will assume your purpose is to remind Balliol and his allies that you have a claim to the Scottish throne should you choose to press the issue," Callum said.

"They will, won't they?" David grinned. "And then there's this business with France." He looked to where Geoffrey de Geneville sat at the far end of the table, currently speaking to Bronwen, who could charm anyone with her smile—though David was pretty sure she didn't know it. She had always been one of his secret weapons at court.

"Don't tell me you're thinking about going to France to meet King Philip as he asked?" Callum said. "The last time you and I boarded a boat together didn't turn out too well."

"It did in the end." David felt suitably chastened about the time traveling, but he was feeling more than a little satisfied about how his day had turned out. He raised his cup to his friend. "France, here we come.".

The End

Acknowledgments

First and foremost, I'd like to thank my lovely readers for encouraging me to continue the *After Cilmeri* Series. I have always been passionate about these books, and it's wonderful to be able to share my stories with readers who love them too.

Thank you to my husband, without whose love and support I would never have tried to make a living as a writer. Thank to my family who has been nothing but encouraging of my writing, despite the fact that I spend half my life in medieval Wales. And thank you to my beta readers: Darlene, Anna, Jolie, Melissa, Cassandra, Brynne, Gareth, Taran, Dan, and Venkata. I couldn't do this without you.

About the Author

With two historian parents, Sarah couldn't help but develop an interest in the past. She went on to get more than enough education herself (in anthropology) and began writing fiction when the stories in her head overflowed and demanded she let them out. While her ancestry is Welsh, she only visited Wales for the first time while in college. She has been in love with the country, language, and people ever since. She even convinced her husband to give all four of their children Welsh names.

She makes her home in Oregon.

www.sarahwoodbury.com

Printed in Poland
by Amazon Fulfillment
Poland Sp. z o.o., Wrocław
18 November 2020

65f44471-840f-4624-956b-5e91c323e52bR01